THE GIFT & THE CURSE

Mark Devlin

The Gift & The Curse
Mark Devlin

Paperback Edition First Published in Great Britain in 2023
eBook Edition First Published in Great Britain in 2023

ISBN: 978-1-913438-76-0

aSys Publishing
http://www.asys-publishing.co.uk

FOREWORD FROM THE AUTHOR

And so, one decade on from the events of '*The Cause & The Cure*,' we catch up with Verity, Keith, Max, Drew, May, and one or two others. This time, Daniela Mots and Aimee Hardwick make their debuts, as do the unholy trinity of Eugene Nicks, Fabian Lucas and Vic Asttok. Again, the story takes place my bornplace, as there are few more fascinating cities in which to base a thriller than in Oxford.

Just as musicians bemoan "that difficult second album," so the same challenge exists for new fiction writers. For '*TGATC*' I've taken my cue from '*The Godfather Part 2*,' which is that rarest of entities—a movie sequel that surpasses the quality of its predecessor. If readers consider '*Gift*' to be superior to '*Cause*' I'll be very gratified. If not, ah well, I tried.

I feel my novels have a great many cinematic overtones. I imagined how each of the scenes would look if being filmed as a movie, and I've even gone as far as to draw up a list of my preferred actors to play each of the characters based on how I imagine them to look.

My novels are probably the only ones in the world to come with their own movie-style soundtracks, and I had a lot of fun curating the one that accompanies this. As before, I've taken music from the story's timeframe, in this case 2001, and interspersed it with news audio of the era, to create an authentic sonic snapshot of what the world was like in those times. This can be accessed via my Mixcloud page at:

iii

https://www.mixcloud.com/TheSoundOfFreedom/
the-gift-the-curse-soundtrack/

Meanwhile, the soundtrack to '*The Cause* & *The Cure*' can be heard here:

https://www.mixcloud.com/TheSoundOfFreedom/
the-cause-the-cure-soundtrack/

I would suggest a new literary genre for these stories—and quite a few others out there. This should be "truth fiction" since, though the surface narrative may come from the author's imagination, so many aspects of it are rooted in reality that it's sometimes hard to tell the difference.

There's certainly more truth here than in any main-stream TV or radio news bulletin, or mainstream "news"paper! In this case, Oxford serves a microcosm for society at large, and so much of what happens within the city can be demonstrated to actually occur—or at least have the potential to—everywhere else. Many accounts of "real world" happenings depicted here are factual in basis.

Though possibly less allegorical than '*Cause*,' there are still many cryptic elements waiting to be decoded by the vigilant reader. Lots of wordplay and the odd anagram. I remain enthralled by the movies of Stanley Kubrick and how, not only was he able to provide an "exoteric" surface narrative to satiate a mainstream audience, there were also multiple sub-layers full of "esoteric" communications, necessitating several viewings to pick up on every clue being offered.

That being said, let's take a trip back to 2001.

Anything interesting happen that year, can anyone remember??

Mark Devlin

Acknowledgements

Huge appreciation goes out to the following:

To Nick Smith for another awesome and
mood-capturing sleeve design.

(www.nicksmithgraphicdesign.com)

To Nicola Mackin of A-Sys publishing for the usual
support and service.
(www.asys-publishing.co.uk)

To Janet and Daniela for their sharp proofing eyes.

And to the various real-life folk who provided the inspiration for some of this story's characters. They may, or may not know who they are!

Also by the author

MUSICAL TRUTH, VOLUMES 1, 2 AND 3

To most people, the music industry represents a source of harmless fun and entertainment. Beneath the glossy veneer, however, lies the devastating truth of who really controls these institutions, and the deeply malevolent agendas for which they're being used.

Mark Devlin is a long-standing DJ and music journalist. The three volumes of Musical Truth are the culmination of his several years' of research into the true nature of the industry and its objectives—from dark occult rituals, to mind-controlled artists, and all points in between. These books show how these agendas fit into the much wider picture of what's really going on in the world, and—crucially—how the power lies with us to bring it all to an end.

All three volumes are available at Amazon and Barnes & Noble. Signed copies may also be obtained direct from the Author, however.

Please e-mail markdevlin2022@protonmail.com to arrange.

THE CAUSE & THE CURE

1990; Oxford, England, and the respectable facade of the City of Dreaming Spires is being shattered by a series of brutal murders. Police chief Neil Lowe needs a quick result, even if it calls for a fit-up, which suits him if it allows him more time in the sandwich shop. Radio reporter Verity Hunter has noticed that the choice of victim suggests a far deeper motive than that of a straight psycho-killer — a particular breed of retribution is at play — and her investigations uncover another aspect of Oxford hidden from view — the world of "elite" secret-societies.

Her boyfriend Keith is on the same page, and his consulting of the direct-talking consciousness guru Max Zeall makes him realise that there are spiritual components dictating the way things are playing out. It's these very same forces which provide the opportunity to restore justice and balance, if understood and employed responsibly.

A crime thriller set during a time of great cultural change, (the last days of Thatcherism, Poll Tax riots, the fall of Communism, the first Gulf War, Acid House and Rave culture,) gets taken to uncharted territories through the interplay with eternal, spiritual truths, and a recognition of the true, illusory nature of life in this realm.

GOOD VIBRATIONS

A free, ongoing series of conversation-based podcasts, covering a huge array of topics within the truth/ conspiracy/consciousness/ spirituality fields.

The entire archive so far is available at:

https://www.spreaker.com/show/good-vibrations-podcast

THE SOUND OF FREEDOM

TSOF is a free showcase of conscious music, old and new, compiled by Mark Devlin. It stands as the inspiring antithesis to the corporate agenda, offering meaningful music by switched-on, awakened artists.

The full archive so far is available at:

https://www.mixcloud.com/TheSoundOfFreedom/

Mark Devlin's main website:

www.djmarkdevlin.com

Mark Devlin's Odysee channel containing his entire (downloadable) video archive dating back to 2008:

https://odysee.com/@markdevlintv:e

To e-mail the author:

markdevlin2022@protonmail.com

PROLOGUE

Saturday 25th August 2001

"Time marches on never ending.
Time keeps its own time . . .

I hope I'm in a better state,
When here and now crumbles and falls."

Kings of Tomorrow Featuring Julie McKnight: 'Finally.'

"Dearly beloved, we are gathered here today to get through this
thing called life."

Prince & The Revolution: 'Let's Go Crazy.'

The scent and smoke and sweat of a nightclub are nauseating at eleven at night.

It doesn't help when the ceiling's sweating either, reflected a disgruntled Drew Hunter as what must have been the thirtieth drop fell onto the rotating slab of black vinyl from which the sounds of Aaliyah's 'Try Again' were blasting through the club's PA system. Frustrated, not to mention fatigued from his fourth night straight of DJing, he watched as the turntable slowly inched the stylus ever closer to the droplet, now more flattened.

Shrugging his shoulders, he turned back to the two metal crates on the chest-level bench behind him as the low-frequency basslines farted and rasped out of the speakers, and the dancefloor of room one of Derby's Pink Pineapple heaved with the weight of the dancers who had been throwing shapes to Drew's selections for the previous 90 minutes.

The bar area was similarly overcrowded, as was the VIP seating on the raised adjacent platform. The club always did good numbers, particularly on a Saturday night, and even moreso when a big-name DJ crew was on the bill as was the case tonight. The combined body heat had created a room temperature akin to that of a sauna, dripping roof included. In a Def Jam T-shirt, black baggy jeans and Lugz boots, Drew was hardly dressed appropriately.

"Not 'til I see what this could be," went the sweetly-sung female vocal blasting out of the sound system—not that anyone would have been able to make out the lyrics amidst the bass-heavy distortion.

"Could be eternity or just a week. But, yo, our chemistry is off the chain. It's perfect now, but will it change?"

The cardboard sleeves to the past several records in Drew's set jutted jaggedly from the record crates, arranged diagonally so he could keep track of what he'd played. There was Missy Elliott's 'Minute Man;' Lil Mo's 'Superwoman Remix;' Outkast's 'Ms. Jackson;' Ja Rule's 'Put It On Me.' As he thumbed through the first few he kissed his teeth as his fingers registered the moisture that had been absorbed from the sweating room.

The covers were in a bad enough state already, frayed at the edges from overuse and neglect, many of the corners little more than powder, and the records themselves badly scratched and worn. He recalled the maxim he had presented to many a club promoter when hustling for gigs. "Never book a DJ with mint-condition records. The ones with knackered vinyl are the ones in demand!"

As he glanced at his watch he noted, mercifully, that he only had 20 minutes or so til he could be on the road back to Oxford in time for his 2am set at The Arena. He considered for a moment which tunes would comprise the remainder of his set, before searching for them using the long-acquired skill of identifying the sleeve from just the top edge, all in the limited light offered by the DJ booth's single anglepoise lamp.

"And if at first you don't succeed, dust yourself off and try again."

The voice continued. Drew had heard the song a hundred times, but it seemed tonight to have an other-worldly feel to it. Aaliyah sounded like a siren. Or a ghost. Drew surmised that he was over-tired. If his eyes could have been clearly viewed away from the 60-watt lightbulb of the pulpit, their bloodshot redness would have confirmed this. Though tiredness wouldn't have been the only explanation for their appearance.

"You can dust it off and try again, dust yourself off and try again, try again."

Instinctively he gave his sore eyes a rub, his thoughts turning to lighting the pre-prepared spliff he had secreted in the glovebox of his Ford Mondeo outside, and absorbing it prior to making the 100-mile journey back. He gave his wildly perspiring brow a wipe also. He swore the temperature had risen another few degrees in the past minutes.

"I'm getting too old for this shit," he mumbled to himself. At 37 he was hardly over the hill, but tonight the impact of two decades' worth of late nights, motorway miles, spliffs, and broken circadian rhythms really seemed to be taking its toll.

The next few records got selected. Drew searched for what he decided would be his set finale and pulled at the orange sleeve, still encased in a few remnants of its original cellophane shrinkwrap, He saw that he had called it correctly when he found a copy of Sunshine Anderson's 'Heard It All Before" in his hand. The dancefloor was heaving with young, nubile females, he had been delighted to notice. A ladies' favourite was the way to go out with a bang.

His pleasurable view of the dancefloor had been hampered not only by his tiredness, but by his angst at the fact that The Wrecking Crew, the three-man DJ group from London who were due to take over deck duties at 11.30, had not yet arrived. Neither had the club's promoter with his pay. The venue being part of the dubiously-named Lucius Leisure conglomerate, and one of the best-known niteries in the Midlands, Drew wasn't anticipating any of the sheisty shenanigans employed by many a fly-by-night promoter at paytime. But still, he didn't relish the prospect of having to scour the sweaty club for his benefactor.

The Sunshine Anderson 12-inch correctly cued up, Drew released the black plastic from his grip with well-practiced precision, the first four beats of the introductory sequence sitting neatly over the last four from Mary J Blige's 'Family Affair' so the vocal kicked in at the desired moment, an enthusiastic whoop coming from the female-dominated dancefloor as the line "coming home late, it seems you barely beat the sun" roared through the speakers.

As the hairs on the back of his neck stood up—a regular reaction to the energy levels in the room changing at such moments—a slight smile came to his lips as he imagined his own lady uttering the same lines to him as he rolled in, pre-dawn. Only he would have been out earning, not cheating like the character in the song.

Further reason to smile came from the two factors he'd most been anticipating as, firstly, the promoter hurriedly climbed the three steps to the DJ booth and handed Drew a small brown wages envelope containing £150 in ten-pound notes. As soon as he'd gone, the welcome sight of The Wrecking Crew appeared. The three pulled open the booth door and began hauling their multiple record cases into the confined space.

Drew lifted his boxes off the bench and bumped fists with each of the three. Something was wrong, however. Encountering each-other regularly on the circuit, Drew and the Crew alike would invariably have grins plastered over their faces when reuniting. The trio hardly had an air of joviality about them tonight. Indeed, Phil Phatt looked ashen-faced.

Drew soon found out why. The words hit him like a freight train.

"Aaliyah's been killed in a plane crash."

"What ... *what*?" Drew requested confirmation that he'd heard correctly.

"I said Aaliyah's been killed in a plane crash."

The hairs on the back of his neck were standing up again. The moment was reminiscent of the one four years previous when he had descended from an upstairs office at Lux FM, in which he had been sleeping it off after a gig, to find the newsroom bustling with frantic activity. He vividly recalled the words of the traumatised journalist.

"Princess Diana's been killed in a car crash in Paris."

"What the *fuck*?" had been Drew's justifiable response.

It was the same response to Phil Phatt's news.

The goosebumps were not entirely from nostalgia. They were also triggered by the paralysing fear of flying that Drew had experienced all his life.

"Bwoy, I've always said, plane travel is not the way to go."

"I know, right?" mumbled Phatt as he and his colleagues busied themselves with opening up their record crates and selecting their first tunes. As the familiar AV8 records logo flashed into his subconscious, Drew noted that Phatt had selected the Crooklyn Clan's 'Ladies' as a way of coming out of 'Heard It All Before.'

Drew struggled to process the information as Phatt, the Crew's MC, pushed open the microphone fader on the mixer, pulled down the levels on Drew's last tune and, with seasoned professionalism shouted, "Yo, Derby! What's going on? Much respect to the man like Drew Hunter. But right now, The Wrecking Crew is in the building! Are you ready?"

As the opening beats to 'Ladies' kicked in, accompanied by more whoops and cheers, Steve B pulled the microphone fader back down. Noting Phatt now able to speak as his colleagues dug through their records, Drew seized his chance

"So what happened?" Drew quizzed.

"It was in the Bahamas. She was out there filming a video with Hype Williams. Her light aircraft crashed. Hype wasn't on it. A few others were. We just heard as we were driving up. That's why we were late. Couldn't believe it."

"Damn!" proclaimed Drew, furrow-browed. "She can't have been more than ... "

"22," Phatt interrupted.

Drew kissed his teeth. "What a waste."

"I know, right?" concurred Phatt. "There's so many others you'd have preferred it to have been!" Several famous faces flashed into Drew's mind.

He stayed for the first ten minutes of the Crew's set, more out of etiquette than a desire to remain in the heaving sweatshop for a minute longer than he needed to.

He cupped his hand around his mouth and shouted into Phatt's ear.

"You gonna announce it?"

"Yeah, we're gonna play a tribute set in a while."

11.47pm. Drew decided it was time to make his exit and bumped fists with the Crew once more, before heaving up his record cases and beginning the slow battle through the teeming crowd towards the main room exit.

His journey to the venue's front entrance took him past room two where, as an alternative to the upfront "urban" styles, older soul and funk from the 70s and 80s got played. As the evergreen sounds of Cheryl Lynn's 'Encore' faded out, a bassline that Drew knew he recognised but couldn't immediately place took over. Very quickly his aficionado's mind had told him it was something by Prince. But which cut?

His shoulders screaming their protest, he placed the two heavy boxes on the floor as he strained his neck to see the DJ. Through a crowd much thinner than the one in the main room, he saw the skinny outline of a character he had the idea he had seen somewhere before—but where?—as his mind continued to process the news of a short while earlier.

"Dyam! Aaliyah dead! So beautiful. So young. What the *fuck*?!"

The lyrics to the song had kicked in.

Drew suddenly placed it. '17 Days.' That was it. The B-side to Prince's 'When Doves Cry.' One of his lesser-known tunes, but one which Drew himself had always liked. He glanced again at the skinny DJ.

"Dyam. White bwoy knows his tunes, star," he muttered to himself with a slight smile.

"Let the rain come down, let the rain come down, let the rain come down, down (17 days)" went the lyrics.

"17 Days," he muttered, registering the portentous feel this night seemed to have—and without even realising that Prince's father, the jazz musician John L. Nelson had himself died that very day. "What could possibly happen in 17 days that could be any worse than Aaliyah dying in a plane crash?"

Picking up his cases and continuing his exodus to the car park, he came closer with every passing minute to finding the answer to his own question.

CHAPTER 1

Monday 10th September 2001

"I can feel it coming in the air tonight.
Well, I've been waiting for this moment for all my life."

Phil Collins: 'In The Air Tonight.'

"Like it or not, everything is changing. The result will be
the most wonderful experience in the history of man, or the
most horrible enslavement that you can imagine. Be active or
abdicate. The future is in your hands."

Milton William Cooper (1943-2001) 'Behold a Pale Horse.'

"I really am convinced we're in danger of the sort of terrorist
attacks that will make the (1993) bombing of the Trade
Center look like kids playing with firecrackers."

Donald Trump: 'The America We Deserve' (2000.)

"Ladies and gentlemen, have you been paying attention to the news lately?"

The authoritative voice rang out through the speakers in the studio, just as it did through the handful of radios across the city of Oxford that were tuned in to Oxford

Freedom Radio, 93.0FM. The voice's American accent had a slight Californian twang. There was swirling interference in the background of the recording.

It couldn't be helped, reasoned Max Zeall as he presided over the broadcast. Anyone too distracted by the noise to focus on the profundity of the words wasn't ready for the message in the first place.

The strangely alluring voice continued.

"After the anniversary of the Oklahoma City bombing, we were bombarded with anti-patriot, anti-militia, anti-constitutionalist...anti-American propaganda...And now we're being bombarded with messages that Osama bin-Laden is planning to attack the United States of America and Israel.

"And I'm telling you, be prepared for a major attack. But it won't be Osama bin-Laden. It will be those behind the New World Order, who once again want to take the guns and the freedom away from the American people, because we're the only ones left in the world who can oppose the destruction of freedom in the world, and the implementation of a one-world totalitarian socialist government. And that is the goal..."

"Do you ever hear of Osama bin-Laden? Before you heard of Saddam Hussein, when did you start hearing of Osama bin-Laden? It was after Saddam Hussein and Iraq was supposedly neutralised in the Gulf War because they needed a new boogeyman...

"...Can you believe what you have been seeing on CNN today, ladies and gentlemen? Can you believe it? Supposedly, a CNN reporter found Osama bin-Laden, took a television camera crew with him, went into Osama bin-Laden's hideout and interviewed him and his top leadership, his top lieutenants and colonels and generals in their hideout...

"Now, don't you think that's kind of strange, folks? You see, because the largest intelligence apparatus in the world, with the biggest budget in the history of the world, has been looking for Osama bin-Laden for years and years and years and can't find him. The FBI has been looking for Osama bin-Laden for years and years and years and can't find him. Then some doofus jerk-off reporter with a camera crew waltzes right into his hideout and interviews him!

"...But they're not looking for Osama bin-Laden because I'm telling you right now, if I were the head of the Central Intelligence Agency, within two weeks I would have him dead or in custody without fail. Without fail! If I had those assets and that money he would be mine. I would own his terrorist ass within two weeks without fail."

As the audio concluded there was a sharp click as Max Zeall pressed the pause button on the Eltax cassette deck. Ever the professional, only then did he push open the microphone fader on the battered radio desk. As he moved his mouth closer to the now-live microphone his beard bristled against the red foam pop shield.

"And there it was, folks. Cautionary words from a man who's in a position to know. William Milton "Bill" Cooper, former US military and Naval intelligence officer turned whistleblower. Author of a landmark book for our times," he glanced across the desk at his copy of 'Behold A Pale Horse,' well-worn from ten years of constant referencing.

Max could have used a producer or assistant, but had never been able to find anyone he could rely on to stay the course. A couple of volunteers early on in the show's history had feigned enthusiasm, but after a handful of absences and unsatisfactory excuses, Max had lost patience and indignantly told them not to bother returning.

Since then, reasoning that the only individual anyone can truly trust is themselves, he'd set himself the challenge of handling the technical aspects of his show single-handedly. This had certainly sharpened many of his skills, yet led to a hectic experience in the studio, one which frequently sent him home with a headache.

The twenty-minute monologue taken from Cooper's 'Hour Of The Time' American radio show dated 28th June 2001, had certainly given him a most welcome break from the usual stress. He had spent much of it habitually rubbing the skin at the very top of his nose, eyes closed, which was as close as he was able to get to meditation. The sensation of the rubbing, he found, gave him the distraction from the 'monkey mind' which would otherwise kick in. It was as close as he ever came to relaxing during his waking hours.

After a few minutes he opened his eyes, replaced the black baseball cap emblazoned simply with the word 'freedom' in white lettering, and consumed from the chrome flask the rest of the vegetable juice he had prepared at home.

With characteristic precision, Max had programmed in enough time to take two or three listeners' calls before the show's midnight end. He rarely received any more than three per session anyway, a weekly reminder of just how few in Oxford cared for the values of Truth and Freedom, and just how much work there was left to do.

As he announced that he would now be taking calls and gave out the phone number, a red light began blinking above the first channel on the telecaster set to his left. As Max pressed the button below the red light he simultaneously pushed open yet another fader on the desk.

"Caller, you're through to '*At Last The 1984 Show*.' What's your name and where are you calling from?"

Max knew the answer before it came.

"Yes, Max, it's Stucky from Rose Hill."

"Hey Stucky, what's up, my friend," asked Max, smiling to himself at the inevitability of it all.

"I'm doing OK, my brother. Just surviving the Matrix the best way I can. You know, like John Lennon said, 'whatever gets you through the night, it's alright, it's alright'."

"Yes, he did, didn't he?" replied Max as the sounds of Stucky exhaling smoke on the other end of the line filled his headphones.

"Those words from Bill Cooper were so prophetic, man," Stucky resumed. "What he said right there is going to be looked back on generations from now and will stand as a historical documentation of these times."

"And so they should," Max interrupted, "because he cares enough to speak truth and do what he knows to be right, regardless of any potential consequences. Fear doesn't figure in Right Action."

"Well, you know what Bill Hicks said, Max," Stucky continued. "Everything is a choice between fear and love. That's it. Those are the two emotional states at each end of the spectrum. Everything between is just derivatives of one of those states or the other. When fear is in control, truth is the casualty. And we need truth more than ever in these precarious times, my brother. I know you know that."

"That's why we do this every Monday night, and will continue to do for as long as is needed, whether that can be measured in days, weeks or decades. As long as it takes."

"As long as it takes," repeated Stucky. There was another pause and the sound of exhalation.

"But yo, Max," the caller continued, "though Cooper seems fearless, I do worry for his safety. He's now got a great big target painted on his back, and his former employers are not going to forget what he's done. I hope nothing happens to him, but something tells me he's not going to see the end of the year. And what he's been predicting and warning against could be coming sooner than any of us think."

"Well, I guess we'll know soon enough.

"OK, Stucky, thanks as ever for your call. You take it easy, my brother, and we'll talk again soon. Next Monday, no doubt."

All his adult life, Max had possessed an uncanny ability to know the time to within a minute without needing to look at a clock. This was a trait attributed to Sirhan Sirhan, the alleged assassin of Robert F. Kennedy. Sirhan had been an MK-Ultra mind-controlled Manchurian Candidate though, and this seemed to have developed the skill, whereas one thing Max could be damn sure of was that he had never been MK-ed himself. Instinctively, he knew it was 11.57pm, giving him enough time to take one more call. Happily, one solitary light blinked on the console.

"Caller, you're through to '*At Last The 1984 Show*'. What's your name and where are you calling from?"

***

As Max pulled down the microphone fader he pressed the Play button on the upper of the two Denon CD decks, firing his forty-eight-second outro music. In the two years he had been presenting his show, he had perfected being able to gather together his personal effects and place them in his backpack by the time the music ended. As it did, Max reached for the mouse to the right of the giant iMac computer monitor housed on its own wooden platform above the desk, and clicked on the mp3 icon named 'Overnight." As he did so he fired off the six hours' worth of monologues, interviews and commentary that would sustain the station's output until the morning host arrived at 6am.

The "studio"—a renovated garden shed—was as dimly lit as ever. An 80-watt bulb glowed in a single uplighter with no shade in the corner, illuminating only that side of the room. All along the wall opposite the door was the equipment from which OFR had been operating as a pirate since its launch on the symbolic date of 31st October 1999.

OFR being his personal vision, Max had been instrumental in the technical side of getting the station set up. Equipment had been acquired from a ragtag bunch of sources—car boot sales, charity shops, donations—and Max had used up pretty much every cable that had previously resided in his garage to connect the various components to the broadcast desk, rescued from a skip outside Lux FM and found, despite its decrepit appearance, to be in fine working order. He had found deep irony in the fact that, to synch the desk's output to the transmitter—helpfully bolted to the balcony of Drew Hunter's flat three miles away in Barton—he'd had to use microwave links, a technology whose health perils had been warned about through so much of the station's output.

Shamim Amed, a Cowley Road restaurateur, had volunteered his newly-renovated garden outhouse to accommodate the broadcast studio. It was run by a small handful of volunteers, all of whom had been closely vetted for their passion, knowledge and potential reliability. OFR had managed to secure reliable hosts for what, in radio verbiage, were the weekday "breakfast" and "drivetime" slots, though *this* content was a million miles away from Zoe Ball or Steve Wright.

The other live shows were scattered randomly through the week, with pre-recorded speech and music content filling the gaps between hosts. Drew Hunter had taken late-night Wednesdays to present 'The Truth Trip,' a showcase of empowering reggae and hip-hop, heavy on the lyrical messages. Max had volunteered to present his 'At Last The 1984 Show' on Monday nights, reasoning that people were in a more serious and sober state of mind than later in the week, so important messages were likely to be better-received.

Despite the "illegal" nature of the station, as the government's Radio Authority would have seen it, OFR had encountered zero visits from any enforcement agencies. The baseball bat housed in the umbrella holder in the corner was a reminder of Max's preparedness for any such visits. But despite undoubtedly being listened into by military intelligence agencies, ensuring a file had been opened on each of the hosts, OFR had never seen any formal challenge to its existence.

Though he admired Shamim's dedication to the cause, the man's lack of tidiness and order always grated with Max.

All the moreso now as he surveyed the overall state of the "studio." Scattered haphazardly around were a half-eaten kebab, two screwed-up Red Stripe beer cans, cocaine debris, tobacco, and a woman's white stiletto shoe. Must have been one hell of a party, Max considered.

Then there was the aroma which perpetually filled the air and which Max always carried with him in his clothes after leaving the building, one so impossible to pinpoint that he could only refer to it as "*Eau D'OFR.*" It seemed to be part-curry, part-marijuana and part-blocked toilet, creating a funky cocktail that had no means of escape from the windowless room.

'I've met a lot of people in my life and I can't to my knowledge recall anyone who wanted a war. Who had any interest in wars."

The words of David Icke from a 1994 speech resonated from the speakers, recorded at a time when the former footballer and BBC sports presenter was regarded almost universally as having lost his mind as he had publicly proclaimed that the world is not run by governments, but by an "elite" class, who operate from the shadows and pull the strings of every aspect of world affairs. The consensus among the British was still largely the same, though Max was encouraged to find evidence of more now prepared to give time to what Icke had to say with every passing week.

He turned down the studio speakers and flicked the light switch as he reached the door. The red and green lights of various equipment winked like stars in the otherwise darkened room.

Max held his breath as he walked into the corridor, adjacent as he then was to the open toilet door, with that room's contribution to one third of '*Eau D'OFR.*' He knew better than to breathe in during the couple of seconds it took him to reach the outhouse's main door.

He stepped down to ground level, slammed the framed glass door shut, turned the key and placed it under the doormat ready for the breakfast show host in six hours' time.

He glanced up at the sky. It was a clear, cloudless night illuminated by the waning crescent of the moon. He knew that it was 12.02am, Tuesday morning, 11th September 2001. He let out a deep sigh as, contemplating the heavens, he wondered how much longer it would take the controllers to truly reveal their hand for all to see; how much longer it would take for humanity to awaken to the peril it unknowingly faced; and just how much longer he would have to dedicate his life to this cause.

Max carefully navigated Shamim's back lawn as he moved towards the house. He'd slipped in that mud with an armful of equipment way too many times. As he passed by the kitchen he heard the sound of sizzling and crackling through the open window, and looking through, saw Shamim presiding over a curry, agitating the pan with a wooden spoon.

"Hey Max. How was your show, man?"

"Portentous!" Max replied with a smile.

"Just another day at the office then. You hungry? Want some of this?"

"I'm good. Thanks anyway."

"Well, the night's just starting for me," said Shamim.

'Sleep needed with me," replied Max. "The days never seem long enough to get it all done. Something tells me tomorrow's going to be a busy one."

As Max moved along the side alley to his car, parked in front of Shamim's 1950s three-bed Cricket Road semi, he was bemused to find the words of Bill Cooper still ringing in his mind.

"There's been a great awakening in this country and and a big backlash against these Marxist, communist, lying, subversive, Nazi, jackbooted Gestapo thugs, that is gaining momentum.

"And so I can tell you with a certainty, they must do something terrible in order to stop this backlash, and regain the sympathy of the mass herds of sheeple out there."

CHAPTER 2

Tuesday 11th September 2001

"Truth comes, we can't hear it
When you've been programmed to fear it."

Lauryn Hill: 'Freedom Time.'

"They must find it difficult, those who have taken authority as
truth, rather than truth as authority."

Gerald Massey.

"When fear is allowed to flourish in its dark and lonely
medium, then any evil that can be conceived by the fearful
imagination will emerge."

Andrew J. Robinson: 'A Stitch in Time.'

Verity Faith Hunter was content.

Leaned against a stack of rocks towards the front right side of Mawgan Porth beach, as she surveyed all around her, she counted her reasons to be grateful. In the first instance it was an uncharacteristically warm September afternoon, making for ideal beach weather at a time when, the school holidays now over, quality time could be enjoyed so much more freely.

Pushing her Ray-Ban sunglasses more firmly to the bridge of her nose, she tilted her glance upwards. The perfectly blue sky wasn't even tainted with the usual myriad of milkily-melted chemtrails.

The bastards must have something more important to do today.

Scattered around her on the wicker picnic blanket were the remnants of an enjoyable lunch that betrayed its family-friendly nature; sandwich crusts, tomato and grape stalks, half-nibbled cucumber and carrot sticks, two plastic beakers and a Tommee Tippee tumbler. The battery-powered mini radio, its ariel extended, relayed the harmless-enough sounds of an extended 90s sequence on Virgin Radio. Though she hadn't cared much for Pearl Jam or Nirvana, Verity was happy enough to detect the feint strains of Gabrielle's 'Dreams' follow those of Tasmin Archer's 'Sleeping Satellite.'

Her spot on the rocks had given her a useful vantage point of the beach which, just two weeks earlier, had been teeming with holiday-makers with barely a spare foot of sand to be claimed. Today, though, the few couples and families were more than amply spaced out, and there was barely an annoying dog in sight.

The unconquerable rocks of ages leered imposingly on both sides of the Porth, as the river inlet, so popular a feature of this beach, meandered haphazardly through the sand and in and out of the rock pools on its way down to the Atlantic Ocean.

As she stretched out her slim, coffee-coloured legs and let out a lazy yawn, happiest of all in Verity's vision was the heartwarming sight to her right, with joyful sounds to match, and she smiled as she retained her gaze in that direction.

There, in the shallow waters, the mild waves lapping against her short, lightly tan legs, was her five-year-old daughter, Hope, in pink swimsuit and white bucket hat, scooping up waves with all the vigour her young arms could muster, and sending the spray in the direction of her dad, dressed far more simplistically in a pair of navy blue Speedos and a black peaked cap.

Feigning a far worse drenching than he was reaping, Keith Malcolm let out soundbites like, "you got me good!" and "right, just you wait, missy!" as he reciprocated, taking care to keep his splashes low and light, with Hope generating ear-piercingly shrill shrieks no matter how benign he kept his attacks.

So engrossed was Keith in his daddy-daughter fun-play—childhood memories of holidays taken on this very beach himself flooding back—that he remained completely oblivious to the number of similarly-playing parents and their offspring who had swiftly moved out of the water and back towards their towels during the previous couple of minutes, as if in the 'shark scare' scenes from 'Jaws,' (the basking ones of British waters posing no such threats as a Great White.)

Keith had been paying equally little attention to Hope's mother, no longer sat with their stuff at the rocks, but instead running towards them, water cascading in all directions as she floundered into the waves with wild abandon. Her presence had now been registered. The silent expression—one which Keith knew his partner well enough to recognise as one of pure trauma—spoke a thousand words of its own. In her right arm, Verity had with her the small portable radio set. 2.11pm.

"V, what is it?" Keith quizzed her. Hope ceased splashing and gave her mother a glance of confused concern.

"America's under attack. Keith." She fixed him a solemn, knowing stare. "I think this is the big one."

***

Much to Hope's bemusement, protests and inadequately answered questions, the trio had hurriedly dried off, piled all their belongings into their holdall, and made for their car on the other side of the sandy road by the cafe and ice-cream stand. They had barely paused to brush them-selves free of sand—something on which Keith in less extenuating circumstances would have insisted before boarding his Navy Ford Orion—and had hot-tailed it around the hairpin bend and along the top road to their ex-council three-bedroom semi in St. Columb Major.

Another break with convention was to have the radio news playing throughout—not out of any delusion on Verity or Keith's part that they were getting any semblance of truth, but so they could simply arm themselves with what everyone else was getting asked to believe.

Pulling up in their driveway, as Keith scooped up Hope from her car seat and carried her though the back gate, there was little need for a still sandy, still bikini-ed Verity to ask the two occupants of their house if they'd been hearing what they had as she burst through the kitchen into the living room.

"Oh my dear, Lord," she heard her mother Joy's voice utter with its omnipresent Bajan twang, as she surveyed what was coming out of the household television.

"Unbelievable ... it's like watching a movie," her companion muttered incredulously.

There weren't many things on which Verity and her mother's new gentleman-friend, Norman Peter Cocker, or

'Norm,' ever agreed, but here at least was some common ground as, after twenty minutes of having to piece together her own idea of the imagery from solely the audio, here at last was her first visual confirmation.

She knew at that moment that the scene on this 24-inch screen would be one which would remain etched into her consciousness for the rest of her days.

One of the iconic twin towers of New York City's World Trade Center was engulfed in flames, masked momentarily by belches of dense, black smoke, while its twin stood precariously by its side. The news reports had consistently reinforced that it had been hit by a commercial airliner which had plunged into its steel framework like a knife into butter, and immediately triggered a gargantuan explosion.

Having managed to engage Hope in some artful activities in her bedroom, Keith now joined the others in the morbid display, and was just in time to watch the next phase in the act unfold. With footage seemingly being shot randomly and in real time, what appeared to be the outline of a second airplane careered rapidly towards the remaining monolith, and just as with the first, slammed into its frame, causing a second explosion of the exact same nature.

"Oh, dear Jesus, save us," Joy whimpered, pure fear in her eyes, as she instinctively crossed her forehead and neck with the four cardinal points of the compass.

"They've done it! They gone and bloody done it! Those crazy Muslim bastards!" blurted out Norm indignantly.

It didn't take much for this man's ways to spark Keith's ire. Something about the dense, heavy atmosphere in the room quickened the process more than ever.

"What do you mean, Muslims, Norm? What possible proof have you got that this was Muslims?!"

"I'n't it always?" Norm protested, his South Yorkshire dialect leaving no doubt as to his cultural roots. "They're known for it. 'Ow many plane 'ijackings have been down to this lot over the decades? Who was it behind that Oklahoma Bombing t'other year? That Usama bin-Laden, whatever his chuffin' name is. And t' news is already starting to say he was the mastermind behind this one."

"Yeah, there's a clue there, Norm. The News is telling you! They pieced that one together remarkably quickly, don't you think, considering this only happened a few minutes ago?'

"Oh please, you two, don't start," Joy appealed, shaky-voiced, tears streaming down her face. Verity fixed Keith a wide-eyed glance, what he called her "black girl glare," but he remained fired up.

"Norm, you remember V and I have been telling you and Joy that something really big is coming down the pike very soon for the past few weeks now? Well, it just went live. You're watching it!"

"Bollocks! Nobody could have foreseen this!" insisted Norm, a slight glob of drool appearing at the corners of his mouth as he kept his trance-like gaze fixed on the low 60hz flicker-rate of their television set. Keith glanced over to Verity. The two shook their heads simultaneously before a movement at the living room door caught their eye.

There stood young Hope, nervously chewing on a favourite teddy bear with anxiety in her eyes. With a mother's instinct, Verity hurried towards her, removing her again from this most bizarre of experiences that none of those in the room—or indeed in the vast, overwhelming bulk of the rest of the world—had had the first clue that they would be waking up to witness that day.

***

Three hours had passed—a time during which they—and the rest of the world—were told that it was even worse than at first thought. The "terrorist attacks" were not limited only to New York, but two other hijackings had been involved—one flight slamming into the Pentagon building in Washington DC, the other—in more scenes straight out of a movie—having apparently crashed after heroic passengers managed to wrest control back from the hijackers—but not soon enough to prevent it from slamming into a field in Pennsylvania, the impact killing all on board.

In an act which went against their entire ethos, but for which they figured they really ought to make an exception today, Verity and Keith had been sat transfixed to the 'idiot lantern' alongside Joy and Norm, taking it in shifts to go and attend to Hope in her room. Despite their best attempts to shield her from the obvious change in atmosphere from anything she'd ever been used to, Hope was more savvy than they might have anticipated. "Why are the bad men trying to hurt people?" she had asked Verity, looking her squarely in the eye as if daring her to offer a patronising response.

"There *are* men who want to hurt people, sweet pea, but it won't be the men we're being told it is."

The cogs seemed to turn in Hope's mind as she contemplated for a moment.

"Will we be safe?"

"Well, me and your dad—and our friends—are going to do everything in our power to make sure we all will be,' came as honest an answer as Verity could muster.

The tender moment was broken by the piercing ring of the hall telephone. Calls had been coming in all afternoon, mainly from Joy and Norm's concerned peers who didn't do mobile phones. Reportedly, many of the cell tower networks had been down all day anyway. Joy had evidently prised herself away from the box for the first time all afternoon as she called through to Verity.

"V. Come quick. It your cousin."

Moments later Verity found herself chatting to Drew Hunter back in Barton.

'V, you have on the news?" There was no playful banter on this call.

"Yeah, the Brutish Brainwashing Corporation is on," confirmed V, peering through from the hall to the lounge.

On the screen, Verity could see a woman reporter, gesticulating enthusiastically as she evidently described the scenes behind her—a Manhattan landscape still enveloped in thick smoke.

"You see the caption in the box beneath her?"

Verity read it out: "The 47-storey Salomon Brothers building close to the World Trade Center has also collapsed."

'Right," replied Drew. "Only one problem though."

"What's that?"

You see that flat, square building to the right of her in the background?"

"Yeah?"

"*That's* the 47-storey Salomon Brothers building, otherwise known as World Trade Center Building 7. Does that look collapsed to you?"

CHAPTER 3

Tuesday 11th September 2001

"The very word "secrecy" is repugnant in a free and open society; and we are as a people, inherently and historically opposed to secret societies, to secret oaths and to secret proceedings."

US President John F. Kennedy, 27th April 1961.

"Freedom is not a gift bestowed upon us by other men, but a right that belongs to us by the laws of God and nature."

Benjamin Franklin.

"In every age it has been the tyrant, the oppressor and the exploiter who has wrapped himself in the cloak of patriotism, or religion, or both to deceive and overawe the people."

Eugene Victor Debs.

It was a far cry from only three days previous when Drew Hunter had been among the hundreds of vinyl enthusiasts digging through the crates at the venue's monthly record fair. Today, the air was sombre as Eugene Nicks, elected

Lord Mayor of the city of Oxford since 1st May, stepped up to the lectern in the assembly room of the Town Hall.

The room was full to capacity, as legions of bewildered and traumatised Oxfordians had flocked to attend this emergency meeting. For many, the atmosphere in the room had brought memories of the funeral of Princess Diana four years previous. The world had felt different that day, and they were getting an unwelcome replay of that low-density vibrational state today.

None were sure entirely why they were there, as there was little that Oxford's Mayor could do by way of assistance here, 3,000-plus miles away from the chaos in the United States. Those who gave it any conscious thought figured they were there simply for the camaraderie; for the sense of commonality that humans tend to feel towards their fellow men and women in uncertain and testing times.

The 6pm meeting had been hastily arranged and announced via the airwaves of BBC Radio Oxford and Lux FM, rivals in the radio game, but showing solidarity on this day of days. The message had simply mentioned that the Mayor and the Bishop of Oxford would be in attendance to offer reassurance to the people of the city.

The assembly room had not received any decoration or refurbishment for decades, but little was really needed. The pine floor panels had proven extremely durable, as had the oak walls, decorated with portraits of some of the most celebrated figures associated with Oxford's history—Winston Churchill; John Radcliffe; William Morris; Lewis Carroll; CS Lewis; JRR Tolkien; Richard Dawkins; Bill Clinton; Tony Blair. If Max Zeall had been present he would have to have fought the inclination to rip several of them down given the true nature of the characters concerned, in stark contrast to the finely-polished PR spin that most accepted without question.

But he wasn't. Establishment Pomp and pageantry and Max did not get along.

Lining the opposite wall were portraits of previous Oxford Mayors dating back to the 1600s. From the 1960s onwards, the paintings had been replaced with photographs. Eugene Nicks' took pride of place on the far left of the row.

Nicks' mayoral trinkets jangled as he ascended the three steps. He felt the weight of the gold-chained medallion, engraved with the emblem of a fox, on the back of his neck, and silently cursed the obligatory regalia. His long, red velvet robe with gold plaited collars bore a sewn-on badge with the same fox sigil discreetly placed at chest level to the left. Underneath, Nicks wore the same checked shirt and jeans he'd had on earlier that afternoon while tending his allotment.

While the rest of the world was recoiling from the shock of the news, Nicks did not share their surprise. His heads-up had come some weeks before.

Nicks tapped the Shure SM-58 microphone and, satisfied it was working, cleared his throat and began to speak.

"Ladies and gentlemen, boys and girls. Thanks you for attending this emergency meeting. By now we'll all have heard the terrible news coming out of America. There is, of course, very little that I can do from here in Oxford to offer any immediate assistance.

"Really, the value of this meeting is for us all to show some fellowship. Times of great distress remind us of how we need one another more than we might imagine.

"Today is no normal day. We'll all remember where we were on 11th September 2001 for the rest of our lives. And this day will remind us that terror attacks can happen at any place, at any time. There are in the world, many who wish to do great harm to others, who will go to unfathomable extremes to achieve their goals. And they come as wolves in sheep's clothing. Those who wish to do great harm operate under cover, and it's often the ones you least suspect."

There was slight nervous shuffling to be heard from the crowd. A scan of the facial expressions would have revealed sadness, confusion, panic and helplessness among the emotions on obvious display. All derivatives of the emotional state of fear. Those who had heeded the call had come to the meeting to reap some comfort from two of the city's most trusted figures.

Some close scrutiny of Nicks' words might have given some cause for concern—had any of the crowd been of the mind to examine them. While they had sought comfort, Nicks had merely reinforced their fears with his cryptic reminder that dastardly terrorists could be walking among them.

As Nicks finished his brief address, his final task was to give a sycophantic introduction to Fabian Lucas, the Bishop of Oxford, nominally the most senior figure within the city's Theologian community. The crowd clapped gingerly as Nicks descended from the lectern and gave a distinctive handshake to Lucas, before he himself climbed down.

Lucas' full-length robes were black, finished off with a dog collar, a small square of white sitting right at the point of his throat chakra, symbolising the purity of what he would speak. Not that any in the audience would have noticed it, but sewn into his robe at the exact same position that Nicks had his, was a badge bearing the sigil of a fox.

***

The press conference had finished by 6.15. If any in the audience had not been numbed by the trauma of the day, and instead been paying conscious attention to the content, they would have noted that it consisted solely of empty platitudes and PR-friendly soundbites. The Mayor had talked of togetherness, the Bishop of forgiveness.

As the attendees slowly shuffled through the large oak doors on to St. Aldates, Nicks and Lucas were joined by four walking clichés—men in black suits and sunglasses, looking like hybrid characters from 'Men In Black,' 'The Blues Brothers' and 'Reservoir Dogs.' Each was fitted with an earpiece extending round their jawline with tiny microphones on the end. They quietly muttered instructions and acknowledgements to each other as they guided the two VIPs through the plushly-appointed chambers to the rear of the main room, through another door into a red-carpeted corridor, and through a back door into a courtyard.

Here were parked two 2001-model Mercedes S-Classes, the black paintwork and chrome wheels and bumpers gleaming from the thorough valeting they had just received. As the rear doors were opened for them, Nicks climbed into one and Lucas into the other, sinking down into the luxurious leather seats as the doors were closed carefully behind them.

One Man In Black took the driver's seat in each car, while the other sat beside him, each muttering into their microphone sets throughout. While both passengers could easily have travelled in one car, this was always the protocol for those of their status. Two targets are harder to take out than one.

Nicks' driver fished in his jacket pocket for a small device, aimed it at the solid wooden gate to the courtyard, and clicked. As he did so the gate trundled slowly to the left. Each car passed carefully through, making an immediate right turn into a narrow alley with high concrete walls. The first driver drew a scornful look from beneath the dark glasses of his colleague as he narrowly missed scraping the S-Class's nearside bumper against the corner, the black paint deposits on the stone indicating that others had not been so precise.

Two right turns later, both cars had emerged into Blue Boar Street. From there, the only option was a right turn on to St Aldates, navigating the Town hall attendees who were still mingling in the area, then a right down Oxford's historic High Street.

Though measures were in place to limit traffic in this part of the city to buses and public transport only, with surveillance cameras installed to identify offending motorists and issue them with fines, the drivers proceeded along the route without concern. Nicks had signed off on this very scheme and knew that the cameras would be picking up their licence plates and liaising remotely with the DVLA database in Swansea, but that the moment the cars' details got flashed up on screen, it would show their diplomatic status.

There were none of the concerns on the minds of regular motorists, either, as the Mercedes', having gathered speed as they emerged into St. Clements and Headington Hill, blazed past each and every yellow-painted speed camera they encountered. Similarly, any tickets which might have been automatically generated, would be annulled when it came to processing.

The two drivers' final flouting of Oxford's Admiralty Law Acts and Statutes was to weave in and out of bus lanes whenever it pleased them to do so. Not that there was much need. The Headington crossroads was unusually devoid of traffic for a weekday rush hour, many too disturbed by the events that continued to unfold on the news to face going about their regular business, or too hypnotised by the images being flashed out of their television sets, like deers caught in headlights, to be able to pull themselves away.

Once over the Headington roundabout the two cars continued to head East, taking the A40, and eventually the M40 in the direction of London. They were at Junction 3 in a fraction of the time it would ordinarily have taken. As their journey continued, it took them through Stokenchurch, past Beacon's Bottom and Piddington, and eventually to West Wycombe. The gravel crunched under the strong tyres as they pulled up on to the side of Church Road and the cars came to a rest.

Inside each vehicle, the occupants checked their watches. 6.47pm. Over half an hour before sunset. All patiently waited for the phenomenon. Flanked by bunches of intimidating grey clouds, the sky began glowing an ominous, almost portentous pink back towards Oxford in the West as, to the East, the shades of blue got gradually darker. By 7.30pm, Nicks decided it was time.

He swung open the rear nearside door of his Merc as the MIB in the front hurried to assist him. Lucas followed suit. They straightened and brushed down their robes as they surveyed the sight in front of them.

They had arrived at the caves of West Wycombe, known colloquially as the Hellfire Caves. The outline of a church structure in the Gothic fashion faced them, the trees behind it appearing as a solid black clump against the rapidly darkening sky.

The warren of caverns which lay below it had been dug in the mid 1700s for Francis Dashwood—statesman, 1st Baronet—a title inherited from his father when he was only 15—Freemason and, though nominally 'Christian protestant,' a dark occultist. These had become the head-quarters for what Dashwood had termed his "Hellfire Club," based upon an earlier institution founded by the Duke of Wharton, and positioned close to the Dashwood family estate in Wycombe.

Dashwood's version was intended as an "elite" secret society, officially founded on the Pagan occult date of '*Walpurgis Nacht*' on 30th April 1752 at nearby Medmenham Abbey, concerned with parodying religions and mystery-schools founded upon arcane knowledge, by instead embracing and encouraging hedonism and debauchery among its members. These, as well as prom-inent 18th-century British politicians, socialites, writers and theologians, had included, on occasion, American president Benjamin Franklin. The motto '*Fais ce que tu voudra*s,' translating roughly as '*Do What Thou Wilt*' had been placed above a stained-glass doorway long before it became adopted as the slogan of Aleister Crowley's Thelema tradition.

Nicks and Lucas exchanged glances as, after taking in what they perceived to be the majesty of the sight before them, they moved towards the church, flanked by their security detail, still finding something to mutter into their headsets. Once inside the stone vestibule they were greeted by two stewards, and proceeded to remove their respective occupational robes, to pass them to the stewards to be hung on wall hooks, and to replace them with the new robes they had been handed. These consisted of a full-length black under-layer, with a blood-red silk cloak draped over the top.

Once robed up, Lucas and Nicks were led by the stewards into the opening to the bowels of the caves. They descended slowly, the smell of damp filling their nostrils. The caverns were illuminated only by candles placed into wall-mounted holders every few feet. An ariel view of the complex, as well as showing occasional similarities with the tunnel layout of the Great Pyramid of Giza, would have shown it forming various geometric shapes as the walkway veered first to the left, through a circle to the point known as Franklin's Cave, into a chamber known as The Skull, then through the Triangle, the Miner's Cave and the Nun's Cave.

Last was a creation in which Dashwood had revelled—a symbolic crossing of the River Styx, the place which, in Greek mythology, separated the earthly realm from that of the Underworld. In the dim candlelight, Nicks and Lucas exchanged smirks. Pausing briefly, and drawing in deep breaths of the dank, earthy air, they strode forward, symbolically crossing the Styx. Once they had, the narrow cavern walls opened out into the last of the chambers, this one circular and domed. By now they were burrowed well within the chalk of the Chiltern hills, and directly above them was what Dashwood had dubbed his 'Mausoleum,' a morbid pastiche of a Christian church. Here, was The Inner Temple.

Lucas and Nicks moved further into the chamber. They were far from alone. Already assembled in two concentric semi-circles, were seventeen additional figures dressed in identical black and red robes. All wore face masks in the Venetian carnival tradition. All clutched steel goblets.

If the characters had all been standing unmasked, an observer would have noted among them the new Chief

Superintendent of Thames Valley Police CID, its newest Detective Chief Inspector, Sam Haine, the managing directors of radio station Lux FM and the *'Oxford Gazette'* newspaper, the Field Marshal from Dalton army barracks in Abingdon, and two prominent judges.

Lucas pulled on the mask he had been holding since he had been handed his robe and joined the left of the front row. This left Nicks as the only unmasked member of the congregation. He walked towards the simple wooden lectern, liberated from the church above decades ago. A thick red candle, caked in melted wax, was mounted on the wall behind. Though the flame was orange, the lectern seemed to be bathed in a distinctly crimson glow.

Nicks cleared his throat and surveyed the sea of macabre masks that stared back at him from the candlelit chamber.

"Gentlemen. *Melius quam deus.*

"Today is a fine day. Today is one for which so many of us have waited so very long. Many of us may have thought that we would never live to see it come. Certainly, those in the Hellfire Club who met in this very chamber so long ago, would have been envious of what we today have been privileged to witness.

"And yet, though the accomplishments made today by our brothers have been magnificent and world-changing, we here have yet to witness *our* finest moment. The time when *we* get to announce to the world that *we* are the masters of our *own* New World Order. That *we* are masters of *our* own destiny, and that *we* can give the world a spectacle every bit as attention-grabbing as those seen today.

"We've all been so very patient. We need only be patient a short while longer. Soon, our time will have come.

"Til then, let us drink to the newest and greatest incarnation of The Order. 11th September 2001, one human

36

gestation period following the symbolic re-birth of the sun on 25th December, is *our* day one."

Nicks put gravitas into his voice as he grabbed his own goblet from the shelf of the lectern, raised it to the air with his left hand, and shouted.

"To The Order!"

CHAPTER 4

Thursday 13th September 2001

"The whole secret lies in confusing the enemy so he cannot fathom our real intent"

Sun Tzu: 'The Art of War.'

"Dani . . . Dani . . . DANI!"

The voice grew louder and more exasperated with each shout until, accepting defeat, it turned into a muttering, as the middle-aged woman began to ascend the narrow stairway. She navigated the handrail, draped with towels and assorted undergarments, with her right hand. In her left she held a dinner tray, on it a steaming bowl of freshly-made spaghetti bolognese and a glass of apple juice.

Reaching the top of the stairs she stopped outside the shabbily-painted white door to the immediate right. Placing it down on the worn, dour, mixed-colour carpet, she rapped three times on the door.

"Dani! Food! I just made it it fresh. *Do not* waste it!"

Her tone took on an air of authority. The woman paused.

"Did you hear?"

There was a mumble which sounded something like an affirmation. The woman knew it was the best she was going to get. She shrugged her shoulders and started back down the stairway.

Most would have concluded from the scene on the other side of the door that it was the bedroom of a student. All clichés were present. Under and around the bed were assorted plates and dishes of food in various stages of consumption. Socks littered the carpet, and it would have been an exercise in futility to try and match any of them into a pair.

The lounge chair at the end of the bed was piled high with clothes in a state of disarray, many of them pulled inside-out and carelessly discarded. The bed itself, the duvet pulled fully back, housed a cereal bowl with a few cornflakes floating forlornly in a puddle of milk, and three books—'*Fingerprints of the Gods*' by Graham Hancock, '*The Bible Code*' by Michael Drosnin, and '*Uriel's Machine*' by Christopher Knight and Robert Lomas.

Around the bed, attached to the wall with Blu-Tack, were various movie posters. Taking pride of place above the headboard was a limited-edition Japanese release for the '*Matrix*' movie of two years previous. Up front was Keanu Reeves' Neo character, as on the regular release, flanked by Morpheus and the others. The text was in Japanese. This wasn't the only difference from the regular poster, however. Instead of the usual generic background, this one had the green zeroes and ones of the plot's key binary code set against a black backdrop.

Lining the blue painted wall to the left of the bed was Kate Winslet's face on the official poster for '*Enigma*,' the film released a few months earlier to chart the cracking of secret German World War 2 codes by a team working out of Bletchley Park, along with one for Darren Aronofsky's disturbing '*Pi*' from 1998, simply featuring the mathematical symbol in red, set against a single eye in mono.

The remaining furniture in the room included an old pine wardrobe, overloaded with coats and blankets to the point that they were spilling out of the doors, and a slim writing desk, assembled from flatpack only a few months earlier but already showing signs of wear, the MBF wood chipping at each joint. Predictably, the desk was cluttered and disorderly, with piles of papers, leaflets, ring-binders and clip files spread about chaotically. Various hastily-scribbled Post-It notes had been slapped on the wall in front of it, along with other bits of paper secured with Sellotape. The wall bore the evidence of others having been hastily ripped away, taking chunks of paint with them.

Whatever space remained on the desk was occupied by a 1998 Apple iMac G3, an all-in-one unit with the computer's hard disk housed inside the same casing as the 14-inch monitor, making for a chunky and unfeasibly heavy machine. The cheap desk groaned daily under its weight, and it was surely only a matter of time before it surrendered fully to it.

For now though, there it sat, and tapping away feverishly at its external keypad, squinting through her National Health reading glasses at what she had written on the screen, was the room's occupant, 21-year-old Daniela Lesley Mots.

She had graduated from Oxford's Brookes University earlier that summer with degrees in psychology and mathematics. Although diagnosed at age twelve with high-functioning Autism—or what at the time was still referred to as 'Aspergers' Syndrome'—this had not hindered her academic abilities. Rather, her compulsion towards retaining detail with an almost photographic memory had seen her fast-track her way ahead of other students on each of her courses. She felt an almost supernatural affinity with numbers, and particularly the transcendental code of Pi—hence her interest in the Aronofsky movie—and could memorise it on cue to 25 digits.

To the right of the desk was an unlikely sight. The last item of furniture was a three-shelved pine bookcase, in which well over a hundred books, all covering metaphysical, mystical or spiritual topics, were arranged alphabetically by author name. Each title had also been given its own catalogue number, printed on to plastic Dymo tape and applied neatly to the top of each spine. Dani had what doctors had described as "selective OCD." Though untidy by nature, she showed intense insistence upon order when it came to certain aspects of her life. She would often place more importance on fine minutiae, than on what she considered "trivial" activities like eating.

Her condition had led to social awkwardness since her early teens, and she had struggled through her subsequent difficult years with few friends. At Uni, her peers had always considered her strange, never imagining that her eccentricities might be down to a condition, and while they would spend their Friday and Saturday nights partying at the Park End Club or The Coven, never caring to invite her, she would settle under her duvet and devour whatever books she had managed to procure that week, usually polishing off at least four in a weekend.

Oddly—at least as far as her fellow students were concerned—she had refused to wear the traditional black cape and mortar board hat for her celebratory photograph. They recalled her mentioning something about the hat representing a black cube and being connected to Saturn and death cults, or something of that outlandish nature.

On a narrow shelf positioned a foot and a half above the desk, sat a radio cassette player. The tuner was set to

99.9FM, from which Lux FM was back to broadcasting its "Better Mix of Music" following two days of solemn and dutiful reporting of events in the United States. The volume was set low. While she mainly concentrated on the content of her iMac screen, Dani gave a small percentage of her consciousness to acknowledging the output—there was U2's 'Beautiful Day' following plays for Tears For Fears' *Mad World* and John Farnham's *'You're The Voice.'*

She glanced at the time in the top-right corner of the screen. 20.57. Not long to go. Would it happen again? If it did she was ready.

Her mind seemed to compute the subsequent minutes in double time. The Lux news bulletin at the top of the hour sped through its now-familiar rhetoric of framing the American terror attacks as the work of 19 Arab hijackers armed with box-cutters led by their ringleader, Mohammed Atta, and part of a "Jihad" organised by the "terrorist group" Al-Qaeda.

Dani scoffed at their constant neglecting to mention that this was in fact a group put together by rogue elements of the CIA, with its chief, bin-Laden, having previously been an agency asset with the codename of Tim Osman, and a close personal friend of US President George W. Bush—and that the Bushes had been dining with members of the bin-Laden family the night before the attacks. The research that her relentlessly enquiring mind had been able to conduct on her iMac—despite the high cost and severe restrictions on bandwidth brought by the Dial-Up internet connection—had opened her up to a whole new worldview that she didn't stand a chance of hearing represented by any mainstream source.

The news was followed by Michael Jackson's *'HIStory.'* The clock registered 21.05. Leonard Cohen's *'The Future,'* with its doom-laden lyrical content, was next. As it drew to a close, Dani stood up and pressed play and record on the cassette machine. The spools on the TDK CD-ing tape whirred into action. As the song faded out, the Lux FM ID tag gave way to an ad break. Since when did this station take an ad break at 11 minutes past the hour? Dani had already asked the question multiple times.

Ads followed for Staples' office superstore, the 'Thirsty Thursdays' student night at The Park End Club, and the new Cowley Road gym. Dani stood in anticipation.

And—as she had predicted—there it was again. The cassette spools slowly rolled as they collected the evidence and printed it for posterity on to the magnetic tape.

But what the hell did it mean?

***

"That's me in the corner, that's me in the spotlight,
  Losin' my religion.
  Tryin' to keep up with you."
REM: 'Losing My Religion'
It was the same as it ever was.

There was a stone, spiral staircase which wound steeply to the right. The steps were thin and the way was narrow. It was tough going, yet she knew that she had to get to the top. The prize that awaited more than justified the effort.

She used all the energy she could muster to run as fast as possible up the staircase. But it was one thing after another. She would lose her footing and slip down a few steps, grazing her shins in the process. Or she would keep hitting the walls with her shoulders, the steps being so slim and the angle being so extreme. Why was it always so difficult? Could what lay at the end really be worth it?

What made it worse was the fact that many others had pushed past her as they were eagerly, and with apparent ease, able to navigate the steep climb far better than she could. Among them was her good friend Verity who was already near the top. She couldn't see her, but there was an instinctive knowing that she had steamed ahead of her, just as she had on previous occasions. Where even was this place? She had a vague idea that it might be Carfax Tower.

A gush of tenacity surged through May Pearce. If others could make it, she told herself, she could too. This renewed sense of determination replaced the dejectedness of before.

She knew that only a few places were available at the top. This might be her only chance to ever claim one. She picked up pace as she navigated the steep steps in the dim and dingy light. After twenty or so, she saw another climber, red-faced as he puffed and panted his way up. May took care not to barge into him as she squeezed past and continued her ascent. Winding continually to the right, she came upon and passed another woman, also evidently struggling. But Verity must surely have ascended the staircase and emerged onto to the ramparts and the bright daylight at the top by now.

May's body ached with fatigue as troublesome thoughts, memories and regrets plagued her mind. Why did others find it so easy? Why could she only ever get so far? It wouldn't be long before the bell would chime again and her time would be up. If only it was as easy to get to the top as it had been to descend to the bottom.

There were 33 flights of stairs. Always 33. A knowing came to May that she was getting close now. Just as they had before, the feint strains of Steve Winwood's *'Higher Love'* could now be heard. She knew it would soon give way to Michael McDonald's *'Sweet Freedom'* as if she were listening to a Lux FM 1986 throwback.

She knew that she had done 30 flights now because there, as it always was, was the stone ceiling that blocked further access, except for by way of a heavy wooden trapdoor embedded in the centre. May braced herself for the physical challenge of pushing it up. Mustering all her remaining strength she heaved upwards with her shoulders, gritting her teeth with the struggle. There was a long, creaking groan as the trapdoor gave way, showering May with the dust of ages as she pushed it fully open. She managed to hoist herself up and through to what lay beyond.

As ever, it was three more flights of steps. Just three more and she would be there and it would all be over.

The same thing was happening, though. The steps here were even thinner than down below. Gaining a foothold was even more of a test. Not only that but, as the staircase continued to wind to the right, May found herself being drawn, as if magnetically, to the left. It was all she could manage to prise herself away from the cold stone slabs of the left-hand wall. She was so close to the top, and yet . . . .

It was too late. The ominous sound of a large church bell chimed its doom. May lost her footing and slipped. Falling down. And down. And . . . .

The dark room loomed before her, the only light coming from the red LED figures on the alarm clock to her right. 03.11. The usual sort of time. The panic that would normally have receded upon the realisation that it was "just" a dream instead remained as May, adjusting to her new state of consciousness, grappled again to recognise the significance of the images she had just experienced. She could just make out the location of the tumbler from the red light of the clock, and reached out to grab it and consume a few gulps of water. She realised she was sweating profusely.

There was a slow, cushioned sound as the bedroom door was pushed slowly and carefully open. A silhouette appeared in the doorway, illuminated by the light from the landing—a tall, stocky man with dreadlocks pulled into a ponytail.

"It's OK. I'm awake." May whispered in a croaky voice.

"Again? Why?"

"Had the dream again. Just woke up."

The man sat down on the edge of the bed and began to undress. "I'm sorry, Maysie. Damn. You can't even get any relief when you sleep."

"I know, right?"

May shuffled herself around so she could watch the man finish undressing.

"Anyway, how was it tonight?"

The man was now in a T-shirt and boxer shorts as he pulled back the duvet and climbed into bed alongside May Pearce.

"You already know. Pissed-up bitches asking for Christina Aguilera twenty times and moaning that they were in the toilet when I played it. Rude boys trying to pick fights. College toffs pretending to be hard and asking for 'some West Coast shit.' I seriously can't take much more of this."

There were no more words. As May Pearce closed her eyes and turned to her right, Drew Hunter snuggled up close to her and pressed his nose into the back of her neck, as his arm reached over to caress her breasts.

Within minutes they were asleep.

CHAPTER 5

Friday 14th September 2001

"When the whole world is running towards the cliff, he who is running in the opposite direction appears to have lost his mind."

CS Lewis.

"What the herd hates the most is the one who thinks differently. It is not so much the opinion itself, as the audacity of wanting to think for themselves—something they do not know how to do."

Arthur Schopenhauer.

It had been as much as Keith could manage to have remained sane over the previous 72 hours...if indeed he was sane any more. From minute one of day one, he had been able to recognise the entire debacle of "9/11," as it had become referred to universally by the mainstream media, as the most brazenly audacious false-flag operation imaginable, to help advance the New World Order agenda which he had studied so precisely over the previous decade and a half.

But even with all that he had come to comprehend about the psychopathic nature of the so-called "elite" ruling class that he instinctively knew were really behind it, he could never have conceived of them being so utterly evil to have gone to such extremes. Even worse than that, though, was the fact that they were getting away with it, and that evidently, 99.9 per cent of humanity had swallowed every fearful word which had spewed forth from the treasonous "news" corporations.

Verity had been able to see it too, and—mercifully—he had at least been able to find an oasis of sanity and clarity through her company. While she shared his exasperation, she had proven much more successful in keeping her mood tempered. He knew that she was doing so because she had to—for the sake of limiting the amount of negative energy to which young Hope would be exposed. He admired that expression of the Sacred Feminine Principle of Care that she embodied, and her selfless inclination to put Hope's needs before her own. He suspected, though, that like him, she was burning inside with a rich, passionate mix of emotions ranging from indignation to dread.

Keith was finding that the older he got—he and Verity were both now 35—the quicker he felt righteous rage rising within him. It was a quality which he used to identify in his old friend and mentor Max Zeall, and it had caused him curiosity and—if he were being honest—occasional amusement to see Max ignite in such a way. Now, though, it was within himself, and others weren't always so amused by some of his reactions.

Relations with Joy and Norm had been particularly testing since Tuesday. With the pair having delayed their return to Oxford indefinitely, and insisting on having BBC News 24's rolling reports on morning, noon and night,

Keith and Verity had been subject to unrelenting psychological torture for two days straight.

While Joy had simply sat in shock, frequently shaking her head while clutching her crucifix and muttering 'dear Lord' on loop, Norm had been more animated, interacting with the TV as if he were watching a football match, yet barking out phrases like "when they find that bin-Laden monster they should cut his fucking knackers off!" rather than "get the ball, you idiot!"

At one point Keith had snapped, literally causing Norm's jaw to drop as he had snatched the remote control from his hand, muted the insufferable tones of the BBC script-reciter, and yelled at him, "you don't seriously believe any of this horseshit do you, Norm?" After taking a couple of seconds to regain his perception of the scenario, Norm had fired a predictable riposte at Keith.

"Oh, so they're lying are they? *Every* TV station, *every* radio station and *every* newspaper? They've all got it so wrong? And yet you're the genius that can see through it all and spot all the things they missed? Just remind me what qualifications you have again, Keith, and what it is you do for a living?"

Joy had shaken her head all the more, while Verity had appeared at the doorway, alerted by the commotion.

Norm hadn't finished. He had risen from his armchair—the first time since breakfast by Keith's reckoning—and had faced Keith head-on.

"And what's more, I find your stance wholly disrespectful! How dare you come with your dumb 'conspiracy theories'," (he mimed the air-quotes he had chuckled at from the first '*Austin Powers*' movie as he said the words,) "when people are dead! 3,000 people are dead, Keith! Where's your respect?"

The gauntlet had been thrown down. Keith had been in no mood to pass it up.

"Right, first of all, 'Norm,' have you ever considered the act of applying critical thought to a situation yourself—*ever*—rather than just blindly swallowing what somebody else is telling you is happening, without question? An example. Yesterday BBC News told us, in all seriousness, that amidst the blazing inferno in New York, which reduced two 100-storey structures of steel, concrete and glass, plus everything contained within them—along with two jumbo jets—to piles of smoking ash and rubble within minutes, the *paper* passport of the lead hijacker *just happened* to not only survive unscathed, but to magically float down to the ground and land where it could be conveniently found to identify the culprit."

Norm had spluttered indignantly. Keith hadn't finished.

"Not only that, but do you remember how they told us they knew the hijackers were all part of this 'Muslim terror gang'? We were asked to believe that 'detectives' found alcohol, copies of the Qur'an and the phone numbers of strippers in the motel rooms where they'd been staying. Does that strike you as very likely, given that these were supposed to be fundamentalists hell-bent on a 'Holy War' with the West? Because all good Muslims drink, cavort with strippers and randomly throw copies of the Qur'an around wherever they go, don't they? *Does* that strike you as very likely? Or does it strike you as the demons behind this plot taking us *all* to be useless-eater morons and openly mocking us to our faces?"

More spluttering. But Norm just hadn't been quick enough.

"To your point about it somehow being 'disrespectful' to question whether what we've been getting told is accurate or not, if I were unfortunate enough to have lost a loved one in what's just happened, I would *absolutely* want to know the truth about the circumstances in which they'd died, and if there was an alternative narrative being offered to the one being peddled on the news, I would *absolutely* want to look at it to see if it had validity and if there might in fact be a different guilty party that would need bringing to justice.

"And lastly...sit back down in that chair unless you want me to do the job for you. And while you're about it, just remind me when you were planning on going home? Because from where I'm standing, you, my old mate, have just about outstayed your welcome. So first thing in the morning you can pack your bags and take your old, dumb, mainstream media-believing lard ass back to Oxford where you can sit and feast on fear porn and governmental propaganda to your heart's content. *That's* not how we get down in *this* house."

"Keith! Enough! Out here!"

Verity had been giving him her vexed "black girl" look. He'd known it would be coming, as any slight against Norm would be taken as a slight against her mother. Verity had reminded Keith that this decision was not his to make, and that the encounter had clearly upset not only Joy, but also Hope.

The pair had considered that some time away from the house would do them some good.

***

The encounter replaying in his mind, Keith resigned himself to making the best of the day that he could as, a few steps ahead of him, Verity and Hope, hand in hand, led the way to the grocery store in Newquay's East Street.

Something's gone *very* wrong with your life when a trip to the local Co-op has become the highlight of your day, he reflected.

Some minutes later, Verity had gathered together the few items they'd needed into a basket, as Keith had taken charge of Hope. As they joined the queue at the single till, the conversation between the two locals directly in front, both sounding like the comedian Jethro—Oxford's perceived "country bumpkin" accent magnified tenfold—made sure all around them heard what they had to say.

"Nearly fuckin' shat myself on the bus 'ere today," said the elder of the two through a mouthful of bad teeth. "I'm sat there reading all about what them bastards did in America when one one gets on. Bold as brass he was. Whole bus froze. He walked right towards me and I was convinced the bastard was gonna shout '*Allahu Akbar*,' pull a cord under his jacket and blow the whole fuckin' bus sky high."

"Can you believe the nerve," countered his slightly younger, but equally yokel ish companion. "You'd think he'd be too ashamed to show his face."

"Probably left a bloody Qu'ran behind on the bus seat too."

The pair's light chuckles abruptly ceased when they became alerted to a new customer, a tall Indian with a long black beard and sporting an orange turban, who had entered the shop.

The younger of the yokels couldn't resist.

"You've gotta be kidding me. 'Ere, Abdul!"

The Indian turned his head in bewilderment.

"You've got a bloody nerve showing your face after what you lot have just done! Honest, decent folk just going about their business, not expecting to be ... "

In an instant, the words gave way to the sound of knuckles hitting skin with great impact. The yokel lurched backwards, grabbing on to his companion for stability. The shoppers around them gasped and jumped aside as both figures crashed to the floor.

The yokel who had been hit instinctively gripped his face as the pain began to surge, and tried to process what had just happened.

Towering above him was the figure of Keith Malcolm, his face red with exertion and his right fist throbbing. "You lot? *You lot?*" he spat venomously. "That man's a fucking Sikh! Different culture. Different religion. Different ethnic group. Different part of the world, you fucking inbred moron!"

In different circumstances, with time to have prepared, the yokel would have been on his feet and coming right back at Keith in retribution. But he hadn't seen this one coming.

The Sikh had already left the shop. Keith's involvement in the fracas was cut short by Verity's intervention.

"Keith!" she snapped sternly. "The Non-Aggression Principle?"

"This man instigated the situation with his supreme *ignorance!*" Keith glared down at the still-writhing figure as he barked out the last word.

"Also," Verity added, "your daughter?"

Standing knee-high to Verity's right was Hope, looking confused and afraid.

"Daddy, why did you hit that man?" she asked with wide, innocent eyes.

A tsunami of sober clarity swept over Keith.

"I'm sorry, sweetheart," he said, peering down at his daughter's tender face. "Daddy shouldn't have done that. It was wrong."

Then, turning to Verity.

"V, we need to get out of here. We need to go."

"You're damned right we do, Keith. This place will be crawling with cops any minute."

"No, I mean, we have to get out of *here*. Of this place. I feel like I'm losing my mind. I can't breathe."

The gaze of all in the shop followed them as Verity, Keith and Hope made for the door and hastened their way back along the street to their car.

CHAPTER 6

Monday 17th September 2001

"The word is about, there's something evolving.
Whatever may come, the world keeps revolving.
They say the next big thing is here,
That the revolution's near.
But to me it seems quite clear,
That's it's all just a little bit of history repeating."

Propellerheads Featuring Shirley Bassey: 'History Repeating.'

"I've been a journalist for 25 years. I was taught to lie, betray and never tell the truth to the public. I was paid by the CIA, secret societies and American billionaires. Journalists are used to manipulate the people."

Udo Ulfkotte, Editor of a leading European newspaper. (He died of a "sudden heart attack" in 2017 shortly after making this statement.)

"God's a comedian telling jokes to an audience too afraid to laugh"

H.L. Menchen

"Hey listen, thanks for all the great work you do, Max. History will judge us all on what we did in these times."

"It certainly will, brother. Thanks again for the call. That one's definitely worth an OAK."

Max Zeall signalled across the desk to Shamim to pause taking calls by slicing the four fingers of his right hand across his throat. Keeping his microphone fader open, he pulled down the fader to the Telecaster unit and reached out towards the right-hand CD player while speaking into the mic. Shamim watched with curiosity at his juggling of so many tasks.

"Some great comments from your calls tonight, people. Remember, we have a special extension of an hour in order to accommodate them all, so stay with us until 1am. A quick music break now while we regroup, and we'll be right back with more of your calls. Remember the number—01865 432432."

Max's finger hit the play button on the CD machine and the opening tones to Bob Marley's '*Get Up, Stand Up*' came in. He pulled the mic fader down.

"Hey, what's an OAK?" Shamim called from across the desk.

"What?" asked Max, turning down the volume on the studio monitors.

"What's an OAK?" Shamim repeated.

"It's an acronym for Occult Arcane Knowledge. It's a compilation of many of the resources I've used for my research over the past eight years—documents, articles, electronic books, pictures, short videos, web links. I copy them all on to a CD-ROM and mail them out to anyone who requests them ... or anyone I think will listen."

Max had known that tonight's show would bring a record number of call-ins, and he hadn't been wrong. Though he normally prided himself on doing everything alone, on this occasion he knew that the show would run far more efficiently with some assistance, so had asked Shamim to come down to the shed to sit with him for the four hours, and had given him the quickest of crash courses in how to handle the telecaster unit. This one, it turned out, had previously been used for call-ins to Lux FM.

He had been particularly keen that this show should be preserved as a historical document of the era, and had checked several times that both the DAT machine and the cassette player he was using to run off a monitor tape were recording efficiently. It was his plan to put his desktop iMac to use in the week ahead, in converting the recording into video format, with the addition of some key graphics, and to burn to CD-ROM.

The red lights on the Telecaster were illuminated like a Christmas tree.

"Calls still piling up," advised Shamim, proud to have been commended by Max for doing a great job on handling the board so far—along with providing a great curry earlier on.

"Right. After Bob Marley we'll do another 20 minutes of calls. Then, find the CD and track number for Manic Street Preachers '*If You Tolerate This*' from this lot. Max handed Shamim a pile of a dozen or so CDs.

Shamim started sifting through the jewel cases, but ceased when Max indicated that he was about to put the microphone live again. The Marley tune had been deceptively short. Many had been kind enough to comment to Max that he had a natural voice for radio. He reflected on this as he began to speak.

"We're back with your calls on this most monumental of weeks." And, with a wave of his hand towards Shamim, "caller, you're through to '*At Last The 1984 Show.*' What's your name and where are you calling from?"

"Hey Max, it's Denroy in the Leys."

"Hey Denroy. Good to hear from you again. What's on your mind?"

"Yo, a few things on my mind that I wanted to share with you and the listeners, my bredren. First off, you remember that speech from George Bush Sr. where he talked of an incoming 'New World Order'?"

"I do indeed. On September 11th, 1990."

"Ah, damn. You beat me to it. That's right. 11 years to the day before the fuckeries of last week, right? A lot of symbolism around the number 11. The twin towers resembled an 11. In Freemasonry it's recognised as a master number—the end of one cycle and the beginning of the next. That's why the armistice for the First World War was on 11/11 at 11am. Three elevens equals 33. They even encoded the Armistice date into the registration plate of the car that Archduke Ferdinand was riding in when he was assassinated, by the way—AIIII18. Decoded as 'Armistice 11/11/18.' These fuckers are so devious and so all-pervasive that they already knew at the start of that event how and when it was going to end, because they controlled it every step of the way. That's truth. And it's elevens all the way.

"Bush is a 33rd-degree Freemason. I'm talking about Poppy Bush, not that bloodclaat village idiot bwoy dem put in the White House ready for all this foolishness. Bush was in Dallas on the day of the JFK assassination—22/11/63, and was involved in ordering the hit. 22 + 11 equals 33. 33s everywhere. Also, construction of those towers started in 1968—33 years before they were brought to the ground in an occult Freemasonic ritual last Tuesday."

Max nodded, impressed with the knowledge of this most regular of callers. "That's right, that's right," he added simply.

"Same way Stanley Kubrick's '*2001: A Space Odyssey*' was released in '68—33 years ahead of the time that its story was prophesying, of all the years it could have been. Kubrick's also a Mason, as is the co-writer of that film, Arthur C. Clarke.

"You know what else? I'm looking at the image of a front cover of '*Newsweek*' magazine from 1967, and that satanic demon David Rockefeller's pictured on the cover. You know he was the major funder of those towers being constructed, right? Why wouldn't he be when that family have been involved in every aspect of the degradation and debasement of human society for the past 100 years? Anyway, in this picture Rockefeller's wearing a wristwatch. And guess what figures the hands on that watch are set to?"

"The 9 and the 11?"

"You're damn skippy. What are the chances of that being by random chance, star?"

"Not a whole lot."

"Right. Guess which day in 1967 this picture appeared? The 93rd. You know, whenever Aleister Crowley wrote an important piece he started with the header '93' to signal that a major message was to follow, and the footnote he wrote was '9393,' like a kind of over-and-out. In Kabbalistic Gematria, '*Thelema*' equates to the number 93.

"And the motherfucker was in his Manhattan penthouse last Tuesday with a ringside view of his masterplan finally coming to pass. Must have given him and all his other New World Order pals a wet dream."

"Just like Klaus Schwab," contributed Max, keen not to be upstaged by his caller, "having breakfast with Rabbi Arthur Schneier at his synagogue."

"Who dat now?" replied Denroy, as Max had hoped he would.

"Head honcho of the World Economic Forum since 1970. They're another of these Non-Governmental Organisations who wield incredible power over governments, like the Bilderberg Group, the Council on Foreign Relations—which Rockefeller founded, incidentally—the Trilateral Commission and all the rest. They've largely operated in the shadows up to now, but I've a feeling they're really going to show their hand in the years to come."

"Seen, seen," said Denroy, before setting off again.

"Anyway, more 'lucky coincidences.' You know when the most recent lease of the World Trade Center was granted?"

It was a rhetorical question as Denroy left no room for a response.

"24th July. Seven weeks ago. It was taken out by Larry Silverstein, known to his friends as Larry the Cockroach, and a company named Westfield America, operated by a Frank Lowy. Both Jewish, like Rockefeller. Well, I call him 'lucky Larry,' 'cause he has to be one of the luckiest motherfuckers in history. He insured those towers to the tune of several billion just a few weeks ago. Then—would you believe it?—they *just happen* to get completely destroyed a few weeks later, netting a very happy payday for Lucky Larry. I mean, this is the kind of motherfucker you'd want to go and spend a weekend on the tables in Vegas with, right?"

"If only there were any flights running," remarked Max, drolly.

"Right, right?" Denroy continued.

"There's more. How about The Pentagon? Did you know that the section that was hit *just happened* to be undergoing refurbishment, meaning there was no-one working there at the time? And it was hit by a plane? Was it *mi raas*! That was a military-grade missile, star. Not the kind of thing some dumb, clueless 'Muslim terrorists' with box cutters could get hold of. Directed by a man in a cave who needed a dialysis machine to keep living! How the fuck do you think you can get a hospital-grade dialysis machine way up into the mountains of Tora Bora? Who's even asking these questions?"

Max smiled a rare smirk at the reference to bin-Laden. Shamim wondered what he could be finding amusing, not realising that Max and bin-Laden had both been born on the very same date—10th March 1957. The Universe is not without its sense of irony, Max had reflected. It had delivered two men with characteristic beards, both passionately devoted to their causes, on the same day. Here they both were, at 44 years of age, diametrically-opposed in their value systems.

Denroy was on a roll.

"Convenient also that no 'security' footage of the hit exists too, don't you think? The cameras that were supposed to be trained on the building *just happened* to be owned by a Jewish 'security' company and *just happened* to not be functioning at the time in human history when their evidence was needed more than at any other."

As Max spoke he considered how, if this were a "legal" station monitored by the UK government's Radio Authority, his show would have been axed long before this one had had a chance to go to air. This only made him prouder of what he had created for this pirate outlet. Though he had been frustrated by the pitiful number of callers most of his previous outings had attracted, the massive number trying to get through this evening reassured him that this was a platform whose time had truly come.

It was just unfathomably tragic that evil and darkness had been allowed to take such a hold as it had during the past week, unmolested. But if that was what was needed to give the wake-up call to humanity that—just maybe—would now take hold and see true cosmic justice put into effect—in some twisted way, maybe it could be considered to have been worth it.

Denroy had one more observation to contribute.

"Hey listen. Just in case anyone's still not fully convinced that this was an inside job fit-up, how about this? Did you know a 'security drill' was being conducted on the very morning of those events, in which the very attacks on the same targets were being simulated? To the point that emergency responders at NORAD, when the drill went live, were uncertain of whether they were still dealing with a hypothetical scenario, or whether it had become 'real world'? There's some dude from NORAD recorded asking just that! I mean—*hello???*"

Max winced at the increased volume of Denroy's voice in his headphones.

"Really, people? What are the mathematical odds of that being a 'coincidence'? What? Several trillion to one? And we're letting them get *away* with this? What the *bloodclaat?!*"

As Denroy took a rare natural pause, Max interjected.

"Minds blown, my brother. Minds blown tonight. Tell me, where do you get access to all this information?"

"Same way anyone else can so long as they have an internet connection and the will to do it, Max. It's all right there on the 'net, man. I'm telling you, this is the resource that has the power to free humanity from the slavery of ages. Babylon invented it to control us—to gather data and surveil our every move. And they plan to push us towards running every aspect of our lives on-line in the coming years.

"But this is a world of duality where the opposite of everything is possible. That's the Hermetic Principle of Polarity, right? Everything has a polar opposite. So the internet *can* enslave us ... if we let it. But it can also free us in enabling us to share information widely that has been hidden from we 'profane' ones for millennia.

"And the truth can set us free. So it can be a gift, or it can be a curse."

Max picked up the philosophical baton.

"That's right. Taking the 'red pill' is one of the most painful and life-altering experiences. Humans naturally seek comfort over discomfort, pleasure over pain, and, sadly, ignorance over knowledge. Our brains and bodies prefer the easy path every time. But our souls demand something more."

Denroy was back again.

"Damn straight. We all have moments of weakness where we doubt our purpose and place in the world. We wish to go back to younger days of nostalgia with few responsibilities. But deep down—if we can be honest—we know we're here for more than just that. That's what Morpheus meant in 'The Matrix' when he said it's like a splinter in your mind."

"Great call, Denroy. Let's take another." Max flashed Shamim another wave of his hand. Shamim didn't catch it. Max reiterated, with more authority in his voice.

"Another call."

Shamim looked up from his well-thumbed copy of '*Asian Babes*' magazine and took his cue, quickly connecting the next caller.

"Caller, you're through to '*At Last The 1984 Show.*' What's your name and where are you calling from?"

"Hello...hello, Max?" The nervous young voice spoke softly.

"Hello. Yes. Please speak up a bit there, caller. Who do we have?"

"My names Daniela...Dani. Calling from Botley."

"Welcome, Dani. What have you got for us?"

There was a slight hesitation. Max and Shamim exchanged puzzled glances.

"I've discovered something. I think it's important. It's hard to explain, but I'd like to show you—to play you—some of the stuff I've discovered. I wouldn't waste your time. I'm a big fan of your work. I'd like to share with you what I've found because I don't know anyone else who would be able to appreciate it. "

"OK, Dani," Max replied. "How would you like to do this?"

"Could I...could I meet with you? I need to play you something, but I don't want to do it on the radio. This was the only way I knew of reaching you."

"OK, Dani. Stay on the line and my assistant will take down your details while we take a quick music break." He snapped his fingers at Shamim.

"I think it's related to everything you've been talking about tonight," said Dani as the opening section of the Manic Street Preachers faded in.

"Only this relates specifically to Oxford."

CHAPTER 7

Monday 6th June 1977

"She had a bad childhood when she was very young,
So don't judge her too badly . . .
And the sins of a family fall on the daughter,
Yeah, the sins of a family fall on the daughter."

Barry Maguire: 'The Sins Of A Family'.

"See, 'cause, if you forget where you come from,
Then you're never gonna make it where you're goin',
Because you lost the reality of yourself.
So take one stroll through your mind,
And see what you will find,
And you'll see your whole universe all over again and again
and again and again and again."

Ghostface Killah Featuring Mary J Blige: 'All That
I Got Is You.'

Charles Street might have been any other Victorian-era terraced street in the nation, with nothing to mark it out as being in East Oxford, but everything to connect it to the scenes being witnessed in every other town in the land. In a show of community spirit not seen since World War 2, the residents had pulled together in an almost military-grade operation to give what they were determined would be the best damned street party in the whole of town.

All cars had been pulled up on to the pavement on both sides of the cross-section with Catherine Street, leaving a central thoroughfare along which rows of tables had been placed end to end. Red, white and blue tablecloths, some plastic, some fabric, had been draped over all of them. Each table place was equipped with a paper plate, white plastic cutlery and a paper cup. Large jugs of orange and lemon squash sat in the centre, amidst plates of party snacks—sandwiches, cocktail sausages, sausage rolls, cheese and pineapple on sticks, crisps, peanuts, and Custard Cream, Bourbon and Iced Shortie biscuits. Glass bowls of trifle, Jelly Whip and Angel Delight sat between the jugs.

Sat at each of the table places, most already tucking into the feast in front of them, was one of the children from the neighbourhood. Their ages ranging from four to fourteen, most wore outfits consisting of red, white and blue. The girls were in dresses, the boys in shirts and hats. They exuded a collective sense of excitement at seeing their normally drab and humdrum home territory having been transformed into such a vibrant mix of colour, sound and activity—not to mention the thrill of having been granted an extra day off school.

As the neighbourhood mums had collaborated on the catering, the dads had come together in solidarity to erect the many strings of Union Jack flags which were hung, a few feet up, from one side of the street to the other. There had been much sharing of ladders, hammers and other tools, and each family had considered their house—along with everybody else's—to be free-range, as the dads wandered into each front garden as required. Many of the men worked shirtless, such was the warmth of the day.

The forces of nature were smiling upon Queen Elizabeth II's Silver Jubilee celebrations, it seemed.

This apparent show of benevolence from the Universe was not, however, extended to one household in the midst of the happy throng.

The facade of number nine was pretty much the same as any of the others in this most uniform of streets. There was the navy blue door with the brass knocker centre-top, the small bay window to its left, and the two slim windows up above as it sat sandwiched between the neighbouring properties.

The door concealed the drama occurring on its other side. Jubilation this was not.

Had the street outside been quieter, the jarring smash of a flower vase hitting the ornamental wall mirror, causing it to expel shards of glass across the room, might have been heard and acted upon. It was as if Hal Hunter had seized the opportunity offered by the occasion to unleash this outburst of violence upon his wife. This was no rare occurrence, however—especially of late—and no measure of calculated planning was possible under the drunken haze that presently consumed him.

For every jug of squash the children in the street had guzzled, Hal had downed a measure of rum or whiskey—sometimes a combination of the two. He was more than four hours into his orgy of intoxication, and one plea too many from Joy, his wife, had resulted in the nearest available projectile, in this case a vase of daffodils, being hurled towards her. Had she not been swift enough to duck it would have hit her, instead of the mirror, full in the face.

The small, humbly-appointed living room was running short on potential weapons. Hal's previous liquor-soaked rages had seen countless ornaments, ashtrays and drinking glasses fall casualty—as well as the portable radio, two clocks, and Joy's sewing machine. The black-and-white television set that was currently broadcasting a volume-less 'Pebble Mill At One' had somehow escaped destruction.

As Hal slumped down into the room's only armchair, emitting a belch and fart simultaneously—and Joy stood glued to the spot, sobbing—cowering meekly at the door frame was their daughter Verity, fifteen days away from her eleventh birthday. She wore the red, white and blue dress that she and her mother had worked on embroidering over the weekend. Her black frizzy hair was pulled back into a pony tail fastened with a red, white and blue ribbon. Her feet were in white knee-length socks.

She had awoken at six that morning, so excited at the prospect of the street party, and had made the mistake of going into her parents' bedroom—as she did each Christmas morning—and waking them early. This had caused Hal to fly into a fury, sparking a morning's worth of arguments, and culminating in his ambitious alcoholic excursion. She hadn't helped herself by asking what "Sex Pistols" meant after hearing what she knew to be their current hit song 'God Save The Queen' playing from over the garden fence, earning both herself and her mother a sharp slap around the back of the head in the process.

As the trauma of seeing her mother so upset and afraid swept over her, little Verity blamed herself for having caused it to happen.

Through a faceful of tears, Joy suddenly remembered her daughter, and turned to the doorway to meet Verity's distraught gaze. The glass scrunched under Joy's slippers as she took the few steps towards the child. She crouched down to Verity's level and threw her arms around her.

"Don't cry, mama," sobbed Verity as Joy blubbed on her shoulder. "It'll be okay."

Over in the armchair, Hal Hunter emitted a chain of deep sighs as he ran his left hand across his face and up through his receding hairline. He put his hands on the chair arms and used whatever effort he could muster to hoist himself up. He wobbled as he sought to stand up straight. A dark, wet stain had appeared at the front of his beige trousers.

Steadying himself against the mantel shelf with one hand, he fished around in his trouser pocket with the other, eventually producing a crumpled pack of Benson & Hedges cigarettes and a small box of matches. After several attempts to find an unspent match he achieved a lucky strike and lit the cigarette. The orange tip glowed as he puffed it into life and the smell of freshly burning tobacco merged with that of the jerk chicken and rice that Joy had been preparing in the kitchen.

Joy and Verity flinched, then moved aside as Hal lurched towards the door and slurred.

"You shee…you shee what you've made me do? Again? I hate it that you make me do this."

Stumbling through the door into the hall, he made a grab for the keys to his Austin Maxi that hung from a hook on the wall. With a slam of the front door as he headed out into the merriment of the street, he was gone.

It was the last time Verity would ever see her father.

CHAPTER 8

Wednesday 19th September 2001

"Goodnight, my little Hopi."

"Goodnight, Lady V."

As Verity offered her nightly term of endearment to her daughter, she received back a surprise rendering of the name that her man had long reserved for her.

"Oh, Lady V, is it? Someone's been listening to their dad, have they?"

Verity playfully pushed against Hope's nose as the five-year old settled further into her rabbit-themed duvet. Verity put away the story she had just read her—the moral of the tortoise and the hare from a collection of such inspirational stories aimed at slightly older children.

"Now, what do we always say?"

Another nightly ritual got underway as Hope recited the message that had been printed out and Blu-Tacked to the wall above her headboard, along with a picture of a karmic wheel—"don't treat others in a way you would not wish to be treated yourself." Underneath, in blue crayon, Hope had scrawled her own addition—"it's so simple."

As Verity kissed the little girl on her forehead and got up to turn off the light, Hope unexpectedly asked, "Mama?"

"Yes, sweetheart?"

"Are these the End Times?"

Verity smarted at the question. "What? No...Why? Why d'you ask that?"

"I heard one of Daddy's tapes where some man was saying that we'd reached the end of days."

Verity returned to crouch by Hope's bedside.

She whispered with all the convincing reassurance she could muster. "I think he would have meant that we'd reached the end of one point in time and the beginning of another. You know, like when Summer turns into Autumn, as it will very soon now. That's all. Are you worried about what you've been hearing on the news?"

"There are bad men in the world, aren't there, Mama?"

Verity felt a mix of emotions sweep over her—angst, uncertainty—and unconditional love.

"Yes, there are. There are." There was no value in lying.

"But there are way more good people than there are bad. And the bad men are going to discover that. Because me and your dad, and all the other good people in the world—like your Grandma and your Uncle Drew and your Auntie Maysie—are going to make them see that. What happened last week was a test. It was a test of where everyone stands.

"And I promise you, the bad ones will not win. We are going to make sure that your future is a beautiful, bright one where things are going to be so much better for everyone than they are now. And then one day, it'll be your job to make sure that gets carried on to your children."

"Eww! I'm not having kids! Yucky!"

Verity laughed at the surprise retort. "Well...we'll see about that, won't we, young lady? Now, that's enough talking for today. Time to get to sleep." As she headed again towards the light switch she glanced back at the cherubic face of her firstborn, and wondered just where her worldly wisdom came from, since it seemed to way exceed her tender years.

Creaking her way down the narrow staircase and into the dimly-lit living room to where Keith was thumbing through his copy of '*Behold A Pale Horse*', brow firmly furrowed, she remarked, "I swear that girl is an old soul. She knows too much for a five-year-old. She's been here before."

"She'd have been better off staying where she was," replied Keith, only half-joking.

Verity slumped into the armchair adjacent to Keith's vantage point on the two-seater sofa. She was quietly grateful that the three of them had their home to themselves again following the hasty departure of Joy and Norm at the weekend. But not as grateful as Keith.

"What kind of world did we bring her into?" she asked after pausing for a few seconds.

Keith looked up from his pages. "The only one we could have done. We didn't make the world the way it is, V. It's our job to make it better."

"I know that. Oh, by the way, you need to be careful what you let her hear. She made some comment about how the world is full of bad men and that we're in the End Times. Heard it on one of your recordings, evidently."

"Well, she's wise beyond her years, V. You said so yourself. She's just got a head start on others of her age, that's all."

"Well, when you know better you gotta do better, right?"

Keith peered back at the book. Then looked up again with an afterthought.

"You don't really feel we made a mistake bringing her in, do you?"

"No," replied Verity, reclaiming the glass of Merlot that she had temporarily abandoned to put Hope to bed. "But I feel we've made other big mistakes."

"Like what?"

Verity took a couple of warming sips before responding.

"Like moving to this place."

A puzzled expression hit Keith's face. The book had been put down now.

"I thought you liked it here?"

"I adore it in the summer. But face it, Keith, Winters down here are desolate as hell. And is this going to be any kind of place for Hope when she's a teenager and wants to go out and have some fun?"

"Oh, you mean like Illuminati Central?" Keith over-exaggerated the phrase, always his favourite term for his native Oxford.

"Well, whatever else Oxford might be, it's never boring."

Keith considered the comment. "Well, OK, I have to concede. Plenty of other things, but not boring."

"Exactly. And I miss my Oxford friends. I miss May. I miss Max. I miss Drew."

"They've been keen enough to visit in the summers. But nowhere to be seen in the Winters."

"My point," replied Verity, before taking a generous sip as she reflected on the pros and cons of their quiet Cornwall life of the previous five years. Though her role as a self-employed investigative journalist had supported them well—augmented by Keith's far less generously-paid position as a private hire driver, mainly ferrying corporate clients to and from Newquay airport and the train stations of the county's larger towns—either of them could just as easily perform their functions in Oxford. She gazed over towards the father of her child, full of contemplation and memories.

Her misty-eyed musings were interrupted by the piercing tone of the household phone ringing. Keen not to let it wake Hope, Verity was up and on it within seconds.

"Hello? ... Oh, Max. Hello, mate. How's it going? ... Yeah, he's here. Hold on."

Keith had been up and out of his seat at the mention of the name. He took the receiver enthusiastically.

"Max! What's up, man?"

250 miles away. Max Zeall spoke with an assertive tone from his one-bedroom flat in Cowley.

"Keith. I've come across something. It's not wise to go into it on the phone, but to put it bluntly, you're needed. You and V are needed back in Oxford. Something's going down here. I don't know exactly what. That's why i need you. I need V's skills and I need your insights. We've got work to do."

Ten minutes had passed. Keith reiterated the main points of Max's call to Verity.

"There it is, then. This is our calling, Keith. What were we just talking about? There's no place for us down here any more. But there's every reason for us to be back in Oxford.

"This is a calling from the Universe. We're needed."

CHAPTER 9

Tuesday 18th September 2001

Twenty-two hours previous, a tall, bearded figure had passed through the garden gate and up to the front door of a two-bedroom council house in Helen Road, Botley. Not that he had realised it, but he had been watched as he had done so. His observer had looked down nervously from the upstairs bedroom, taking care to stand far enough back that she would not be seen in the evening dusk.

Finding neither a doorbell nor a knob, Max Zeall had rapped vigorously with his knuckles. After a few seconds the door had opened ajar, and a middle-aged woman had peered cautiously through the gap.

Before Max could speak, a voice could be heard in the background. "Mum! It's for me. Leave it!" There was the thunder of feet hurrying down the stairs.

"She'll be with you in just a moment," said Mrs. Mots with a courteous smile.

"No worries," said Max, exchanging the same.

The woman opened the door wider. Her daughter was standing behind her.

"Hi ... Hi, Max." Her smile was just as awkward as her mother's.

"Hi there. Daniela?"

"Yes ... Thanks for coming."

The woman now wore a cheesy grin.

"Mum!" Dani murmured through gritted teeth, flashing her mother an animated glare.

"Oh ... oh, right. Well, I'll be back to the kitchen then. You let me know if you need anything." Max knew that it was code for "you shout if you get into any trouble." What he knew, but the woman obviously didn't, was that any such fears would be unfounded.

The woman disappeared out of the hallway. Satisfied that she had left, Dani said, "come on up."

Max followed the girl up the thinly carpeted stairway. Her national health glasses in place as ever, she was dressed in a lime-green T-shirt under denim dungarees and white socks, her light-brown hair pulled back and tied with a scrunchie.

She turned around suddenly at the threshold to her room. "Err ... excuse the mess. I'm ... uhh ... I've got a, ... uhh, I'm a bit untidy."

"Don't worry about it," said Max politely. "It's your home, not mine."

As Dani invited him in and switched on the light, he surveyed the sight before him. The room was in pretty much the same state as a few days before, give or take a few more socks littering the floor. The only major difference was that now, taking the place of the '*Pi*' film poster, was a wooden-framed corkboard of the type regularly found in police incident rooms, recently purchased from Staples office superstore in Park End Street. Post-It notes of various colours containing scrawls in Sharpie marker pen were being held in place by map pins, many of which were connected to each other by threads of wool liberated from her mother's knitting basket.

"Err .. sit down . . . if you'd like?" offered Dani, beckoning towards her unmade bed.

"Thank you. But I'm fine standing."

As Max discreetly surveyed the room's contents, his eyes fell on the EMac machine, its cooling fan gently whirring away within its bulky white casing.

"I have the same machine. They're great aren't they?" he smiled, pointing with his eyes.

Dani followed his gaze, then, thinking to check the time display on the screen, stated, "we're just in time actually."

It was 8.59pm. Max had arrived a few minutes before their 9pm arrangement.

He watched curiously as she reached towards the radio cassette and switched it on. Lux FM had just begun broadcasting another insufferable bulletin from Independent Radio News, the host dutifully reading out yet more state-sanctioned propaganda. Beyond the lead story about letters containing traces of Anthrax having been mailed to various American news outlets, there was yet more of what by now had become predictable puff about how the Bush regime was "continuing its hunt" for Osama bin-Laden and the Taliban leadership of Afghanistan, whom they believed guilty of harbouring him—along with accounts of the weakening of the US dollar, and the increased security checks that would now be routinely put into place in airports around the world.

"The usual bullshit," Dani instinctively commented, before remembering herself. "Oh, sorry!"

"No, don't apologise," offered Max. "Bullshit is exactly what it is."

"It'll be on soon," said Dani. "If they're following the same pattern."

"So, what are we listening to?" Max asked, feeling to take the weight off his tired feet but not feeling right about sitting on the bed of an obviously nervous stranger half his age.

The news gave way to the usual Lux idents, then Eminem's 'Stan.' To kill time over the next few minutes Dani gushed about what a fan she was of Max's radio show and how instrumental it had been in her making sense of the world: "I realise because of you that the world is sick, insane and unjust because it's been *set up* to be that way. It didn't all just happen by accident, or because human beings are pre-disposed to be cruel and evil to each-other." Max had smiled at the compliment, recognising the words as his own from one of his previous broadcasts.

Dani had been trying to find the way to tell Max about her condition, but there was no need; Max could recognise it within her. He could sense that, beneath all of her social anxiety, there was a good soul. And, truth be told, he found some of her awkward mannerisms to be quite endearing. There was no bullshit with her.

Ian Brown's 'F.E.A.R' was beginning to fade out. Dani surveyed the clock. 9:10 and 50 seconds. "Here we go," she said, firmly pressing down on the play and record buttons on the radio cassette.

"Listen up."

There were the opening chords to Kate Bush's 'Army Dreamers'—just as before—with its gun-cocking click effects, before the smarmy radio-esque voice came in.

"Coming to Oxford soon, an explosive event you'll never forget. Things will never be the same again!"

The voice of Prince from the end of his song 'Alphabet Street' followed as he whispered various letters—"'I . . . A . . . A . . . B . . . A . . . ' Finally, out of nowhere—and out of place—came Will Smith's lyric from DJ Jazzy Jeff & The

Fresh Prince's '*Boom Shake The Room.*' "Tick, tick, tick, tick . . . BOOM!"

As the bizarre sequence ended, the first strains of Robbie Williams' '*Life Thru A Lens*' came in.

Dani turned down the volume knob on the radio. She glanced at Max for a reaction.

"OK," he said. "Well, that was a bit weird."

"What was that even an ad for?" she asked.

"Exactly. I mean, I've heard of 'teaser' campaigns, but they usually give some indication of what's being teased."

"That ad's been running for several days now. And always at the same time, morning and evening. Did you notice?"

"9:11, right?"

"Right!"

They stared at each other for a few seconds. Suddenly feeling the awkwardness, Dani turned to press stop on the radio cassette.

"I hope I didn't waste your time in bringing you here to hear this," she remarked.

"No, not at all. I'm very grateful that you did. This clearly means something. It's just a question of what."

She smiled sweetly. "I didn't know if you'd come. I'm very glad that you did. I had an image of what you'd look like from your voice."

"And . . . do I look like how you'd imagined?"

"No." She let out a slight giggle as she blushed lightly. "Totally different."

"Well," said Max, breaking the awkward silence that followed. "Leave this with me and I'll give it some thought. Maybe speak with a couple of friends of mine."

He headed to the door. Pulling it open, he was started by the presence of Dani's mother on the other side. She quickly straightened her posture.

"Oh . . . hello. I was just .. I was . . . " Then, calling to her daughter, "everything OK, love?"

"That's why Max came here, mum," was the reply. "To make sure it is."

CHAPTER 10

Thursday 20th September 2001

"A man is known by the company he keeps."
Aesop.

"Every day I walk alone,
And I pray that God won't see me."

The Blow Monkeys: 'Digging Your Scene.'

Grey clouds hovered ominously over the dreaming spires of the medieval city as dusk began to set in and choke the last vestiges of daylight away. Outside of St. John's College on St. Giles, two figures sat in the back of their respective black Mercedes' awaiting the full onset of darkness. Once satisfied that the time was right, they exited from either side of the vehicles. The drivers, having been given their pick-up instructions, slinked slowly off towards the fast food takeaways of Jericho.

In matching long black overcoats, the former wearing a fedora, Eugene Nicks and Fabian Lucas moved wordlessly towards the security gate at the college's front entrance. Lucas pressed the intercom. As the security guard responded Lucas spoke a phrase discreetly. After a brief pause there was an electronic buzz and the heavy cast-iron gate popped free of its lock. As soon as the pair were through it was remotely restored to its former position.

Nicks and Lucas marched purposefully through the ancient college's cloisters. Grotesque gargoyles glared down at them from the edges of the imposing buildings, many heavily discoloured with the grime and mildew of ages.

Reaching the far corner, and not having encountered anyone since leaving their drivers, Lucas brandished the mottled brass doorknob of a navy blue door, turning it to the left. As they knew it would be, the door proved to be unlocked. They passed into an imposing corridor which felt chillier than it was outside, the cold seeming to get exuded from the grey flagstones in the floor. They watched clouds of their own breath appear as they moved towards the rounded oak door in front of them.

There was no need for them to knock. There was the click of a latch and the slow groan of the heavy door on its un-oiled hinges. Behind it was the room's regular occupant who had known they would be coming. No words were exchanged, only knowing glances, as the two visitors descended into the room beyond, and the door was promptly closed behind them.

They were inside the office of Vic Kostta, the descendent of an Aristocratic Hungarian family sent to Oxford to get his system entrainment, and now the Director of Social Sciences within the University. The three stood surveying each-other as if in a movie-style Mexican stand-off. Suddenly, as if psychically connected, grins appeared at the corners of each of their mouths as an air of geniality became established.

"Eugene...Fabian," said Kostta with a plummy, Etonian cadence as he reached out to take the pair's over-coats and Nicks' hat. Both coats were adorned with the fox logo which had received an airing at the town hall meeting the previous week. The same logo was embroidered into Kostta's own beetroot-coloured velvet blazer, right next to the college's coat-of-arms.

The visitors took their seats in the leather chairs angled to either edge of Kostta's mahogany desk. Kostta himself poured three tumblers of whiskey from the cut-glass decanter on the left-hand shelf. He placed the three glasses in their respective positions and took his own seat in what resembled something of a masonic throne behind the desk. Only then did Nicks speak.

"Greetings, Vic. And so … what's the latest?"

"We've located all the cells," their host responded straight away. "However … " His eyes darted from side to side as he considered how best to phrase his message. "We've hit something of a snagging issue."

"And that would be … ?" Nicks' piercing gaze—the one Kostta had been keen to avert—quizzed him just as much as his words.

Kostta looked to Lucas who, he noted, was registering the same inquisitive glare as his colleague.

"We're lacking the trigger phrases."

"How can this be?" enquired Nicks after a couple of moments of reflection.

'We thought they had been logged, but it would seem that they were retained by your predecessor," Kostta's eyes went to meet Nicks' as he spoke, "who apparently is the only one who knows them."

Nicks and Lucas exchanged concerned looks.

"Nomas?" asked Nicks.

Kostta nodded in the affirmative.

Coming from London with a BA (Hons) in Psychology and Behavioural Sciences, he had taken up his position in Oxford six months previous. Nicks had used his influence to see him awarded the role. Kostta's initiation into The Order at the Caves had come only a short while later, where he had taken his oath of allegiance to the fraternity through participating in a ritual sacrifice, followed by an anything-goes Roman-style orgy.

Kostta had been under no illusion that his new-found day job would come with its price to be paid, and was not surprised when, only a few weeks into his extremely well-remunerated position, the pair who sat before him now had visited and made it clear that they wished to tap into his deep understanding of the human psyche, and how the vast majority of the population could be coerced into thinking and acting in certain desired ways through the application of what, in his field, had come to be known as 'behaviour modification.'

Great secrets had been revealed to Kostta, and Nicks had not been troubled by any concern that he would ever divulge them, given the penalties for such treason which had been made abundantly clear to him.

Among such secrets was the revelation that, embedded deep within various strata of regular Oxford society, were a handful of 'sleeper cells'—individuals who had undergone mind-control programming of the type practiced by the CIA under its far-reaching MK-Ultra scheme, to create what were termed 'Manchurian Candidate'-style assassins. Naturally, given the interplay between the US and the UK, where mind-control had been perfected through organisations such as the Tavistock Institute in London, there had been a British counterpart.

Their programming had been achieved through the application of techniques including electro-shock 'therapy,' systematic exposure to extreme trauma, and the administering of mind-altering drugs—not least LSD. While such treatment was often applied to the offspring of military personnel—always head of the queue for any human experimentation that might be needed—the ingenious thing about this particular scheme was that it involved regular members of society from all walks of Oxford life, those who would never be suspected of such involvement. It had been a long time in the planning. Most of the subjects had been selected and programmed from early childhood; they were now into their 30s or 40s.

These methods—so devoid of any moral justification that the programmes had to operate below radar and 'off the books'—depended on the subjects maintaining a 'front alter,' the aspect of their personality which would interact within society on a daily basis. The other 'alters'—the compartments within their minds which would include the one programmed to kill—would only be brought forward through the successful application of a "trigger" phrase which would have been allotted at the time of programming.

Though carefully guarded, these would usually be known to at least three separate 'handlers' in the know. It had been a severe oversight on the part of the ordinarily thorough Order that, in the case of the Oxford sleepers, there appeared to be only one individual who had knowledge of the words that would need to be spoken in order to unlock these secret compartments of their minds and set them on their missions.

Kostta's affirmation of this fact came as especially unwelcome news considering Nicks' predecessor, former Detective Chief Superintendent Nomas, had been removed from both his 'cover' position day job and his post atop The Order some ten years earlier, and had been subsequently deemed clinically insane and shuffled off to a lonely cell in Littlemore Mental Health Hospital.

It would not be easy to retrieve the information that they needed, Nicks considered.

It would not, however, be impossible.

The Order always had its ways.

CHAPTER 11

Saturday 22nd September 2001

"You must give them fair warning, you see."
Jimmy Savile.

"All is numbers; numbers rule the Universe."
Pythagoras.

"Some people laugh all day.
Some people cry, cry, cry, in the night."

The Kane Gang: 'Closest Thing To Heaven.'

"The Taliban must act, and act immediately. They will hand over the terrorists, or they will share in their fate. Every nation, in every region, now has a decision to make. Either you are with us, or you are with the terrorists."

"Said the village idiot who can barely tie his shoelaces on his own without his daddy there to do it for him."

Keith Malcolm grimaced at the words spoken by George W. Bush through the car radio's speakers. Verity, in the driver's seat, rolled her eyes, anticipating another of the daily rants for which Keith had now become famous within his own household.

"Why are we even listening to this horse-sh..." he remembered the presence of his daughter playing with her dolls in the back. "...this rubbish anyway? Mainstream news bulletins just grate with me. I swear there's something in the sound frequencies designed to put you on edge."

"Doesn't take much with you, does it?" said Verity snarkily, as she squinted behind her sunglasses and navigated the Ford Mondeo into Abingdon Road from its junction with the Oxford Ring Road.

It was all Keith could do to keep from swearing again as the voice of British Prime Minister Tony Blair oozed slimily out of the speakers.

"We stand side by side with you now, without hesitation. This is a struggle that concerns us all, the whole of the democratic and civilised and free world."

"What the hell would that sickening abomination know about being civilised?" scoffed Keith with venom in his voice.

"I need to keep a handle on what the masses are being told so I can try and work out what's really going on with all this," Verity added patiently, but not telling Keith anything he didn't already know.

"That's not hard to work out," Keith snapped back. "They're already banging the war drums, as you just heard. Watch them use this as an excuse to launch wars of occupation in the Middle East. They'll probably go into Iraq and finish off Saddam Hussein as Junior's daddy didn't get the job done properly last time."

"Who's Sad Man Insane?" Hope piped up innocently, sending Verity and Keith into fits of laughter.

"You got that about right, sweet pea," said Verity.

The three had spent the previous two days packing up all their belongings and piling as much as they could into the Mondeo's boot space, and next to Hope's child seat in the back. Only the furniture and some bulkier items had remained behind in Cornwall. With only five weeks left of their current rental, and still with the option to renew or relinquish, they had decided to cut their losses.

An emergency family meeting had resulted in Keith and Verity agreeing, following Max's call, that their presence was required back in Oxford. The danger of Keith being arrested for the supermarket attack had provided additional justification, as had Verity's innate reticence towards spending another bleak Winter in a region which, she felt, only felt alive for six months of the year.

Fortuitously—or was it down to cosmic fate?—their old house at 216b Abingdon Road had been available to rent for some time, and was being offered fully furnished for an initial period of six months. As the young family neared the address, Keith and Verity found themselves experiencing mixed emotions; warm nostalgia for the happy times spent there, including the conception of their daughter, along with some trepidation.

The circumstances which had caused them to leave back in '91 had been ominous to say the least. For Hope's part, she was deliriously excited to be seeing the place her parents had called home before she was born, plus excited at the prospect of making some new friends at school, as her parents had assured her she would; certainly, some of those she had encountered back in Newquay had been mean.

Verity had kissed her teeth many times at the evidence that the city's notorious traffic situation had only worsened, and did so again at being reminded of how difficult parking still was. "You're not in Kansas any more, Dorothy," she whispered under her breath. "What, mummy?" came a small voice from the back. "Oh, nothing sweetie," Verity replied, negotiating the tight turn into Vicarage Road.

Twenty minutes later the trio had met the new landlord and picked up the keys to the house. It felt to Keith and Verity as if they'd never been away. As she stood in the hallway by the front door letterbox, eyeing up the armchair in the simply-appointed lounge, that fateful night of ten years previous felt like it could have been only last week. Keith walked over to the hall table, instinctively running his finger along the top of the bakelite telephone and blowing off the resulting dust. It was the same rotary-dial phone as before, complete with the same number.

***

A curious paradox gazed back at May Pearce as she examined herself in the bathroom mirror. She stood sideways-on in her underwear as she inspected her body. She could see that she had lost a fair amount of weight. Standing closer to the frame, she scrutinised her own face. There, clearly, were traces of the little child before she became a woman; the innocence, the vulnerability, the well-meaning-ness.

Simultaneously, however, her face bore all the traces of the mistakes that she had made—not least her misguided years unwittingly serving satanists, freemasons and paedo-philes on the force, and some ill-judged relationships which had seen her, at 37, still devoid of motherhood. The crows' feet and wrinkles were staying away, thankfully, and there was no trace of grey in her dark brown bob cut. But her face bore a kind of weathered-ness that was difficult to put her finger on. Something in her eyes?

There, too, was the disappointment of not having made a go of her business as she'd so hoped. And, if she were really honest with herself, as she so tried to be, a nagging resentment towards her good friend Verity and how far ahead of her she seemed to have progressed—both in having found the right man and begun a family, as well as in her personal and spiritual development. It wasn't that that she begrudged V any of this; she was just a long way from where, ten years earlier, she had imagined she would be by this age.

Her relationship with Drew had surprised everyone, none more than herself. Verity had been the catalyst, having invited May to a night out at the Park End Club where Drew had been DJing. With drinks freely available on Drew's tab, May had been well-oiled on red wine by midnight, and had begun flirting with Drew behind the DJ booth, playfully bumping her backside against his crotch in a figure-hugging navy blue dress and making it extremely difficult for him to concentrate on his job. Indeed, the bar staff had commented on how sloppy the second half of his set had been.

The night had ended, post 3am, in a way that would have surprised few, with May's dress no longer hugging her figure but carelessly discarded on Drew's bedroom floor. May had questioned her drunken choices upon coming to her senses the next day, but, staring at a still-sleeping Drew, had decided that she could do a whole lot worse, that he was quite cute and the night had been fun, and—as everyone had been telling her for so long—it was about time she found herself a man. Open to the possibility that Drew could fit the bill, their relationship had begun. Within a few weeks she had moved into the single-bedroom flat in Barton that he had occupied for most of his adult life.

Now, eight months later, she emerged, still in her bra and panties, into the living room. The smell of burning marijuana melded with that of a sandalwood incense stick.

Drew had not acknowledged her entrance, engrossed as he was—and had been for most of the day—in obsessively flicking through the 12-inch singles and albums in his record boxes. Several of them were strewn across the rug, itself fashioned in the form of a vinyl record. He was holding another, tilting it towards the daylight of the window.

His concentration was broken by the chime of the doorbell. He looked up, noticing that his girlfriend was now in the room. "See who that is, will you, Maysie?" he said nonchalantly while reaching for the half-burned spliff in the ashtray to his right.

"Err, hello? Have you noticed that I'm half-naked?" May replied.

Drew kissed his teeth. "Put some clothes on then, 'oman!" he replied, putting down the album in his hand and hauling himself up to answer the door. Doing so, he found his cousin on the other side.

"V? What da bloodclaat?" The familiar vernacular was underway. "What's going on, cuz? I didn't know you were in town."

"Dat was de idea, fool!" Verity smiled back. Then, reverting back to regular-speak. "We thought we'd surprise you."

"Yeah, you did that," replied Drew, making way for Verity to cross the threshold, then bumping fists with Keith.

"Wh'appen, breddah?"

"All good in the hood," said Keith following in Verity's footsteps and using a 'street' phrase by now several years outdated.

"Where likkle Hope?" Drew asked Verity.

"She's with Mum."

"An' dat dyam fool Norm?"

Keith smiled at Drew's shared evaluation of Joy's choice of partner.

"May in?" asked Keith.

"Yeah, she ran off to get dressed when she heard the doorbell."

"Oh? She shouldn't have bothered on our account" Keith joked.

"Hey, watch it, bwoy, else I'll take you out into North Way and kick your raas!"

"Then I'll do the same!" called Verity displaying her remarkable ability to hear everything Keith ever said, as she rapped on the bedroom door.

"Oh, May! Guess who's here!" she called.

The door opened swiftly. May, now dressed in blue jeans and a white T-shirt, greeted Verity with a light smile and a tight embrace.

"I heard it was you! What are you doing here?"

"Well, let's just say that we're going to be in Oxford for the foreseeable, so sorry, but you're going to be seeing a whole lot more of us!"

As May invited Verity into the room, and herself sat at the dressing table, she received a filling-in on the circumstances surrounding their return. May commented that she shared Verity's dismay and concern at world events of the past few days. As her friend spoke, though, always facing away from her, Verity's finely-honed detective skills sensed that there was further cause for May's distinctly melancholy tone. Though she worked hard to stifle her tears, Verity had picked up on them.

She knelt down at her friend's side and put her arm around her.

"Hey, hey...what's up, mate? Come on."

May broke down into a full flood of tears and threw her face into Verity's shoulder. Verity caressed her hair as she invited her to share what was on her mind.

"Is it ... Drew?"

"No ... not exactly. He's a good man and he's doing his best. It's me. I just ... I just don't know who I am or what I'm doing here any more."

"I think we all feel that way from time to time."

"This is more. I feel ... I feel it's a mistake that I'm even here. I've always felt it."

***

In the room next door, both men were oblivious to their partners' conversation. Kneeling on the floor, Keith was paying Drew his full attention as he sat, almost open-mouthed, at what he was revealing to him.

"I remembered this just the other day. The music ain't exactly my thing, but this was in a garage sale collection that I bought off this geezer in Cowley the other year."

Drew was holding a copy of the album '*Breakfast In America*' by the British group Supertramp. Keith saw a cartoonish image as viewed from an aeroplane window of a plump woman in an orange waitress outfit mimicking the Statue of Liberty. A tray with a glass of orange juice was replacing the torch. In the background was a breakfast selection made to resemble the Manhattan skyline. The name of the group was emblazoned across the top of the sleeve.

"Now, watch this," said Keith, reaching for a mirror liberated from the bathroom. He held up the sleeve to the frame and glanced at Keith for a reaction.

"What am I looking at?" he asked, not getting it.

"What do you see above the twin towers?"

Keith squinted. He saw it. Now, inverted, the U and P of 'Supertramp' looked distinctly like a 9 and an 11.

Drew smiled. I know you of all people are *not* going to tell me that's 'just a coincidence'!"

"I'm not the man to tell you that!"

Keith was more than familiar with the concept of what one of his favourite broadcasters, the Scottish researcher Alan Watt, had described as 'predictive programming.' This, Watt had explained, denotes the act of placing visual depictions of real-world events known to be coming into works of popular culture, where they will be viewed by, potentially, millions of people. The reasons for doing so were threefold.

Firstly, the images will be subliminally absorbed by the subconscious mind of the viewer, thus creating a familiarity with the narrative that will later be peddled. So when the mainstream news outlets—owned and controlled ultimately by the same forces which would have made the event happen—dutifully report the official story, it is far more likely to be accepted as "truth."

The second reason comes from the observation that 'energy flows where attention goes.' A colossally-sized audience all unwittingly giving their attention to the representation of an as-yet unfulfilled event, can actually help bring that scenario into physical manifestation, drawing on the unique ability of humans to be the co-creators of their own experienced reality.

The third—and, in Keith's view the most likely reason these things get done—goes into metaphysical realms.

The dark occultists who control entertainment, along with everything else, grudgingly acknowledge the reality of Karma; of what is expressed in '*The Kybalion*,' the book teaching Hermeticism, as 'The Principle of Cause and Effect.' They realise that this physical realm is governed by a set of conditions often expressed as 'Natural Law,' chief among these being the Non-Aggression Principle. This teaches that no individual should initiate harm against another. They are free to do so if they choose, as Free Will is humanity's greatest gift—but if they do, they will bring upon themselves appropriate experienced consequences.

The dark occultists—many in conspiracy research chose to refer to them as the "elites"—in their utter hubris and arrogance, seem to believe that they can cheat the workings of Karma by pre-announcing their dastardly plans for humanity. This, as they see it, takes away our ability to claim we weren't given fair warning. Any harm or loss that we then suffer is on us because we didn't say no. To *not* say no is as good as saying yes in their sick, twisted mentality.

Of course, no absolution from rightful consequence on their part can be claimed to have been achieved, since they were never open and transparent about their plans. They are only ever communicated symbolically and cryptically. How could anyone viewing a depiction of planes being flown into the World Trade Center in a movie in the 1970s or 80s, possibly have been expected to know that they were being told what was going to happen in reality decades into the future?

And of course, this dynamic dictates that those forces placing these depictions into popular culture vehicles *must* be working in conjunction with those who cause the events to happen. Otherwise, as Drew was fond of pointing out to naysayers, the odds of it all being coincidence must surely be at several billion to one.

As Keith mused on this point Drew appeared to have read his mind as he remarked, "that's very far from an isolated example, trust me."

Reaching for the pile of CDs on the coffee table next to him, Drew removed the first one and handed it to Keith.

He found himself looking at an album titled '*Party Music*' by an act he had never heard of—The Coup. In the background were the twin towers exploding in *exactly* the way they had been seen to on TV earlier that month—except that this album had been released in June, three months previous. In the foreground was the group's frontman holding what appeared to be a remote-control detonator, suggesting that the towers came down *not* as the result of an aeroplane strike, but because they were pre-wired for demolition.

"What possible reason is there for an album titled '*Party Music*' to feature a scene of mass destruction on the cover?" asked Drew rhetorically.

"I knew they do this shit routinely in movies," added Keith. "You know the date given on Neo's passport in '*The Matrix*' is 9/11/01, right? Also in TV shows and music videos. But I didn't know it extended to record sleeves as well."

"Plus release dates. Guess what date Jay-Z's latest album was released? September 11th 2001. And what's it called? '*The Blueprint*.' Who uses blueprints? Architects who design buildings, right?"

"Or destroy them."

"Exactly. And records are normally released on Mondays, not Tuesdays. And you know another one released the same date? '*God Hates Us All*' by Slayer. Track number 9 is titled '*Bloodline*' and track 11 is '*War Zone*.'

"And remember the lyric from Notorious BIG's '*Juicy*'? 'Time to get paid, blow up like the World Trade.' That was a reference to the explosion that happened in the basement of one of the towers in '93. Makes you wonder if this event was planned for that year but somehow went wrong. 93's an important number within Crowley's Thelema tradition."

"But then again, it could have been a way of priming the public for the idea of 'Muslim terrorists' attacking the towers, so it was still in their consciousness when they came back to do the job properly in '01?"

"Seen, seen. Oh, one last thing. I saw this on the chat forums on David Icke's website. Prince played a concert in Utrecht in December '98. At the end of it he says something like, 'we got one more and I gotta go. I gotta get back to America. Osama bin-Laden's gettin' ready to bomb, Osama bin-Laden's gettin' ready to bomb.' Then one of his band members adds, 'America you'd better watch out. 2001—hit me'!"

"So, that suggests Prince and his band were given an advance heads-up on this event, doesn't it?" Keith responded as Drew nodded, "you know, given that they were specific enough to mention this year."

The pair looked at each other, all out of words for the moment. Drew suddenly remembered the spliff that he had left burning in the ashtray, now little more than a barely glowing paper stub. Spontaneously, they both burst out laughing at the profundity and farcicalness of their observations.

"And what do you think those two are talking about in there?" smiled Keith, indicating with his head towards the bedroom.

"Oh, hair and make-up probably!"

CHAPTER 12

Monday 24th September 2001

"Number nine ... number nine ... number nine ... "

The Beatles: 'Revolution No. 9.'

"Rainy days and Mondays always get me down."

The sweetly-sung voice of Karen Carpenter could be heard only faintly through the car radio, but it was loud enough to generate a reaction from Eugene Nicks in the back seat. "I know the feeling," he mumbled as the car snaked its way through Littlemore, its windscreen-wipers squeaking as they scraped back and forth. The smartly-suited driver remained silent.

In the identical Mercedes directly behind, Fabian Lucas also remained silent as he considered what the pair were about to encounter, and how best to handle the various ways things might pan out. All possibilities were on the table.

As miserable-looking folk scurried around under umbrellas and hoods, the car careered through a large muddy puddle, spraying an old lady wheeling a shopping trolley in the process. Continuing along Sandford Road, it reached the imposing facade of Littlemore Mental Health

Centre. Though not quite as sinister-looking as the more notorious Broadmoor in Berkshire, Littlemore still exuded a far from happy air. In decades past it had been known as Littlemore Mental Asylum, its construction dating back to the 1840s.

The gravel crunched under the tyres as the car slinked its way along the drive to the front entrance. There, they were immediately met by a white-coated orderly. Nicks' driver wound down the window as the orderly asked for credentials. He was invited to peer in to see the back seat passenger. Immediately satisfied, he opened the offside rear door for Nicks to climb out, then hurried to the car behind to do the same for Lucas. Scuttling inside briefly, the orderly re-emerged with umbrellas for the pair.

They were escorted around the back of the main building, passing through the garden area as they went. On a fairer weather day they might have encountered inmates deemed of appropriate mind to be permitted exercise or recreational activities, such as potting plants or tending to shrubs. Not today, though.

They were led to a section of the institution adorned with a high, flat-topped tower. The orderly punched a six-figure code into the panel on the tower's metal door. There was a deep buzz as the gate popped open.

"No biometrics yet?" snapped Lucas, seemingly perturbed.

"Should have had them by now, sir," replied the orderly. "Budget cuts."

Lucas turned to Nicks.

"Better see to that."

Nicks nodded.

Shaking their umbrellas and hanging them on the coat hooks at the entrance, they were led along a narrow, vinyl-floored corridor lit by fluorescent strip lights and smelling of bleach and boiled cabbage. Each side of the corridor housed heavy metal doors, numbered, and with a letterbox-sized slot at eye level, all currently closed.

They reached the door marked Number 9.

"You can leave us here, orderly," barked Nicks authoritatively.

"Oh, I'm supposed to stay to supervise, sir," he replied nervously. "And in case you should need anything."

Nicks' response was wordless, consisting of a dagger-like glare, and a drawing of the orderly's eye to the silver lapel pin which he had now revealed by opening his overcoat. It showed a fox in mid-jump. Seemingly as an afterthought, he then reached into his trouser pocket and pulled out a crisp £50 note which he handed to the man. An understanding had been reached.

From his own pocket, the orderly produced a heavy collection of deadlock keys on a ring. Selecting two of them, he undid the door's two locks. Finally, he punched another six-figure code into the keypad on the handle. The door buzzed and clicked open.

"Bang three times on the door when you're ready to come out," he said. The two men nodded, then carefully pushed open the door and went inside.

The door closed heavily behind them.

The room was a perfect square and very basically appointed. There was an Armitage Shanks ceramic toilet with a wash basin on a pedestal beside it. A faint smell of urine filled the sterile air. The narrow window was fitted with iron bars. Two wooden shelves bore an untidy selection of very old books. On the bed itself, wearing the loose-fitting light-blue uniform of the hospital was a man who, a decade previous, had been arguably the most powerful and influential figure in all of Oxford.

How the mighty have fallen, thought Lucas silently to himself as he surveyed the tragic figure that former Chief Superintendent CC Nomas of Thames Valley Police CID had now become. Wiry white hair protruded from either side of his otherwise bald head. As he looked up at his visitors, there was a dissociative-ness to his gaze. It was what psychiatrists referred to as 'the thousand-yard stare,' a look often exhibited by military veterans suffering from post-traumatic stress disorder.

"Hello, CC." said Nicks, still to this day wondering what the initials stood for. "Do you know who we are?"

"Don't fucking patronise me!" Nomas spat belligerently. "I might be in this place but I still know what goes on in this city. Of course I know who you are."

"Okay, well, that helps," replied Nicks.

"You're where I should still be to this day," Nomas continued.

As Lucas remained standing, Nicks uninvitedly took a seat on the metal-framed hospital bed next to the patient.

"Well, that's not entirely true, my friend. If that were indeed the case we wouldn't all be here today, would we?"

The thousand-yard stare had become a little more focused as Nomas tried, with what was left of his mental capabilities for such a task, to anticipate the true nature of the visit. They were few and far between these days, his family having abandoned him early during his enforced stay. Few of his former colleagues or underlings in The Order had graced him with any visits. There had to be a damned good reason for the top dog of the fraternity to now be sat in his cell.

"You see, CC, we have a bit of a problem. If you're still as connected as you imply, you'll be aware that a major mission is imminent, and we need to activate the sleeper cells for it. I don't mind telling you as, even if you repeat it or to warn anyone, no-one will believe you. Remember where you are.

"Anyhow, due to a *severe* oversight, it seems the only one with knowledge of the trigger codes is your good self. And we need those codes."

A slight smile came to the corners of Nomas' lips as he looked across at his intimidator. Nicks tried to assess whether there was enough mental capacity left in the man to be able to give him what he needed.

"Such an oversight would never have occurred in my day."

"Maybe so. But it's not your day any more, is it?

"So ... we need those codes. You're not doing it for us, you're doing it for The Order."

The visitors smarted as Nomas let out a loud, unexpected laugh. "The way The Order fucked me over? You honestly think I have any sense of allegiance left after that? After they put me ... in here!"

"You took an oath, remember? And you know our penalty for breaking the oath. Now ..." Nicks signalled with his eyes to Lucas, who promptly put his hands into his jacket pocket and pulled out two small accessories.

"We can do this the easy way, or the less easy way. Either way, we *will* get those codes."

As the orderly waited patiently in the corridor, praying his serious breach of protocol would not get discovered, a bloodcurdling scream penetrated from behind the heavy metal door of cell number 9.

CHAPTER 13

Friday 28th September 2001

The brakes on the X90 double-decker screamed as the driver pulled in to the side of St. Clements Street, fatigued after an arduous journey from London's Victoria Station which had taken twice as long as scheduled due to a bad accident in the cut-through section of the M40.

A ragtag selection of passengers began to disembark at this, the last stop before the bus's termination at Gloucester Green. Following closely behind two Chinese students, an elderly lady with shopping bags and a Bohemian-type in beads and a kaftan, was a 27-year-old woman. She wore a turquoise tracksuit and white trainers. On her back was an extremely overpacked rucksack, and in her hands a plastic-shelled suitcase. Her frizzy blonde hair was tied back in a ponytail. Her bronzed skin tone betrayed the location in which she had spent the summer that was just coming to an end—Ibiza, in a non-stop whirlwind of drinking, buying and selling drugs, blagged VIP clubbing, swimming, snorkelling and spontaneous sex with strangers.

Happy memories of getting loved up and blissed out to the sounds of Paul Van Dyk at Amnesia, Judge Jules at Eden, Carl Cox at Pacha and Pete Tong at Space had replayed in Molly Lowe's mind during the tedious journey home. As she struggled with her bags, and the coach driver impatiently closed the doors behind her and veered off towards the city centre, reality dealt Molly Lowe a harsh blow. It was all over for another year, and, unless fortune would smile on her in some miraculous way in the coming months, there was little chance of repeating the experience in 2002—not now she was back in a city where she had long since burned all bridges and called in all favours.

The girl she had been sharing a room with for the entire summer had betrayed her by robbing her of both her gear and her stash of cash as she had lain out-cold from yet another all-night bender. Molly had used her open flight return to get herself back on Ryanair to Stansted, but had then been forced to beg passers-by for the bus fare on to central London, then the X90 to Oxford.

Utterly dejected, she dropped her case to the floor and watched as the bus trundled away. Festooned along its left side was an ambiguous ad. which appeared to be for nothing in particular. "Picture this. An event Oxford will never forget. Not long now," read the slogan in newspaper headline-style font, followed by the number 105. The only graphic was a close-up of an index finger held against a pair of lips.

Her immune system already compromised, Molly Lowe coughed as she inhaled the exhaust fumes of the vehicles now gridlocked in Friday rush-hour traffic battling their way towards Headington on this unusually balmy late afternoon.

Boxed in by another X90 behind her and a Chris Hayter haulage truck in front, was Verity Hunter's Mondeo. Strapped into the car seat behind her was Hope, whom she had just picked up from her mother's. What should have been a quick hop back to 216b had already taken three times as long as it ought to have done. As Verity glanced in the rear-view mirror to check on Hope she instinctively turned down the volume on the car radio. The ads had just given way to the top-of-the-hour news bulletin on Lux FM.

'The five-o-clock news. This is Aimee Hardwick."

'Bimbo," whispered Verity under her breath, unconsciously scrunching up her nose. Though she had now been absent from the station for a decade, she had remained in the habit of casting a critical ear over its output whenever she had been back in town. Every aspect of the station had been degraded in her view; the music—a view shared in no uncertain terms by her cousin Drew; its local reputation—debased by its having been bought out by the Cohen & Bloomberg media conglomerate, resulting in more than 50 per cent of its programmes now being syndicated from London; and, in particular, its news reporting.

Verity rolled her eyes as she registered the robotic tone of Aimee Hardwick, dispassionately reading—badly—from the script so obviously prepared for her. Though she had never seen her, Verity maintained a vision in her mind—early 20s, blonde, top heavy, lots of make-up.

The national news—more sabre-rattling with Tony Blair announcing how Britain was standing shoulder-to-shoulder with its American cousins in what had become known, in sickening news-industry soundbite talk as the "War on Terror"—had now given way to the local headlines.

Hardwick was relating how tensions in East Oxford were running high with the local Muslim community coming under attack from "right-wing thugs." The proprietor of the El-Halal fast food eatery in Cowley Road was bemoaning the arson attack on his shop which had occurred during the previous night. Alim Salaam, the Imam of the area's largest mosque, (Verity had rolled her eyes yet further as Hardwick had pronounced the word "eye-mam") had been invited to comment. Far from offering any words of encouragement, he had instead predicted an "inevitable" bloodbath between the opposing communities in the city "within the next couple of months."

Hopeful news, it seemed, was thin on the ground in this new millennium.

Finally—mercifully—Verity pulled the car in to Green Place and unstrapped Hope from her car seat. Holding her daughter's hand, she walked her through the alleyway into the back yard of 216b and in through the back door, which had been locked; evidently, Keith was still out. Before she had had a chance to remove her coat and hang up her bag, the phone by the front door had begun to ring.

"Take your shoes off and hang up your coat, sweetie," said Verity. "Let Mummy see who this is.

"Hello?" she asked, hurriedly yanking up the receiver.

No reply.

"Hello?" she repeated.

Still no reply. As she listened intently, her journalist's ear thought it picked up a feint sound in the background. It seemed to be the general hubbub of a large crowd. Was that some some kind of market . . . or bazaar?

But still no reply.

"Hello? Who's there?" asked Verity one last time. Her patience wearing thin she replaced the receiver, cursing under her breath, before attending to far more important matters. Hope was hungry, and Verity was more than ready for tea herself.

***

Some streets away in Manzil Way, a Friday prayer session at Oxford Mosque was drawing to a close. A couple of hundred of the faithful had gathered for the second of two special addresses by Alim Salaam. At the pulpit, the Imam's two assistant clergymen had appeared alarmed when a bustle had begun to erupt among some of the young men in the congregation following the previous evening's attack.

Seemingly, this faction was threatening to take affirmative action against the perpetrators, though not yet having established how they could be found. Their stance was being met with resistance by some of their elders. Salaam remained calm as he began to deviate from his script to remind the dissenters of the demands their faith placed upon them for tolerance and dignity in the face of oppression.

"Trust in Almighty Allah, for he alone knows all things and looks inside the hearts and minds of all men. We need not seek vengeance upon the wicked dogs who perpetrated these attacks upon our community, for Allah will surely deal with them himself. And there will come a day when these insurgents will feel his full wrath. We may not know when that day will come... but what we *can* know is that it *will* happen."

Following Qu'ran readings from two of the women in the congregation and further prayer, the throng, appearing as a sea of white head coverings from point of view of the pulpit—began to slowly dissipate. As Salaam himself bade goodbye to his aides and gathered his belongings into his bag at the foot of the pulpit, a plummy Etonian voice brought him back from his own world.

"Hello, Alim."

The geniality that had been conveyed in Salaam's eyes switched to a look of disdain.

"What do you want?," demanded the Imam sharply.

"That's none too friendly for a man of faith," replied Vic Kostta. Salaam noted that he was not alone, instead flanked by two of the security officials armed with earpieces who had been present at the Town Hall meeting. Kostta would surely not have undertaken such a visit without them. The arrival of the three, who had stood out like sore thumbs, had turned many a head as they had made their way through the departing crowd.

"So . . . *what* do you want?" repeated Salaam impatiently.

"Well, that's simple enough, old boy," came Kostta's absurdly out-of-place response. As he took a step towards the elderly Pakistani his security detail robotically did the same.

Kostta rapped on a copy of the Qu'ran with his fingers as he spoke.

"A mission is about to go down. A very important mission. Certain assets need to be deployed. Two of them are within your congregation."

Salaam was glowering at Kostta with pure malice. He knew what was coming.

"I know you know better than to deny them to me, Alim," continued Kostta. ""Don't forget how beholden you truly are to The Order."

Even in spite of his assured personal safety, and the sociopathy that had been burned into him through years of sexual abuse at the hands of both his father and his prefects at Eton, Kostta's voice was beginning to quaver. Tough-guy talk was not his natural state.

"I need to know where to find two young men from your community. You are going to give me their addresses and telephone numbers."

No further implicit threats were required. The few seconds in which the Imam paused served only to prolong the inevitable as Kostta revealed the names of the men he sought, and the Imam proceeded to leaf through his pocket address book, then, sighing, to write down their addresses on a page ripped from the front of a battered Qu'ran.

"Thank you, Alim. It goes without saying that I must now ask you to turn a blind eye to what is about to happen."

On the other side of the not-quite-closed door to the storage area, where he had been stacking chairs until noting the arrival of the visitors, Shamim Amed had remained deathly still, straining to hear the conversation.

He had heard enough. Now, he knew he must remain silent, wait for everyone else to leave, then exit with stealth himself, taking what he had just learned out into the East Oxford night with him.

CHAPTER 14
Tuesday 26th December 1967

"There's something happening here.
What it is ain't exactly clear."

Buffalo Springfield: 'For What It's Worth.'

"There's nothing in the street,
Looks any different to me,
And the slogans are replaced, by-the-bye.
And the parting on the left,
Is now the parting on the right.
And the beards have all grown longer overnight."

The Who: 'Won't Get Fooled Again.'

The lighter clicked once more. The end of yet another spliff glowed orange as the pungent aromatic cocktail of marijuana and tobacco flowed forth. No longer able to breathe in anything other than smoky air, young Max Zeall began to cough and splutter, as his older sister had some time earlier.

To their right, sat on the cold, wooden floor of the Cowley Road squat flat, were their parents. Both were seated in the lotus position. Roy Zeall sported long, flowing locks and a bushy, dark brown beard. He wore a homemade tie-dye T-shirt with a Peruvian kaftan over the top, and ripped and faded denim jeans.

Max's mother, June, was in a long, flowing Indian-style gown. Three sets of beads hung from her neck, while her braided, mousey brown hair contained a ring of dandelions plucked from the grass verge of the roadside, in the seasonal absence of any daisies. Once Roy had taken a few pulls from the spliff, he closed his eyes to exhale as he handed it to June.

Though ten-year-old Max and twelve-year-old Claire were the only minors in the room, their family were far from the only ones in attendance. All seated on the floor, despite the availability of a dilapidated sofa and three hard wooden chairs, were a ragtag bunch of adults, most in their 20s. Having had their children whilst themselves still in their teens, Max's parents were still under 30, yet were among the oldest in the room. Next to them were their childhood friends Jeff and Collette, sporting similar fashions, right down to the facial hair and flower decorations. A thick grey fug had hovered continuously in the air since the family had arrived around two hours earlier.

Max and Claire were more than familiar with the surroundings and with the activity in the room. Momentarily, various of the adults, usually the bearded men, would explode into fits of uncontrollable giggles. The remnants of assorted snacks—sandwiches, bananas, cupcakes—lay strewn across the floor, amidst several empty beer bottles.

In the corner yet another bearded male, this one wielding an acoustic guitar, occasionally strummed on it. Sometimes the other adults would recognise the tune—regularly a Bob Dylan, Rodriguez or Phil Ochs composition—and begin singing the lyrics with varying degrees of melodic skill. Bouts of conversation would spontaneously ensue from time to time.

The females seemed more culturally clued-in than their male counterparts, often referencing literary works from the likes of Aldous Huxley, CS Lewis, Jack Kerouac or Carrol Quigley. One woman had brought baffled looks from the others when she'd announced that the first two had both died on the very same day—22nd November of four years' previous—their stories having been overshadowed by the shock assassination of President John F Kennedy. "Thank God Bobby's still with us," she had added. "And MLK."

As Max considered the bored and sad look of his quiet sister—then surveyed the expressions and mannerisms of the others in the room—his young mind began to consider, not for the first time, just what it was that had changed their parents so radically.

Back in '65 they had been a young, struggling couple raising their son and daughter in the two-bedroom council flat allotted to them in Cowley. While his mother had stayed home, looking every part the 1960s dowdy housewife, his father had worked his way through various labouring jobs—scaffolder, bricklayer, construction worker. He had worn his hair short and was clean-shaven. Both had been enthusiastic music fans, with the Beatles as their favourite band. Max recalled his mother having referred to their "rivals," the Rolling Stones, as "ruffians," far preferring the clean-cut, besuited "Fab Four," with '*I Want To Hold Your Hand*' and '*Twist And Shout*' as her favourites among their songs.

As 1966 had set in, however, Max—unusually astute to such matters for his age—had noticed the entire demeanour of both of his parents change. The first such indicator was his father beginning to grow out his hair. His mother's fashions, in the style of the "hippie" culture of the time, weren't far behind. Max and Claire had been shocked to see both begin to bring home and to smoke strange-smelling cigarettes, neither of them having smoked before. There was also their experimenting with some mind-altering compound which they had heard referred to as "LSD."

Their music tastes were changing, too. Albums by the likes of The Byrds, the Mamas & The Papas, Buffalo Springfield, Captain Beefheart, Frank Zappa & The Mothers of Invention, the Doors, and from British shores, the Pink Floyd, Small Faces and The Who, were now taking pride of place on the living room gramophone where the Kinks, Dave Clark Five, Herman's Hermits and Gerry & The Pacemakers had previously.

Even their mother's taste in Beatles music had changed. With the freakily-sounding *'Tomorrow Never Knows'* from the *'Rubber Soul'* album having been a particular '66 favourite, by the time of the group's landmark *'Sergeant Pepper's Lonely Hearts Club Band'* in June of '67, at the onset of what Max had heard endlessly referred to on Radio Luxembourg as "the Second Summer of Love," the Beatles sounded—and looked—like an entirely different band to the one which had publicly emerged just five years previous. By this point his mother had memorised, and frequently sang, the lyrics to *'Lucy In The Sky With Diamonds'* and *'A Day In The Life.'*

Through '67, Max had watched his father transform from a hard-working labourer, into a frequently-stoned dropout. Having previously held little interest in politics, by this point he had begun embarking on frequent rants, with apparent passion, about the various civil rights causes being championed in America, and the illegality of the Vietnam war.

Now, at the tail end of the year, Max and his sister found themselves once again brought to this place to hang out with Jeff, Collette and their freakish friends. It was either come along or stay by themselves in their own flat, cold and foreboding at this time of year due to Roy's reluctance to run the heating given his severely reduced income. Max and Claire caught each-other's gaze, each seeming to say to the other, "what are we doing here?"

Though today was Boxing Day, there was nothing in the squalorly squat to mark out the Christmas season—though the close-to-zero temperatures served as a reminder of the overall time of year. Max's mother had remained sufficiently sharp to check her watch from time to time. Noting it to be 8.34pm, she broke one of the extended periods of silence by announcing, "it's nearly time, guys."

Surprisingly for a room so devoid of features, nestled in one of the corners was a black-and-white television set. Somehow, despite the flat having been used as a squat for several weeks, the electricity had remained connected, the room being illuminated by a single light bulb dangling from the yellowed ceiling. The adults in the room looked around for a volunteer to shuffle over to the set and fire it up.

Young Max watched in quiet fascination as, sighing and exhaling marijuana smoke simultaneously, Jeff crawled over to the set, punched the On button, and selected the first of the three circular channel buttons. As the television flickered into life, the public school-voiced BBC1 announcer hastily introduced what was the world premiere of the new film featuring the Beatles—'*Magical Mystery Tour.*'

Over the next 55 minutes, the room's occupants watched in captivated silence a succession of scenes and songs which, to Max and Claire—and anyone else *not* under the influence of LSD—made no sense and had no connectedness nor purpose whatsoever; a formerly formidable pop group on a coach travelling to Cornwall, messing about on an airstrip, dressed up as army personnel, donning animal suits, and latterly, performing music hall dance steps wearing white tuxedos.

Something had happened to society. Nothing was as it had been. Closer to home, something had happened to all the people in this room and, most crucially, to Max's parents.

Max was too young to be able to know exactly what it was. What he did know is that it felt artificial. Contrived. As if having been engineered by some unseen force. All he could do at this point was to resolve to discover exactly what—or who—had been responsible for society having been turned on its head in such a way.

And with all the power within him, and with the same level of passion exhibited these past few months by his father, he vowed to oppose it.

CHAPTER 15

Saturday 29th September 2001

The fully-laden tea tray shook ominously as Mrs. Mots sought to find a safe foothold on each of the rickety stairs. The voices from behind the door at the top right grew louder with each new pace. Having finally reached the top, but not daring to let go of the tray to knock, she called out to her daughter.

"Dani.... DANI!"

The voices paused as the door was wrenched suddenly open. Daniela's deep green eyes scrutinised her mother from behind her spectacles.

"Tea," said Mrs. Mots, somewhat stating the obvious, the weight of a fully laden pot, a jug of milk and six cups really starting to take its toll.

Keith was up off the bed in an instant. "Here, let me get that for you," he said, reaching for the tray.

"Oh, thank you, dear," said Mrs. Mots. 'Dani, clear somewhere on your desk for this tray."

Dani's response was to brush a haphazard pile of papers, books and assorted stationery from the computer-free side of the desk. Some of them ricocheted off the fully-laden waste paper bin and the rest on to the carpet. Keith placed the tray down on the spot which had been cleared.

Mrs. Mots remained standing at the doorway, grinning inanely at the group. "Bye, Mum!" remarked Dani loudly, fixing her a glare. "And do *not* listen outside the door!" Mrs. Mots departed. She knew her place.

Never before had so many people—five—been squeezed into Dani's bedroom. Inevitably, the scenario was causing her some anxiety, yet she would never have trusted any of the others enough to go to their homes. The meeting was taking place on the condition that it be here at Helen Road. The presence of Max Zeall offered her the reassurance she needed, and he had vouched solemnly for the other guests in the room.

Sat beside him on the un-made bed were Verity and May. Keith had moved from the desk back towards the window where he was now standing. Max had called the group together for what, in corporate terms, would have been considered an Extraordinary General Meeting. He had assured Dani that these were the sharpest and most trustworthy minds for the job in hand, and all came with more integrity than he had found in anyone else during his 44 years. They were now awaiting the arrival of the final attendee.

The convivial chat that had been struck up prior to the tea's arrival had descended into something of an awkward silence. Presently, there was the feint creak of an un-oiled garden gate. As Max instinctively looked towards the window, Dani turned her head to watch him. Though Keith and May were seemingly oblivious to this minor act, it had not gone un-noticed by Verity, her own razor-sharp gaze going towards Dani's. Yes. She had been right, she told herself.

As the small talk re-ignited, there was a polite knock at the door before Drew Hunter, all smiles, opened and peered round. "Sorry I'm late!" he half-whispered.

Verity kissed her teeth. "So what else is new? Dani, say hello to my cousin Drew, so late he generally meets himself coming the other way." "Hush your mout', 'oman!" came Drew's playful response.

There was an awkward exchange of courtesies as Drew extended his hand towards a nervous-looking Dani who, rather than take it, forced a smile instead. "Err...sorry there's so little room in here," she said, looking towards the floor.

Max stood up. "Drew, come and sit here next to May, man."

"Word up. Thanks. Max," replied Drew, placing himself down on the bed next to his woman. Experiencing some discomfort, he reached around to his back jeans pocket, fished out a padded brown envelope, and passed it to her. "Oh, this arrived for you after you went out, Maysie. Another one." There was a slight rattle as he passed the package to May who hurriedly placed it in her handbag. Verity quietly observed.

Wanting no more time to be wasted, Max took control of the meeting.

"Right, folks. Here and now is where we put our minds together to figure out just what the hell is going on and what we're going to do about it. Because we're the only ones in this entire city who can. I suggest we start with Dani's latest radio recordings. Dani, do you want to play us what you've got?"

The denim dungaree-wearing 21-year-old took a second or two to register that Max had finished speaking and took her cue.

"Oh...yeah, OK, so, let's see."

Raising up from her well-worn office chair, she reached for the pile of TDK tapes stacked next to the radio-cassette. Selecting the top tape she jammed it into the right-hand-side player, rewound it to the start, and pressed play.

The five sat in anticipation as they waited for the few seconds of leader tape to pass the machine's heads and for the audio to kick in.

They found themselves listening to the final twenty seconds of Coldplay's '*Yellow.*'

"So, this was recorded from Lux FM yesterday evening at 9.11pm, right, Dani?," prompted Max, recognising Dani's apprehension at addressing the group.

"Err, yeah, that's it."

"Since when have you known a radio station take a break at 11 minutes past the hour?" chipped in Verity. "Never happened during my time at Lux. It was always quarter past and quarter to the hour."

The song began to fade out as she finished speaking, and a by-now familiar voice-over came straight in.

"Coming to Oxford soon, an explosive event you'll never forget. Things will never be the same again!"

Again, the voice of Prince from the end of his song '*Alphabet Street*' followed as he whispered various letters—"'I...A...A...B...A...'

This time, the excerpt was followed by the Lux voice-over man's own contribution.

"One...zero...five."

Again, the Will Smith lyric: "Tick, tick, tick, tick...BOOM!"

This time, the ad gave way to another full song, '*Waiting For A Photograph Of You*' by A Flock of Seagulls.

"That group was signed by Steve Blacknell, the one-time boyfriend of Kate Bush, supposedly the inspiration for '*The Man With The Child In His Eyes*," offered up Drew. Max flashed him a glare which said wordlessly, "not the time or place, man."

Dani spoke, quietly.

"This one's from 9:11 this morning."

The Flock of Seagulls cut off abruptly as the tape continued playing, replaced by the final strains of '*Have A Nice Day*' by the Stereophonics. The same ad played again, this time immediately followed by Bucks Fizz's '*My Camera Never Lies.*' Verity and Drew simultaneously winced as its opening bars cut in.

Dani shut off the tape.

"Right...so what do we make of that?" asked Max, assuming ringmaster status again.

"That Lux has gone further downhill than even I thought, playing bumbaclaat Bucks Fizz!" said Verity.

"That's the point though, isn't it?" said Keith from over by the window. "They wouldn't normally, but they have as part of...whatever this is. This is all signalling. What do you notice about both of those songs? They're both about cameras and photographs, right?"

"Another one played was '*Life Thru A Lens*'," added Max.

"Right," said Keith. "More camera business."

A voice joined the conversation for the first time.

"The Radcliffe Camera."

All heads turned towards May Pearce. The five awaited her elaboration.

"It's one of the most iconic buildings in Oxford, right? These have got to be clues pointing towards it."

Dani had grabbed a chocolate biscuit wrapper and was scratching something on the back of it with a blunt pencil.

"Could be," said Drew, stroking May's left leg through her jeans.

"She's right." All heads turned towards Dani in the chair.

"You remember the guy saying one...zero...five for no apparent reason? There's a reason. Err...have you guys heard of gematria?"

"Sure," May responded. "It's the allotting of numerical values to letters of the alphabet so words can be spelled out in numbers.

"Right," affirmed Dani. "So, check this out—'Radcliffe' sums to 64 and 'camera' to 41. Together that makes 105."

"The bastards are warning us!" gasped Verity. "But of what?"

"The part where the dude says, what was it, 'coming soon to Oxford, an explosive new event you'll never forget'?" said Keith. The motherfuc...excuse me, the sickos are planning to blow up the Radcliffe Camera."

There was silence as all in the room paused to absorb Keith's assertion.

"Max?"

Keith invited his mentor to comment on his suggestion.

"It would be just like the sick bastards in The Order to pull a stunt like that. And they love their symbolism. The Camera is somewhat similar in style to the Capitol Building which is designed to resemble a human skull. I can just see them wanting to blow to the top of it off, symbolising the destruction of the pineal gland in the centre of the human brain—the portal to higher states of consciousness. It would be their way of saying 'we've completely destroyed the consciousness and the very minds of this city'."

"The Order was never put to bed back in the 90s the way it should have been," added Keith.

'Exactly. Organisations like that don't just go away or stop being sick, twisted psychopaths if you ask them nicely. If you leave them merely wounded, as we did, it's never long before they recover and regroup. You cut off a tentacle, it'll grow a new one. It has to be completely TAKEN OUT!"

The others smarted as Max smacked his left fist into his right hand for emphasis.

"We failed to destroy The Order, and so it's back with a reminder of what it's capable of."

"But isn't the Camera a representation of that very control system?" asked Drew. "One of their favourite icons?"

"They'd destroy it in a heartbeat without giving it a second thought if it suited their plans," said Max. "It's the same with the Twin Towers. They represented the twin pillars of Freemasonry and were an expression of that control apparatus, yet they were happy enough to bring those down in an occult ritual. Those who made that happen will be affiliated to those running The Order."

There was a sudden movement over at the window as Keith jerked his head sideways to get a better look at the scene that was unfolding in Helen Road. A black Mercedes S-Class had reversed into a vacant space on the opposite side of the street, its shiny exterior standing out like a sore thumb among the small and mainly old cars of the street's residents. The rear windows were tinted. Keith was unable to see the driver properly.

Verity had noted Keith's behaviours and got up from the bed to join him.

"We have company," he commented.

"Don't we just?" she added. "What's the old World War 1 phrase? 'If you're copping the flak you're over the target'?"

"Looks like we're all going to have some company going forward, folks," warned Max with a grave expression. "We can't talk about any of this stuff over the phone. Only in person."

"Is that really what we think is going on here, then?" asked Verity. "If we're correct, why the hell would they place warnings in those ads? Is it mockery? They just like messing with us, like a cat playing with a mouse before it kills it?"

Drew answered the question. "Predictive Programming." He proceeded to regale the group with what he had shared with Keith the previous weekend—how, according to their spiritual belief system, the 'elites' consider it essential to pre-announce their plans. The fact that they don't just come out and reveal them in no uncertain terms, but instead veil them cryptically in symbolism and code, is testament to their psychopathy, he explained. But also, they consider that only the worthy will be able to correctly interpret what they are laying down. The masses will be too profane and spiritually ignorant to be up to such a task. And so—according to their beliefs—they're entirely deserving of their own fate.

Max had nodded consistently in confirmation of what Drew had conveyed.

"It's starting to look like we six in this room are the only ones who are 'worthy' according to their standards then. And it's not as if there's anyone we can write to nicely and say, 'Dear Sir. As a law-abiding citizen of this borough I object most strongly to your stated plans to blow up the Radcliffe Camera.' Max affected a comedic public school accent to accentuate the sarcasm.

"No. It never works like that. There's no-one we can ask to prevent it. The only way it gets prevented is if *we* prevent it.

A solemn silence fell upon the compact bedroom for a few seconds.

"I wonder how long we've got?" a visibly perturbed Dani half-whispered.

"About six weeks."

All heads turned in Verity's direction.

"These sickos might be smart and cute with their little tricks, but they're also highly predictable. Because they do everything according to their rituals and on special dates and such, you can often second-guess them. 9/11, as well as providing the excuse for an orgy of warmongering, was also a psychological operation, right? Designed to traumatise the entire world. Fear-based mind-control. Nothing controls a population more effectively than putting them into a collective state of fear. And who specialises in concocting psy-ops of that nature?"

"Tavistock."

May took the proverbial baton from Verity right on cue.

All in the room—even Dani in her youth—were familiar with the notorious reputation of the Tavistock Institute in London, an offshoot of British 'military intelligence,' (Max had frequently pointed out that the phrase was an oxymoron.) For decades they had employed behavioural scientists to advise on how the collective mindset of the general public could be shaped and moulded in line with social engineering agendas; mass brainwashing by any other name.

May proceeded to embellish her point.

"Mind control may be alive and well in America but it was perfected on British shores. So wouldn't it be just like them to want to pull a British version of 9/11? And when might they do that? 9/11 means September 11th in the way Americans render the date, but in British date format it means 9th November."

"Right," came Dani's agreement. Prince is telling us that."

All looked wordlessly in her direction. Dani's cheeks flushed red.

"In the ad...the voice whispering the letters at the end?"

"Right," said Drew. "That's Prince from '*Alphabet Street.*'"

"Listen again." Dani's fingers fumbled clumsily to rewind the cassette. At the end of the most recent recording of the ad could be heard the voice of Prince: "'I...A...A...B...A...'"

"Nine, one, one, two, one," said May without hesitation. "The ninth of the eleventh, 2001. They're even giving us the date."

A moment of silence engulfed the bedroom again as the group let the new-found revelations sink in.

Keith broke the silence.

"So, where from here?"

"We need to start by finding out just who commissioned those ads," replied Max.

"I can suggest a first step in that direction," said Verity. "The voice-over is Cas Passendale, one of the Lux presenters. Smarmy bastard. He was doing fill-in shifts when I was still there."

"Sounds like he might need a visit," suggested Max.

Outside, the driver of the black Mercedes muttered into his microphone in response to an order from his unseen passenger in the rear. Slowly, carefully, the car pulled out of its parking space and slinked back towards the main road.

Intermission

Mawgan Porth beach in Cornwall. Keith spent childhood holidays here, and this is where news of the terrible events of the 9/11 attacks first reaches Verity, shattering their idyllic afternoon.

Oxford Town Hall. Drew used to buy vinyl from the record fairs held here. Mayor Eugene Nicks uses it to host the "emergency" meeting.

The Radcliffe Camera. Originally a reading library, and always one of Oxford's most iconic buildings. The ideal choice for the "terrorists" to gain maximum shock impact from their "event."

The Broad Street vantage point from which Nicks, Lucas and Asttok plan to survey the devastation of "Oxford's 9/11."

The college cloisters leading to Vic Asttok's office.

Cowley flyover, with the famous car works lying beneath,
site of the culminating action.

The former HQ of Lux FM radio, (now a tile and bathroom store,) where Verity used to work, and where she and Keith visit a nervous Cas Passendale.

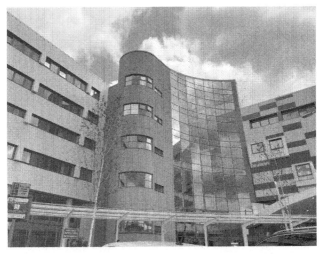

The John Radcliffe Hospital in Marston; the Intensive Care Unit, where one of the characters ends up, is on the first floor.

The rail tracks alongside which the 1980 flashback takes place.

The Bridge nightclub, where Aimee and Molly are partying as Drew DJs on Bonfire Night.

A portal to the underground. A clue…?

The City of Dreaming Spires.

The "classified" section of Littlemore Mental Health Hospital, out of sight from the main facility. A mind-control manipulator's playground.

Shamim's house at 94 Cricket Road. Oxford Freedom Radio operates from the outhouse in the back garden.

Central Oxford Mosque, where the Imam receives some unwelcome visitors.

The Angel & Greyhound Inn, formerly Parkers Wine Bar on St. Clements, scene of the New Year's Eve gathering.

216b Abingdon Road (to the right.) Home to Verity, Keith and Hope.

Helen Road, Botley. Dani lives at No. 2.

Bicester Police Station. Scene of the 1979 flashback.

Drew and Maysie's flat in Barton

Zeall's parents' squat from the 1960s.

The "Illuminati" obelisk near Temple Cowley, one-time base of the Knights Templar. One of so many reasons why Oxford remains a fascinating city in which to base a story!

Alim's Deli, (to the right,) Cowley Road. Hakeem is on-shift here when he is "recruited."

92 Charles Street, Cowley. Verity's 1970s home

139

And finally ... the table in my local social club where around 90 per cent of this story was written. Don't let anyone tell you that an author's life is all glamour!

CHAPTER 16

October 2001

"The journey of a thousand miles begins with a single step."

Chinese philosopher Lao Tzu.

As Autumn had edged ever closer to Winter and the darkness had closed in a little more with every passing day, so the advent of October had seemed to symbolise the growing sense of foreboding that Verity and Keith had been experiencing. The more they had considered what clues and evidence had been made available to them, the more they had remained convinced that they had called the date of "the event" correctly.

This had been reinforced by a new spate of bus-side advertisements which had appeared early in the month. Now, these bore a new slogan hinting yet more at a connection between the events of September in the United States, and those which seemed to be getting portentously predicted in the City of Dreaming Spires. "From New York to Oxford," they had read, "an unstoppable force has been unleashed." With each subsequent viewing, Verity recalled the dreadful sense of anxiety she had experienced at the point of her sacral chakra the first time she had seen it.

The number 105 had now disappeared and had been replaced by 313. Assuming this to be another expression of gematria she had consulted Dani, sure that she would be able to deduce its meaning. She had, but not in the way Verity had anticipated. Dani's remarkable mind had straightaway recognised the reference to the 313th day of the year—9th November. By this point they had all the confirmation of the timing that anyone could have hoped for.

The architects of...whatever this was, had also got cuter with the Lux radio ads, Dani had added. Though the songs following the announcements no longer bore any obvious camera-related lyrics, each one lasted for 3 minutes and 13 seconds. The level of precision that had gone into this whole campaign indicated high-level collusion on the part of Lux senior management and programming. Verity wondered just how many in the organisation were in full knowledge of what this broadcast platform was really being used for. Though really, the hierarchical structure of the station meant only one or two needed to be complicit.

Verity, Keith, Max, Drew and May had been meeting each Saturday, usually at 216b, to compare notes and consider potential plans of action. Dani's social anxiety had kept her away from most of the meetings, but, unexpected to all, she had accepted the offer of a pick-up from Max to attend one of them. This was where she had unveiled her revelation on the meaning of the 313, resulting in her accruing a sage-like status in the minds of the others.

May's attendances had been somewhat reluctant ones also, her having become increasingly reclusive. On the two occasions that Drew had been able to persuade her to get out of her pyjamas and join him she had remained distant and withdrawn, though had made two invaluable contributions to the conversations.

Her behaviour had not escaped the attention of Verity, who had taken advantage of a quiet moment alone with Drew to raise her concerns. He had brushed them off, stating that if there had been anything seriously wrong he would have known. He had put May's demeanour down to her being tired through often waiting up for him to return from gigs, but then waking too early in the morning as he slept in. He had also concluded that she struggled in the darker months with 'SAD'—Seasonal Affective Disorder. May was someone who thrived so much more during the Spring, he had said, as reflected in her name. She seemed to be getting herself through it via on-line shopping, with brown paper packages arriving endlessly. Some kind of make-up or other "women's stuff," he had assumed.

Drew had seemed far more interested in sharing some more examples of 9/11 "Predictive Programming" that he had discovered. At one of the meet-ups, he had excitedly played a VHS promo tape of the video to the 1997 Roni Size Reprazent song '*Brown Paper Bag*.' At another, he had obtained a collection of Depeche Mode videos, and had played the group an alternative promo for the song '*Enjoy The Silence*.' This, they had noted, had been filmed atop one of the World Trade Center Towers, and early on contained the lyric "come crashing into my world." This video was from 1990, 11 years before the attacks.

Predating that, Drew had added, was U2's '*The Unforgettable Fire*' which, for no apparent reason, opened with night-time scenes of the WTC Towers. "Note the title of the song," Drew had reminded the others. He had also presented as evidence a borrowed copy of the Oasis album '*Standing On The Shoulders of Giants*.' Though the Twin Towers were occulted in the Manhattan sleeve design, he had noted, if the lettering of the title were viewed 45 degrees to the right, a case could be made for it then resembling two tall towers, along with a shorter third—Building 7?

Max had judged that his radio audience must have increased tenfold if the volume of calls he was now receiving each Monday were anything to go by. He had granted himself an extra hour each week, and had taken to restricting his Bill Cooper-inspired monologues to only a few minutes, allowing the whole of the rest of the shows to be devoted to phone-ins. The quality of knowledge displayed by all callers—not just the ones he had been hearing from weekly for months—had been filling him with cautious optimism that many were catching on to the terrible truth of the power structure which really presided over all of society. There was still an exceptionally long way to go, but—as he himself had reminded one of his callers, "the journey of a thousand miles begins with a single step."

Finally, an event which Keith had been anticipating for weeks had occurred towards the end of the month, as another "phantom" call had been received at 216b. He had picked up this one himself, remaining silent as his instincts had dictated, and had found himself listening to the same thing as Verity had when such a call had last been received—no verbal response, just a light background ambience, sounding something like a crowd in a street market.

Though he could just as easily have dismissed it as the antics of a prankster, something told him that these calls were significant, and linked somehow to what the group had come to discover. He had decided that he needed to be ready for the next one. Having been consulted on the matter, Max had mentioned that he was in possession of technology which could allow any further such calls to be tracked to a rough geographical location. When Keith had asked him how he had happened to come by such a device,

Max had merely smiled and commented, "the fewer questions you ask, Keith, the less I need to tell you." Adding, "so do you want to know where these calls are coming from or not?" Pausing only briefly, Keith had said, "well, there's only one real response to that, isn't there?"

"That's what I thought," Max had replied.

The following day he had dropped by with a device—a small, saucer-shaped disk with a couple of wires. Keith had watched with quiet fascination as Max had unscrewed the speaker end of the phone's receiver, carefully inserted the disk and, using a jeweller's eye glass and miniature screwdriver, connected one of its wires to one of those inside.

The other, protruding from the phone's receiver, he had connected to a unit which looked to Keith something like one of the portable DAT recorders he had seen Max using at the radio. "When the next one happens, press this," he had told him, indicating towards a red button.

"Whoever the bastard is, we'll be ready for them. Anonymity no more."

CHAPTER 17

Friday 2nd November 2001

A task which had remained outstanding for over a month was about to be fulfilled. Ever since Verity had placed the voice on the ambiguous Lux FM ads, she and Keith had intended to pay the individual in question a visit. It having been more than a decade since Verity had worked at the station, however, she had become bemused when her detective work revealed that only one of her former colleagues remained in employment there, all others having been poached or having left to pursue alternative careers.

The pair had decided that the best course of action would be for this old trusted ally to facilitate their entry to the Lux building, as any attempt to go through official channels would undoubtedly get blocked by an appointed gatekeeper. Verity knew only too well that former employees quickly become *personas non grata* in the radio game.

This ally had advised the previous day that Cas Passendale had finally returned from an inconvenient—at least from their point of view—extended backpacking trip around South East Asia. Acting on this intel, and acutely aware of how time really was running out, Verity and Keith had set off to Horspath Industrial Estate during what should, apparently, be Passendale's lunch hour.

Pangs of bitter-sweet nostalgia swept over Verity as they turned right into Pony Road, and the Lux HQ loomed before her. It could have been 1990 all over again, except for the former furniture warehouse having undergone something of a makeover. It was still adorned in the red with which she was so familiar, but it was now a deeper shade, and the old logo of an illuminated lightbulb had been replaced by a new motif—the rays of a rising sun.

After sandwiching the Mondeo into the only remaining visitor's space, the pair walked reticently towards the glass-fronted entrance. Remaining out of sight of the receptionist, Verity took out her mobile phone and dialled a number, saying merely "we're outside," before waiting.

A minute later, Mateo, still the sports editor, buzzed open the front door.

"Hi guys," he said, flashing them a smile and a wink. "Glad you could make it. Let's do the interview upstairs. Follow me." The receptionist, evidently falling for the subterfuge, barely blinked as the pair followed Mateo out of reception and through the connecting door to the stairs.

Little had changed cosmetically since Verity's day. But the energy certainly had. In some inexplicable way it felt denser, more palpable. One thing which hadn't changed was the dank, grey fug of cigarette smoke which still hovered ominously throughout the open-plan working area. As they walked through Sales, none of the strangers they encountered batted an eyelid, assuming the visitors to simply be interview guests of Mateo's.

"Just wait here a sec, guys," said Mateo, putting an index finger to his lips. Keith recognised it as the "shhh" secrecy sign within Freemasonry denoting the the telling of no secrets, but doubted Mateo had joined the ranks or recognised its occult meaning.

As Mateo headed towards the Presenters' area, Verity surveyed the newsroom in which she had previously spent so many hours of her life. Apple Mac computers and e-mail had replaced the typewriters and fax of her day. Two males sat tapping away at their keyboards, one taking occasional puffs from a cigarette.

Standing by the online printer which still received the news feeds from Independent Radio News was a young woman. She ripped off the sheets that had spewed out and turned around.

"Anything doing, Aim?" asked one of the males nonchalantly.

"The usual. She read robotically, "US probes Saudi cong…conglom…conglomerate for links to Islamic militants."

Verity recognised the voice. So that's Aimee Hardwick! Her appearance was exactly as she had imagined.

Aimee's bleach-blonde hair was pulled tautly into a pony-tail, the dark roots revealing her natural colour and the need for a touch-up. The black sweater was tight-fitting, accentuating, by design, her cleavage. The blazing red skirt—what little there was of it—continued the figure-hugging theme. It stopped so high that the gusset of her black 15-denier tights was on full display. Below it, her long, slender legs were encased in nylon, and her feet in black leather patent high heels.

Keith had noticed her too, before Verity had, when Aimee had been standing with her back to them. He had wondered how she got away with turning up for work more suitably dressed for a nightclub than for a newsroom, but felt sure that few of her male colleagues would have objected. As Keith proceeded to mentally undress Aimee he felt the inevitable stirring in his trouser region, and worked to conceal it by pushing out his pockets. He chuckled to himself at the irony of her name. The Universe—or whatever—certainly wasn't averse to a bit of '*Carry On*'-style humour, it seemed.

Keith's reaction had not escaped Verity's attention. As Aimee stepped towards her desk she became aware of Keith's gaze and gave him a knowing smile. Keith felt Verity's 'black girl look' scorching itself into his face, and knew that this would not be the last that he would hear of the matter that day.

Mateo re-appeared and beckoned Verity and Keith towards the presenters' office. Without knocking, he pushed open the door.

Seated at the computer desk, as Mateo had said he would arrange, was Lux's newly-returned early evening presenter, Cas Passendale.

"Couple of friends of mine to see you, Cas. Have fun, you guys," said Mateo.

Though there would surely be some playful banter later, there was none of it now as he exited and pulled the door shut behind him.

Again, Verity's mental imagery was spot-on as Passendale appeared just as she had expected. His bleach-blonde hair accentuated the Asian tan all the more, though she suspected some topping-up had also gone on. The Hawaiian-style shirt suggested he was still fixed in vacation mode.

Keith let Verity lead.

"Hi Cas. We have a few questions for you about the ad that you voiced a while back," she began.

"Right . . . sorry, who actually are you?" came the defensive response, bearing a slight lilt of effeminacy.

149

"Let's just say we're an interested party. Interested in what it is that those ads were alluding to—this 'explosive event that you'll never forget'." Verity used air-quotes.

"Look," Passendale rose from his seat, "I have no idea who you are or how you got in here, but I've got nothing to say to you. That's private business. Now, you need to leave, or do I have to call security?"

It was Keith's time to step in. "There's no security here, Cas. And if I were you I would start being co-operative. We're short on time so let's get this out of the way straight off."

Keith reached his inside jacket pocket and pulled out a folded sheet of A4 paper. He opened it out and placed it on the desk in front of Passendale. It showed a screenshot taken from the presenter's desktop computer at work. The top left of the image clearly displayed his name in the login section. The image on the screen was taken from a "specialist" gay porn site.

Passendale's expression turned to one of sheer horror as he surveyed the sheet. "How . . . how did you get this?"

It was a good question. The answer lay in a masterful collaboration between Max Zeall and Verity.

Among his various technical accomplishments, Max had perfected a way of remotely hacking into local area networks, such as the one employed at Lux. To have accessed Passendale's individual account he had needed the overall corporate password. It had been a long shot, but Verity had provided him with the one at use during her time there, and they were astounded to discover that it had never been changed in over a decade.

Once in, Max had been able to scroll through the browsing data, which Passendale had carelessly neglected to delete. Max had found plenty of evidence of the type they'd hoped they might, Keith's screenshot page forming only part of it. Though highly "illegal," and perhaps morally questionable an action, Max was satisfied with his justification that it was serving the greater good, and that no harm, damage or loss was being caused; in fact, quite the contrary. Potentially, many lives stood to get saved.

"This isn't legal!" protested Passendale, his campiness now over-written with anger.

"Neither's what you've been looking at on your work computer, fella. Now, Lux management don't need to know about any of this just so long as you co-operate with us. So what do you say we head down to the Chequers, we'll buy you a lunchtime drink, and we can iron this whole thing out?"

Ninety seconds later the three emerged from the office. Through a puff of smoke Mateo signalled an 'OK' sign. Verity would have given anything to hear his impersonations of Zippy and George from '*Rainbow*' just once more, but this was hardly the time. Keith stole himself one last look at Aimee Hardwick's backside as she put on her coat.

"Where you off, Aim?" asked the male colleague.

"Off to interview DI Sam Haine about the ongoing conflict between East Oxford's muslim and white communities," she replied in what Verity had already dubbed her 'bimbo voice.'

Aimee's heels click-clacked as she hurried downstairs to reception, followed closely by Verity, Keith and Passendale.

***

Fifteen minutes later, Keith put a Bacardi and Coke for Verity and a lager each for himself and Passendale on to the circular table in the Chequers, Horspath, drinking hole of choice for Lux staff since the station's inception in 1989. There had been an awkward silence from the radio host, who had been warned that it would be against his best interests to try and leave, while Keith was fetching the drinks. Verity was grateful for Keith's return, and equally, for his taking the lead in the conversation that must now follow.

"So, this can go one of two ways, Cas. Either you tell us all you know about who commissioned that radio ad and what you were told about it, or..." Keith again fished the crumpled sheet of A4 out of his pocket. "This no longer remains a best-kept secret between the three of us."

Passendale fished around in his own pocket, producing a packet of 20 Dunhill and giving one a nerve-steadying light. He took a couple of desperate pulls before he spoke.

"Look...I want to give you what you need, but I really don't have much to tell. I was e-mailed out of the blue and asked if I would lend my voice to an ongoing ad campaign. I was offered £666 for the full set."

Verity and Keith exchanged raised-eyebrow glances.

Passendale continued.

"I had to run it by Lux management. They said they knew all about it, that they were going to produce the music clips to go with the voicers, and that they were happy for me to use the studio to do them." He paused to take a drag and accommodate a thought. "You know, you should be asking them about this, not me."

Verity spoke for the first time. "D'you really think they'd talk to us, Cas? Look at what we had to resort to with you. Now...who did the commission come from?"

"The name given in the e-mail was a Mr. A. U. Akbar."

Another raised eyebrow exchange.

"Classy," said Verity.

"They..."

Passendale considered whether to continue with the sentence.

He did.

"They promised me 'a seat at the table' if I read out everything they sent me."

"You wouldn't want one if you knew what they would be serving," quipped Keith, only half-joking.

"Wait … what? Look, that's honestly all I know."

"And, tell me … have you been paid yet, Cas?"

"Actually … no," said Cas, looking suddenly confused.

"Hold that thought," said Verity, raising up ready to leave. Keith followed her cue.

"You're embroiled in something bigger than you could possibly understand, Cas."

"What about …?" Passendale beckoned with his eyes towards Keith's jacket pocket. Keith once again produced the paper, this time tossing it down on the table. Passendale quickly grabbed it and screwed it up.

"Every boy needs a hobby," said Keith. "Next time, make a better choice."

CHAPTER 18

Friday 2nd November 2001

"Three things cannot be long hidden; The sun, the moon and the truth."

Buddha.

With dusk coinciding with rush hour, Farouk, the proprietor of Kochi's Halal Delicatessen, situated right beside the Jamaican Eating House, was finding business had picked up versus the first week of the previous month.

The middle section of Cowley Road was log-jammed. This was the case on any given evening, but this particular one benefited from it being Friday, and from the dreary drizzle which had evidently driven some who might have otherwise walked or cycled, into their cars. It being payday weekend was always a bonus too, he reflected—an observation shared by the proprietors of all the bars and clubs in the city centre who would benefit from this dynamic as the night would wear on.

Turning back from the door to the counter, Farouk was satisfied to see his two staff, Mina and Hakeem, hurriedly taking orders from the customers and passing them through the hatch to the kitchen. His look of contentedness turned to one of consternation, however, when Hakeem's mobile phone suddenly started ringing, and, glancing at the display, instead of ignoring it as per business protocol, the young employee proceeded to abandon the order he had been taking and to head quickly for the kitchen to answer it.

"Hakeem! Where are you go . . . "

But the old man's protestation had evidently fallen on deaf ears. Noting Mina to be still tied up with a complex and plentiful order, Farouk had little choice but to step in and continue taking the order from the bald, tattooed white man who looked like he could be trouble if he were to get upset.

As he appeased the man and apologised for his employee's walk-out, Farouk continually turned his head towards the hatch to see what was going on.

But Hakeem was already out of view. He had stepped down from the kitchen into the narrow alleyway which connected Kochi's with the back of the Eating House and several of the other businesses in that stretch of the street.

Hakeem strained against the backdrop of assorted kitchen noises and shouting to hear the voice on the other end of the line. The number on the display had already told him that this was a call he could not, at any cost, afford to miss.

A plummy, Etonian voice spoke.

"Would you have a wond'rous sight, the midday sun at midnight?"

Hakeem froze, as the early evening drizzle landed in tiny drops on his hair, beard and hands. Had anyone else been in the alley to witness it, they would have noted a glazed expression fall across his face; a veritable thousand-yard stare.

The voice repeated its simple phrase.

"Would you have a wond'rous sight, the midday sun at midnight?"

His gaze remaining fixed on nothing in particular, Hakeem ended the call, placed his phone back in his left trouser pocket, and stepped back up into the chaotic kitchen.

"Hey, you! Where the hell have you been?" Farouk squared up to him, the drama attracting the attention of the other staff. Wordlessly, now with a look of steely resolve in his eyes, Hakeem pushed the old man out of his way, sending him sprawling into a table, and the saucepans it contained crashing to the ground.

As two of the chefs rushed to help their floundering boss off the floor, Hakeem kicked open the connecting door with the shop, wrenched off his apron and, hurling it at the counter, charged out of the front door into the dark, drizzly East Oxford night.

***

"It always works better in French."

Observing what appeared to be genuine interest in the eyes of his friend, and always welcoming an opportunity to enlighten a student, Max Zeall patiently explained the origins and naming of the days of the week to Shamim, who faced him across the radio desk. Though laden with a ton of preparatory work for that coming Monday's show—most notably cross-correlating predictions and warnings from Bill Cooper with mainstream news recordings of the past few weeks—Max was happy to take some time out to satiate Shamim's curiosity.

"So, *Lundi*, comes from '*la lune*'—the Moon. Monday is really Moonday. Tuesday is *Mardi*—that comes from Mars. Wednesday is *Mercredi*. The clue's always in the first part. It's Mercury. Personified in the Norse traditions as Odin, or Woden. So 'Wednesday' is really '*woden's day*.'

Max was on a roll, but Shamim stopped him in his tracks.

"A question. You mentioned '*la* lune.' This is something I never understood in French class at school. How they'd describe something as masculine or feminine—le or *la*. Something like a friggin' table or chair. Whereas in English everything's just 'the'."

"Great point," replied Max. "That's because English is a bastardised language. It's not even fit to be called a 'language,' being a ragtag hotch-potch of Latin, German, French and other influences. It's no accident that it's become the official 'business' language of the world and one of the most widely-spoken. The days of the British Empire saw to it that it got exported to every corner, because the occult controllers, exactly the same class that we still have running things today, wanted people speaking a satanically-corrupted imposter 'language.'"

There was now little difference between Max's delivery in this private conversation, and the way he sounded when delivering a diatribe on the airwaves.

"It's all word magic. That's why it's called '*spelling*.' We create magic spells when we speak. That's why stage magicians use the phrase '*abracadabra*.' It translates very roughly as, 'as I speak I create.' Remember the teachings of the Bible, along with so many other ancient cultures, that 'God' literally 'spoke' the world into existence?' 'In the beginning was the Word, and the Word was with God.'

"Everything we experience is sound vibration in an endless array of different frequencies. So, imagine for a moment that you were a sick, diseased abomination that was hell-bent on enslaving and subverting all of humanity. Wouldn't a really great way to achieve that be to have the hordes of 'useless eaters' helping to perpetuate their own slavery by the very words that come out of their own mouths?"

Shamim was starting to look confused and was evidently a sentence or two behind, (there's another one, Max thought quietly to himself — a prison term is described as a 'sentence' in recognition of how English literally shackles and binds its users.)

Max proverbially backed up.

"I pity anyone learning English as a second language as it makes absolutely no fucking sense. It's completely illogical and completely inconsistent—by design. And it's a world away from the so-called 'romantic' languages from which it's derived.

"So to go back to your point; the reason why languages like French, Spanish, Italian and German ascribe gender to inanimate objects is a reflection of how everything in nature is an expression of duality and polarities. So you can't have up without there being down. You can't have light without there being dark. You can't have masculine without there being feminine.

"So the sun, for example, embodies masculine principles, that's why it's 'le soleil,' whereas the moon is its feminine counterpart—la lune.' Everything has to have an equal and opposing value. You can't have good without there being evil.

'Then, between these extremes of polarity, there's an endless array of graduations. That's what offers us our free will choice. To take the good and evil example, we can make the choice to come in at any point on the scale between those two extremes. And, through the workings of Natural Law, we then get to experience the consequences of the decisions we've made."

"Yeah, you know I follow that part."

Max had been methodically chipping away over many weeks at the dogma which had been instilled in Shamim through a lifetime raised in a nominally Muslim family.

"Right. Anyway. Where were we?"

Max habitually stroked his beard as he re-traced his train of thought.

"Yeah, days of the week. So, *Jeudi*. That's derived from the Greek god Zeus which is a personification of Jupiter. In Pagan Norse it's Thor, the son of Odin, and that's been bastardised into Thursday—Thorsday. Then *Vendredi*. It's right there in the first part—Venus. Again, in the Norse it was represented by Freyja, or Frigg, hence Friday."

"Friggin' 'ell," grinned Shamim, his puns not getting any better.

Max ignored him.

"Then Satur(n)day and Sunday speak for themselves. Saturday has long been the holy day, the Sabbath, in many cultures. That's why it's '*sábado*' in Spanish. But Western 'civilisation' has turned it from a day of worship to one of football, shopping and getting pissed."

"While the faith I grew up on thinks it's been worshipping Allah, when really it's been a Norse goddess archetype based on the feminine attributes of Venus."

Max smiled and pointed at Shamim, conveying wordlessly 'you got it,' adding, "commonly known as the Morning Star or the Light Bringer, or, to give it its Latin interpretation, *Lucifer*."

"Holy sh…well, you know what I mean." Shamim stopped short of another pun, this one unintentional.

Right on cue, almost as if they were being listened into, though alone in the shed, Shamim's Nokia handset began to ring. Max observed as his friend examined the number on display. His brow furrowed and—was it Max's imagination?—no, his whole energy field seemed to change as he pressed the answer key wordlessly.

Shamim held the phone far enough from his ear for Max to be able to discern the voice on the other end.

"Would you have a wond'rous sight, the midday sun at midnight?"

Again.

"Would you have a wond'rous sight, the midday sun at midnight?"

A glazed expression took Shamim's eyes.

"Everything okay?" asked Max, already knowing that it wasn't, and recognising with great reluctance what was going on.

Shamim replaced his phone and pushed noisily back on his metal-framed chair. Without a word he grabbed his rucksack from the floor beside him, and made towards the door of the makeshift studio.

Max raised up from his own chair and watched as Shamim walked, trance-like, across his lawn, into the side alley alongside his house, and out into the drizzly East Oxford night.

CHAPTER 19

Saturday 3rd November 2001

The heavy keys rattled loudly as Vic Kostta fumbled to find the correct one and, identifying it, turned the lock to what all staff understood was the "classified" section of Littlemore Mental Health Hospital. One of the oldest parts of the facility, and fashioned in the style of many a Victorian-era asylum, it was only a stone's throw from where CC Lomas had spent the previous unhappy decade.

Being a Saturday morning, what few staff were on duty were mostly over in the more public-friendly mainstream facade of the institution, along with the inmates. There was only one in this section.

Kostta was not quite alone, however. Trailing a few steps behind him was a security guard who would have looked at home on the door of one of the clubs or bars which had been buzzing with activity just a few hours earlier. Turning to check the guard was still behind him, Kostta let his keys jangle as he paced towards the cell on the far left of the sad, dimly-lit corridor.

Pausing first to check on the cell's occupant by peering through the letterbox-sized slat, and satisfied with the result, Kostta unlocked the cell. He signalled wordlessly

161

to the security guard to remain in the doorway and stay vigilant. Having done so, Kostta walked slowly over to the prison-style bed.

On it sat a sleepless, dejected-looking Shamim Amed.

Kostta drew encouragement from Shamim's wearing of the "thousand-yard stare" look that was so familiar to those in his trade.

"How was your night, Shamim? Did you get any sleep?" he asked him with insincerity.

Shamim turned his head to face him, appearing distant and withdrawn.

He didn't answer.

"Well, no matter," continued Kostta, now with a duper's-delight smile on his own face. "You'll have plenty of time to sleep after your mission."

Not before looking to the security guard for some reassurance, Kostta removed the small black rucksack he had been wearing on his back. Placing it on the bed, he fished around inside it.

Shamim's gaze remained a thousand miles away.

Kostta's left hand found what it was looking for, and he removed a device which looked not dissimilar to a nail gun which could have been procured from the average DIY store. He placed it in Shamim's lap.

"Do you know what this is?" he asked.

No reply.

Little surprise.

"You've come across these before, Shamim. Remember what you were taught? Remember what they can do?"

This time, there was a glimmer of recognition in the young man's eyes. He turned his head slightly left to meet Kostta's gaze.

"And you know who you need to use it on? This man who is our enemy? This man who needs to be removed, for the greater good? Remember?"

Shamim spoke for the first time.

"For the greater good."

"Right," Kostta replied. "Now, when we let you out of here, you know what you need to do...right? And you know what will happen if you fail to complete your mission?"

More recognition in Shamim's eyes. He nodded.

Kostta smiled.

"Would you have a wond'rous sight, the midday sun at midnight?"

Kostta carefully placed the device back in the rucksack. This he passed to Shamim.

Kostta raised up off the bed. The security guard stood aside to let him pass.

"Come on then, Shamim," Kostta said. "The clock is really ticking now, and it's time to go to work."

CHAPTER 20

Saturday 3rd November 2001

"The function of man is to live, not exist. I shall not waste my days trying to prolong them. I shall use my time."

American novelist Jack London.

The squat flat on Cowley Road in which Max Zeall's parents had spent so much time getting stoned in the late 1960s had long since been converted into a much more agreeable dwelling. The block had been purchased by a developer in the 1970s, among whose first tasks were a thorough fumigation, and a ripping out of all fixtures and fittings.

Now, in 2001, the same facilities which had been installed back then were still in place in the ground-floor flat which Max had, for more than two decades, called home. The place was far from anyone's idea of luxurious. "Humble" was the word which most visitors had allotted to it, though "quirky" also figured. It was sparsely-appointed, though what it lacked in decor was compensated for by an impressive array of technology.

Where most might have positioned a TV or a music system, Max had a makeshift studio set-up on a grey metallic desk procured from the Army Surplus store near Abingdon. On it sat his two heavy iMac computers, one of which he used for video and audio editing, the other for e-mails, internet browsing and archiving. Arranged around them were various devices which a layman might have recognised—a DAT player, a Minidisc player, an iMic audio interface—along with several more exotic items which they almost certainly would not.

As he laboured at editing together a compilation of all the inconsistencies in the mainstream news accounts of what had happened almost two months earlier for his upcoming radio show, his concentration was broken by a forceful knocking on his front door. As someone who, as a blanket rule, was not at home to unsolicited calls, Max was not impressed at this infringement. His curiosity had been sparked as to who could be bothering him on a Saturday morning, however, and his glance went to the baseball bat he always kept in an umbrella holder by the door. Just in case.

Closing his left eye, Max peered with his right through the peep hole in the door. In fish-eye lens mode on the other side stood Detective Inspector Sam Haine of Thames Valley CID. Though Haine was in plain clothes, a tracksuit and trainers, no doubt attempting to blend in with the weekend joggers, Max recognised him immediately. His reputation preceded him.

Haine had seemingly sensed movement on the other side of the door. "Mr. Zeall?" he called loudly. "This is DI Haine of Thames Valley Police. Could you open up, please? I'd like a word."

Max was in defensive mode. "Callers to this address are by prior appointment only. This is private property and I hereby give notice that you are trespassing. I have no wish to engage with you and I would ask you to leave."

Max's reputation was also known to Haine, who showed himself to be equally combative.

"That's not your choice, Mr. Zeall. I'm conducting an enquiry following a complaint made against you by a member of the public and I need to ask you some questions. Now, we can do this by screaming at each other through the door and alerting all your neighbours, or we can do it the easy way by you letting me in."

"It seems you're forgetting your place as a public servant, 'officer'," came the less-than-genial response.

" ...paid for by taxpayers' money. Yes, I've heard that one many times, Mr. Zeall. Though somehow I doubt that you fall into the 'taxpayer' category yourself."

Any concerns Max might have had about his neighbours being alerted—not that he did—had already fallen by the wayside as the young student who occupied the ground-floor flat to his right pushed open his front door to wheel his bicycle out. Under the pretence of attending to the chain, he crouched down to eavesdrop on as much of the conversation as he could.

Haine continued.

"As you wish, Mr. Zeall. I'm here to inform you that a complaint has been made against you by a Mr. Cas Passendale of Lux FM radio. He claims that you achieved a method of hacking into his work computer and of compromising his personal password. As I'm sure a man like you is aware, this is a highly illegal crime. Further investigations will be conducted, and if Mr. Passendale's allegations turn out to have any substance, you will be arrested under the Computer Misuse Act 1990."

"Is that right? Well, I guess we'll get to see about that, *boy*! Now, like I said, this is private property, you have not been invited here nor are you welcome. That constitutes trespass. Furthermore, I charge £500 per hour in the case of unsolicited conversations at my door. So unless you want me to serve you in your *personal* capacity as a living man, and *not* hiding behind that uniform and badge that you *think* gives you any kind of power, my suggestion is that you leave immediately and do not return, you scraping, fawning, bowing little order-following goon!"

If Haine had been a regular listener to Max's rants against all expressions of Establishment, he might have realised that his visit would have triggered him in this way. In the event, he had been unprepared, and was not used to being spoken to in this manner by anyone. Apart, perhaps, from his wife.

Through the peephole Max saw Haine's hands form a downward triangle in his sacral area in what appeared to be an involuntary action.

Haine himself had been triggered, as he let his professionalism slip for a moment.

"I'll nail you, you supercilious bastard. You can bank on that!"

Still apparently tending to his bicycle chain, Max's nosy neighbour looked up surreptitiously as Haine stormed angrily away from the red-brick building and replaced his baseball cap ready to blend back into the flow of Saturday morning Cowley Road joggers. Before long, all in the block would have been made aware of the event.

CHAPTER 21

Saturday 3rd November 2001

"As long as Man continues to be the ruthless destroyer of lower living beings, he will never know health nor peace. For as long as men massacre animals, they will kill each other. Indeed, he who sows the seed of murder and pain cannot reap joy and love."

Pythagoras, C. 570bc—C.495bc.

"If you think there is such a thing as 'humane slaughter,' I'm curious—do you also think there is such a thing as 'humane' rape? 'Humane' child molestation? 'Humane' slavery? How about a 'humane' holocaust?

Gary Yourofsky.

"If slaughterhouses had glass walls, everyone would be vegetarian."

"Paul McCartney."

If life as they knew it was about to end, she might as well get in some last-minute retail therapy, Verity had reasoned as she had set off for the city centre. The Mondeo had stayed in Green Place. By the time she would have found a place to park it would have been quicker to walk. Besides, with funds in short supply, (not that this was hindering said retail therapy) she had not yet re-joined her old gym, and so welcomed the exercise.

Her woman-on-a-mission excursion had taken her to various stop-off points in the Westgate Centre. As she navigated her way through the hordes she recalled the Virgin Megastore and Our Price Records from which Drew used to procure his vinyl, both having long since been replaced by clothes shops.

Swinging her shopping bags full of new tops by her side, she headed in the direction of George Street to check the event listings at the Old Fire Station theatre. Maybe there'd be time to take in one last show. Her journey took her past the druggies and dropouts who seemed to permanently occupy Bonn Square. In their midst was what might have been described as a "bag lady"—all wide eyes and wiry hair—holding a raggedy piece of cardboard bearing the handwritten message, "Prepare, for the end is nigh."

"That might be truer than you think, love," Verity whispered under her breath as she fought to ward off the sense of foreboding that was hitting her again in her base chakra area.

Passing the boutique Kate's Cafe to the right, Verity did a double-take as her keen eye, still not missing a trick, registered a figure sitting alone at one of the tables near the window. Yes, it was her.

The bell above the cafe door jangled as she entered and made a headway for the table.

"Hey, Dani."

The young woman snapped out of her apparent daydream and gave Verity a puzzled look. She pushed her glasses closer to her eyes.

"Oh, Verity. Hi," she replied in a non-committal monotone.

Ordinarily, the two of them would have been together at 216b earlier that morning for their weekly group meet. This weekend it had been decided to instead convene on Sunday. Drew had suggested it with bleak humour, inspired by the title of one of his favourite albums, Mary J. Blige's '*What's The 411?*' 4th November is 4/11, he had pointed out, and the phrase translates as "what's going on?" A suitable question indeed. The group had agreed on the basis that it would free them up for what might be the last Saturday as they would know it. They all knew what was at stake.

"Mind if I join you?" asked Verity out of etiquette, knowing that Daniela had her "ways."

"Oh, sure. Feel free," Dani replied.

Verity pulled out a chair, dropped her bags, and seated herself opposite.

"Shopping's exhausting work."

"Oh … right. Umm, yeah."

"Have you ordered?" Verity asked, noticing the bare table.

"Oh, I'm waiting to. Normally they come around."

No sooner had she said it than a silver-haired waitress appeared at their table.

"Take your order, ladies?"

"I'll have a pot of Earl Grey, please," said Verity.

"A soda and a chicken sandwich, please," said Dani.

The waitress smiled and hurried off.

"Oh … you eat meat?" said Verity, rather asking the obvious, but unable to mask her surprise, having assumed anyone of her tribe's ilk to be non-carnivorous.

"Umm … yeah?" The girl's confused eyes sought clarification.

Many years previous, social etiquette would have prevented Verity from taking things further. But many moons under the influence of Keith and Max had brought a direct candidness rooted in Natural Law morality.

"You really should think about not eating meat, you know. It's not good for your soul—not to mention for the chicken."

It had been challenging enough for Daniela to face Oxford's Saturday crowds. Now she found herself having to figure out the motives of a woman she thought she'd had a firm handle on over the previous weeks.

"Well . . . I only really eat chicken and fish."

"But they're still living, sentient beings just as much as any other animal—or any one of us. They still have the capacity to feel love, fear, pain, terror—just as we do.

"One of the reasons organised society has been coerced into consuming animal flesh as one of its "norms" is because the satanic controllers rely on that constant supply of "*loosh*" energy flooding the morphic field in which we all have to live. That's why slaughterhouses are so often sited at key points on Earth's energy grid—so that all that dense, fear-based energy gets amplified out as widely as possible. They built the United Nations building in New York on the site of a former abattoir. You can imagine what the energy in that place is like as a result."

Dani was taking it all in. "I do want to go vegetarian," she said, convincingly.

Verity considered her next approach. "Look, I'm not trying to have a go, mate. You're a wonderful girl. Lord knows you've come so much further than most of your age. You could just be doing so much better for yourself and for Creation itself if you could just spare the chicken and fish."

Right on cue, the drinks and the chicken sandwich arrived. Dani looked with new-found trepidation at the plate.

"Would you forgive me if I drop a Gandhi quote on you?" added Verity with a reassuring smile, and not waiting for an answer.

"He's supposed to have said that the greatness and morality of a nation can be judged by how it treats its animals ... or words to that effect. If that's the case, what does that say about our nation? Or this city? Animals are a soul test. They live alongside us to facilitate our moral choices. If we can't grant freedom and compassion to fellow living, sentient beings, how can we expect those same values for ourselves?"

Dani kept her eyes on the plate as she spoke.

"Do you raise Hope as vegan?"

"Keith and I are vegans," Verity answered. "We're raising Hope vegetarian until she's old enough to make her own choices. It's a compromise. Then it'll all be up to her."

"I have actually been giving some thought to these subjects myself. Nature is so cruel and barbaric. I read somewhere that one bat can eat up to 3,000 bugs in a single night. Just think of the horror of that! Could it be that way because we—as supposedly a more highly-advanced species who should know better and be setting the moral precedent—are cruel and barbaric ourselves? Could everything have turned out so different if *we* had all behaved differently?"

Verity smiled as Dani did her soul-searching. Yes, this girl surely had all the wisdom of an old soul.

"I think you just answered your own question."

After pausing to contemplate, Dani pushed the chicken sandwich aside. "I've suddenly lost my appetite," she said with the hint of a smile.

Verity smiled herself. "Well, then let me at least get that for you," she said, fishing a five-pound note out of her purse and tossing it on the table.

"I'll save the conversation about the Aspartame in her soda for another time," she reflected silently.

***

An hour or so later Verity had transported her purchases back to 216b. A note from Keith on the telephone table confirmed that he had taken Hope out to play at Cutteslowe Park. Before she'd had a chance to unzip her imitation-leather boots, the telephone started ringing. Was it . . .? If it was, it was as if the caller was watching and knew when she'd just arrived home.

Before answering, she did what she and Keith had now entrained themselves to do as a matter of course and pressed the red button on the DAT machine-like device that Max had installed. Only then did she pick up the receiver.

"Hello?"

No reply. None of the usual ambient noise this time, either. Remembering what Max had told them about needing as much time as possible to trace the call, she styled it out.

"Hello? Can you hear me? It's a bit of a bad line. Could you speak up, please?"

Still no reply.

"We've been having a bit of trouble with the phone. The landlord's still not fixed it. Keep trying and it may connect. Are you still there?"

Verity cursed as a continuous tone filled her ear, though got a welcome surprise when she glanced down at the LED display on the device.

173

It had managed to detect the overall region from which the call had originated.

Goa, India.

CHAPTER 22

Sunday 4th November 2001

"Never underestimate the power of a small group of committed people to change the world ... In fact, it is the only thing that's ever done so."

Margaret Mead.

"Say bye-bye to Mummy then, and we'll see her later, won't we?"

Hope did as instructed, as her grandmother took her tiny hand and led her towards the front door of 216b. The living room was cramped at the best of times, and felt especially claustrophobic with six bodies already there. No sooner had the number dropped by two, as Joy and Hope headed out and in the direction of Hinksey Park, than it got replaced by the two late arrivals to the meeting.

No-one was surprised that it was Drew and May.

"Sorry we're late, guys," offered up Drew in a predictable weekly ritual. "I'm ... "

"Drew?" Verity finished his sentence.

"The girl knows me," he replied, high-fiving Verity as he went to grab a seat at the table next to Keith. May followed in his wake.

"Hey," said Verity, causing May's gaze to raise up from the floor. "You alright, mate?"

May forced a smile. "I will be." But her depleted aura spoke for itself.

"Let's talk afterwards. Don't dash off."

May forced another smile and occupied one of the garden chairs that had been placed on the edge of the four-seater table. Drew took the seat opposite. Verity sat down to face Keith. Max and Dani faced each-other in the remaining seats.

Drew broke the silence. "You think the Bilderberg group do this every week?"

"We're a bit like them, actually," Keith responded, " …only with added truth and integrity…and less Satanism." Then, assuming ringmaster status. "Right then. Where are we at?"

"We're at the most critical juncture in history that this city will have ever seen."

All eyes turned to Max as he answered.

"If we're right about what's scheduled to go down on Friday—and let's be real, we know we are—then this little get-together will go down in history, because it's whatever plan of action we put into place right here, right now that will determine where human society goes from here. Because, let's be clear, it may be Oxford today, but it'll be everyone else's hometown tomorrow."

While everyone else's look had averted away from Max towards the table—or to nowhere in particular—one of the table's occupants was still staring intently at him. While the others seemed to have missed it, Verity had not. Yes, there it was again.

Max continued, seemingly oblivious.

"I've learned a thing or two about The Order over the years, and it's clear that they would only plan a stunt as audacious as this one if it were intended to bring about the *ultimate* New World Order masterplan that's been their wet dream for decades—their "final solution," if you will.

"This has been timed to capitalise to the max...excuse the pun...on the fear and paranoia created by 9/11. I'm sure they would have acted sooner if they didn't love their dates and numerology so much. At least them wanting to pull off "a very British 9/11" has bought us a few weeks.

"But, make no mistake. This event—if it happens—will be used to plunge Oxford into a dystopian "lockdown" that would make George Orwell say, 'my god, I didn't go far enough!' All kinds of natural rights will be rescinded in the spirit of 'keeping everyone safe.'

"And the saddest thing of all is that the vast majority will blindly go along with curbs and dictates that would have been considered outrageous and unacceptable just a week before, all through the blind fear that will have been cultivated. As Alistair McLean observed in the title of his novel—rightly—'fear is the key'."

An air of dejectedness befell the table.

"We'd never be able to get the masses to accept it for what it really would be," said Keith.

"Notice how you spoke there," offered Verity.

Keith looked puzzled.

"You said 'what it really *would* be. *Would.* The conditional tense. Meaning something's possible but not a definite. This event going off the way it's planned to is *not* yet a foregone conclusion."

"And the only way it won't is if—when—we stop it."

All eyes turned in May's direction.

Though she had said less with every passing week, what contributions she had made had always been invaluable, even to the point of causing Keith to ask "what would May think?" in a couple of private discussions with Verity.

"That only leaves the question of how exactly we do that, Maysie," said Drew.

As if anticipating May to have the solution, the others paused to allow her to respond.

"We're all familiar with The Order's tenet of 'revelation of the method,' right? This aspect of their spiritual belief system which dictates that they must pre-announce what they plan to do?"

"Well, we ought to be. Max has mentioned it on the last 500 of his radio shows," said Drew, with a tone of good-natured mockery. Dani jerked her head in his direction as he spoke.

"Well then," May continued, "what we need to do is call them on their bullshit. Send an abundantly clear message that we do *not* consent. Even if we're not speaking for the rest of the city, if we can make it clear that even our small group has figured out what they plan do do, and we're not with it in any way...wouldn't that be something they would have to observe? Wouldn't they consider themselves to be in contravention of Natural Law if they didn't have the unspoken consent of the rest of us, leaving they themselves to stand fully accountable?"

Keith responded first.

"Absolutely...I see that...but how? How would we send that kind of message in a way that we'd know had been effective? The Order don't exactly invite you to write in on a postcard."

"There is a way."

All attention was back in Max's direction.

"We don't need to go to them, but we can be pretty sure they come to us. I'm under no illusion that "they" don't routinely listen in to my show. There's no way they wouldn't by now. I have one more left. Tomorrow. Fireworks Night, appropriately."

The group paused to process Max's words.

"Ladies," he nodded towards Verity, May and Dani, "gentlemen ... tomorrow night, a very clear message will be sent to 'The Order'," (Keith smirked as he recalled Max's comment during one of his epic rants that 'they're "the order" of the sludge and the slime that gathers at the bottom of a cesspit,) "that we do not consent, and that *they alone* will stand fully exposed for the harm, damage and loss that they plan to cause, and that *they alone* will have to face the very God of Creation that they most despise and fear."

"Yeah, man," remarked Drew, offering up his fist to bump with Verity's.

"True dat," she added. Then, turning to her right, "respeck, Maysie!"

Drew and Keith smiled in May's direction as she herself continued to look down at the table. Verity looked towards Max as he gazed pensively at the wallpaper opposite.

"You da man, Max."

The attention of the others was drawn immediately to the scraping of Dani's chair on the wooden floor as she raised herself up.

"I'm sorry," she exclaimed breathlessly, "I just ... I need to get some air."

Quickly and awkwardly, she hurried towards the kitchen and out into the compact back yard.

"It's okay, I'll go," volunteered Max, raising up from his own chair.

"She's having a panic attack," said May.

"I know."

Through her spectacles, Dani's face was flooded with tears as she faced the plum tree that bordered Keith and Verity's garden. The figure of Max loomed large as he drew towards her.

Of all in the group, he was the one she had hoped would come.

"Dani," he said with a concerned tone, placing his hand on her right shoulder.

She turned quickly around. His sadness at registering her tears was replaced quickly by shock as she used both her hands to draw his head towards her much shorter frame, and, navigating the way between his beard and moustache, proceeded to kiss him full on the mouth.

Max recoiled—not from any unpleasantness, but from an instant sense of propriety.

A mixture of shock and hurt appeared in Dani's reddened eyes.

"What's the matter? Don't you ... don't you like me?"

Max paused to find the right words as he instinctively brushed his hand across his lips.

"Dani, I think you're great. I really do. You're a wonderful girl. But this isn't ... right. I'm old enough to be your father!"

Dani glared daggers. "What does age matter when it comes to love?" Then, unconsciously channelling the lyrics of the recently-departed Aaliyah. "Age ain't nothin' but a number. Isn't that what they say?"

"But ... but ..."

"I thought we had a special connection. I've felt it since I first called in to your show."

" ... I'm sorry."

The message had been made clear as Dani ran, in her panicked state, back though the kitchen and living room and through the front door of 216b.

As she hurried along Abingdon Road in the direction of the city, a black Mercedes which had been sitting in Green Place slowly slinked away from its parking space and followed in her wake.

***

A couple of miles across town, in a 'special operations' room of Littlemore Hospital, two middle-aged men in white shirts and black glasses, with listening devices clutched closely to their ears, strained to make sense of the confusion which was ensuing back at 216b.

The spools of a Denon DAT machine turned silently on a shelf to their left, creating a permanent record of everything they themselves had heard that afternoon.

CHAPTER 23

Monday 5th November 2001

"The people who were trying to make this world worse are not taking the day off. Why should I?"

Bob Marley.

Endless explosions of colour lit up the night sky, each ejection of sparks preceded first by a crackle and whoosh, then a deafening bang.

Never one to be coerced into "celebrating" festivals of this nature as dictated by society, Max Zeall had done his best to avoid the spectacle as he had driven his Ford Transit van the short distance from his Cowley flat to the house in Cricket Road. Shamim having been missing since Friday night had understandably caused major concern for his wife, and Max had offered her whatever support he had been able to through the weekend.

She had been very insistent that the radio station should continue operating, however, and particularly keen for Max's show to air on this all-important occasion.

His attention was immediately caught, as he turned in from Ridgefield Road, by the larger than usual amount of vehicles on either side of the house. Parking some distance away on the opposite side, he proceeded cautiously towards the house, his early-warning system fully engaged.

His concern proved well-founded when, seconds before he could reach out and open the side gate, it was kicked violently in his direction. As it smashed against the side of the house, a middle-aged man bowled through, his arms brandishing various equipment from the studio in the outhouse.

The man stopped in his tracks as he regarded Max.

"Boss! He's here!"

Max battled his primary instinct to lamp the man, more out of concern for the equipment which would doubtless fall crashing to the floor than for any other reason. Instead, he barged past the man and through the gate.

A shocking sight awaited him.

With arms fully laden like the first man, leads and cables trailing in the mud behind them, two others were carefully navigating the walk across the lawn from the outhouse to the gate, the constant flickering of light in the night sky illuminating their path helpfully.

Behind them, emerging from the outhouse, but without having stooped so low as to pick up any paraphernalia himself, was Detective Inspector Sam Haine of Thames Valley CID. The sound of his radio crackling away at his waist was being drowned out by the booming in the sky.

"Mr. Zeall." Haine smirked as he acknowledged the look of rage which became more evident with every new step he took towards him. "I believe I mentioned the last time we met that I would nail you one day. It seems that day has come. I am confiscating this equipment under the DTI's Broadcasting Act 1990 Section, which prohibits the establishment or use of a wireless telegraphy station or apparatus for the purpose of making an unlicensed broadcast.

"The financing or participating in the day-to-day running of unlicensed broadcasting is also a criminal offence, as is the supplying of a sound recording for an unlicensed station, and advertising through unlicensed stations."

Again, it took every ounce of will within Max's being not to land his fist in this man's face—particularly as no equipment stood to get damaged in the process.

Instead he clapped.

"Well done, Detective Inspector. You managed to recite the whole passage. Aren't you a good little automaton? You'll make Level 33 in no time at this rate."

The two were a foot apart looking each other directly in the eye.

It was clear to Max what was happening. The timing was no surprise. Without the means to broadcast it, so the theory seemed to be, the absence of consent could not be logged. The logic was as flawed as the idea in the first place that karmic responsibility could somehow be dodged through duplicity.

"You *know* how explosive this broadcast was to be tonight, don't you, *boy*?" Max snarled menacingly. "You really think this is all it takes to stop me from doing what I need to do? If so then you really don't know me at all. I have a will of cast iron, and only the breath leaving my body will stop me from achieving what I set out to. Nothing less will get it done."

Haine continued to smile, derision in his eyes. Max sneered as he considered the authority that this man believed he had, purely as a result of his job title, and just how far that mistaken notion was from the truth. He wouldn't even be aware that the very word "police" is derived from "policy," he considered, meaning the policy of the satanists and paedophiles that he serves—unknowingly or otherwise. Or of the occult mockery that the black-and-white checkered design on police-issue hats represents, this symbol of Freemasonry sitting right at the point of the third-eye chakra, indicating that their very consciousness has been bought and paid for.

"If you were the proprietor of this station then charges would apply," the policeman recited faithfully. "As it is, we don't know where he can be found. Either way, this equipment will now be impounded, and possibly put out for resale.

A firework exploded right above Haine's head as he spoke.

CHAPTER 24

Monday 5th November 2001

"Look around, everywhere you turn is heartache.
It's everywhere that you go.
You try everything you can to escape,
The pain of life that you know."

Madonna: 'Vogue.'

"The world ain't all sunshine and rainbows. It's a very mean
and nasty place, and I don't care how tough you are, it will
beat you to your knees and keep you there permanently if you
let it."

Sylvester Stallone in 'Rocky.'

"Sometimes I look up to the stars and analyse the sky,
And ask myself, was I meant to be here?
Why?"

Ghostface Killah Featuring Mary J Blige: 'All That I Got
Is You.'

"I don't smoke cigarettes, I don't smoke cigars, I don't smoke a pipe . . . pipe, pipe, pipe, pipe, pipe, pipe, pipe, pipe . . .

"I don't smoke de reefer!"

The sampled dialogue was followed by a devastating bassline which caused the speaker stacks in each corner of the small, sweaty room to rasp and fart with reverberation. A collective whoop went up from the crowd.

Drew Hunter wasn't used to such a reaction, being somewhat a stranger to the genre of UK Garage. It still wasn't entirely his bag. Yet, he had to admit, his having been asked to fill in for the regular DJ for this Bonfire Night special at the Bridge nightclub did represent a breath of fresh air from the "urban" fare of which he was becoming increasingly tired. Working his way through the CDs which had been burned for him by the regular DJ, he had already found Pied Piper's '*Do You Really Like It*,' So Solid Crew's '*21 Seconds*' and Zed Bias's '*Neighbourhood*' to have brought spine-tinglingly energetic reactions from the crowd.

He surveyed the vista as he looked out from the vantage point of the DJ booth. Most in attendance appeared to be university students. There was an over-abundance of Caucasians, with little of the ethnic diversity one might have expected from such a music genre.

Not that he would have known either of them, but throwing shapes in front of each of the room's speaker stacks were Molly Lowe, evidently not letting her new-found poverty prevent her from partying, and a just-off-shift Aimee Hardwick.

The latter was perfectly attired for the club. Other than her tights having been removed, she was still dressed the same as she had been for her work shift, a fact which had drawn the attention of countless male onlookers.

One in particular had been fixated, slobberingly, on her form as they had danced together, evidently anticipating the night's titillations continuing once the club was done, but having no idea that he would be discarded as readily as the handful of other young males who had already been in his place that evening. Even if he hadn't, his name would surely have been forgotten by the next morning as readily as any given Lux FM news script was as soon as Aimee had robotically read it out.

***

The scene across town in Barton couldn't have been further removed from that at The Bridge. There was none of the noise—save for that of the muffled fireworks overhead. There was none of the sweat—only a Winter chill. There was none of the over-crowdedness, only a single individual, lying in her underwear on top of the covers of a double bed.

The subdued light from the 40-watt bulb of a small bedside lamp provided the room's only illumination.

May Pearce stared up at nothing in particular as she let out a deep breath, then turned to the items on the bedside table to her right. Arranged there were the contents of several brown padded envelopes, accumulated over the weeks. There they were—multiple blister-packs of small, white pills. By their side, a 1-litre bottle of Co-op budget vodka.

To her left were items to which she had given careful consideration to displaying. A 12-inch vinyl copy of '*Goodbye Cruel World*' by Shakespears Sister, and a manila envelope.

May paused and allowed herself to breathe deeply for two minutes flat. As she did so, she ran over in her mind one last time—the millionth?—the reasons. The reflections. The repercussions.

It was the same as it had been every other time she had been there. Nothing had changed. The reasons to go through with what she had planned for so long, outweighed those to abandon it by a million to one.

She turned again to the bedside table. "It's time, Maysie," she whispered quietly to herself. " ... it's time."

Bringing the fifteen or so blister-packs on to the bed beside her, she proceeded to pop all of the pills out of them, discarding the packs to the floor as she went.

Left with a substantial pile, she reached out for the bottle of liquid so clear it could have been water.

Another pause for reflection.

She reached for the other item on the bedside table. A photograph of her mother from when she was around the same age that May was now. Holding it at eye level, she whispered quietly, "I'm coming home, Mum."

With little further hesitation, the 37-year-old began to pile handfuls of the small white pills into her mouth, then to wash them down with generous gulps from the bottle. The phrase "there's no turning back now; it's too late" reverberated in her own voice through her consciousness as she continued.

Presently, she reached the end of the pile, and swigged another gulp from the now half-empty bottle, shuddering as she did so.

Had anyone been present to scrutinise the contents of the envelope to her right—and able to decipher May's distinctive scrawl—they would have read:

"To Drew.

"To Will.

"To Verity.

"To The World.

"First, let me say, I'm so very sorry for whatever pain and grief I may have caused. Though really, I can't imagine why.

"Perhaps it's best expressed in the words of Whitney Houston from her song '*My Love Is Your Love*':

"If I should die this very day,

Don't cry, 'cause on Earth we wasn't meant to stay."

"What more can I say? This place—whatever it is—is clearly not our natural home. I've known this for so long. That's why some of us struggle so much to operate within it. I always have. I learned to mask it. Because that's what we do, isn't it? We entrain ourselves to act as if it's all good and we fit in here just fine.

"But the truth is, some of us just don't. Some of us know that we don't. That we belong somewhere else. We've always known it. We do our best to blend in. To be a part of "the crowd." To act "normal." But deep down, there's that knowing.

"This is not where we belong.

"It's been getting harder and harder to keep pretending otherwise. So I've decided not to. Not any more. I've decided that enough is enough and the time has come to go home.

"It's a shame that this will cause sadness to many of those I care about. But really it shouldn't. This is my choice. This is my decision. And anyone who truly cares about me should want to respect that, and should want to be happy for my release from the pain.

"So, this is my wish. Don't be sad. Don't mourn me. Instead, celebrate. Because this is what I've chosen. I alone am responsible for this decision. No-one else. And I alone will face the consequences."

"I hope I at least put some good into this world during the time I was here. I hope whatever I was able to contribute towards preventing something terrible from happening in Oxford, will have had value.

"Goodbye to all those who I knew, loved and cared about through these 37 years.

I'll see you all again when you get here.

"Maysie.

"XX."

As the words that she herself had written rang again through her mind, May Pearce closed her eyes. Tiredness was taking her.

She was tired.

So very tired.

There was a sudden explosion of white light, as loud as that of the fireworks outside. Through the dazzling display, May was sure that she could make out a profile.

A figure.

A woman.

Yes. There it was. Wasn't it?

It had to be.

Was she home?

She had to be.

Didn't she?

Whether she was or not, it was too late to turn back now ... too late ... too late.

And then ...

CHAPTER 25

Saturday 13th October 1979

"And school's out early,
And soon we'll be learning that the lesson today is how to die."

Boomtown Rats: 'I Don't Like Mondays.'

"And as we sit here alone, thinking of a reason to go on,
It's so clear that all we have now are our thoughts of yesterday."

Strawberry Switchblade: 'Since Yesterday.'

"And so I face the wall.
Turn my back against it all
How I wish I'd been unborn.
Wish I wasn't living here."

Eurythmics: 'Sexcrime (1984)'

"Right, come on then, you two. Let's get this to your mum."

The tall, middle-aged man swung the sandwich bag with his left hand as his children trailed behind him in Bicester's Sheep Street. Stops at WH Smith, the Fine Fare supermarket and the local deli had ensured they had what they needed, and they headed towards the far end of the street.

15-year-old May Pearce had a copy of the new '*Smash Hits*' magazine under her arm. A youthful Bob Geldof, lead singer of the Boomtown Rats, adorned the cover, which advised that Kate Bush, The Damed and Boney M were featured inside, while May anticipated putting up the poster of Blondie's Debbie Harry on her bedroom wall when she got home. Her 17-year-old brother Will, though not immune to the charms of Debbie Harry, was used to more mature reading matter, and clutched the copy of the '*Daily Express*' that his father had purchased from the newsagent.

"'*I Don't Like Mondays*' is about mind control," Will piped up out of nowhere, in reference to the Boomtown Rats' hit single of that year's summer.

"What? No, it's not. It's about a girl who went crazy in America and shot all her classmates," countered May.

"Yeah? And why d'you think she went so 'crazy'? You remember the line 'the silicon chip inside her head gets switched to overload?' It's talking about brain implants. It's real. The CIA does these experiments in the States. It's called . . . something-or-other Ultra. Ben at school knows all about it from his Dad, 'cause he works on similar stuff at Oxford University."

May took the magazine and perused the cover image again as she quietly considered Will's words. The image of Geldof hunched in a corner stared menacingly back at her.

The three turned left at the end of Sheep Street on to St. John's Street, and left again on to Queens Avenue, May and Will struggling to match the rapid pace of their father. Turning off the main road into the Police Station car park, they quickened as they neared the building.

David Pearce wore a contented smile. He had been proud of his wife's achievement in becoming one of very few female constables employed by Thames Valley Police, and one of only two in Bicester, straight after completing her training at Hendon five years earlier. She had taken inspiration from her own father who had worked his way up to the rank of inspector. Despite his pride, David reserved a quiet gratitude for the fact that his wife had been posted within the relative tameness of the small market town where they lived, rather than in the much more dangerous Oxford just a few miles to the south.

As he trotted up the three steps to the main door and up to the front desk, his life changed forever.

The first indication that all was far from well was the ashen look on the desk sergeant's face upon spotting him. The expression "you look like you've seen a ghost" would have been apt. Two constables in the reception area exchanged glances as Will and May followed.

The smile on David Pearce's face switched to an expression of concern.

"Hi, Stu. Is everything ...?"

Before he could finish, the desk sergeant had interrupted.

"David, thank God you're here. We've been phoning you for the past hour." Then, noticing May and Will and the puzzled expressions on their faces. "Could we .... could we just talk back here?"

The desk sergeant ushered Mr. Pearce towards the office to the rear of the desk.

"Bob, could you ...?" Addressing his colleague, he signalled towards the teenagers.

'What is it? What's wrong?" demanded May of the officer.

"It's OK. The sergeant just needs to speak to your dad for a moment. He won't be long."

Will and May had refused the constable's invitation to take a seat, and instead paced around the reception area while they awaited the return of their father.

Very soon afterwards the door to the back office swung violently open and David Pearce re-emerged.

In the previous two minutes he had learned that his wife had been acting erratically since arriving for her shift that morning. Certainly, she had been quiet and distant with her husband when he had seen her last, yet this had been a common occurrence since she had started on her latest course of pharmaceuticals prescribed by her GP.

Her colleagues had become concerned when she had started snapping and swearing at them, entirely out of character, and even moreso when she had suddenly pushed the entire contents of her desk to the floor, put her head in her hands and begun sobbing bitterly. Recovering, she had taken the keys to one of the Panda patrol cars parked outside, and sped off.

David paced over to where his children stood, confused and scared. He placed a hand on the back of each of their heads, pulling them towards his chest, and swallowed hard as he fought back tears.

During his two-minute conference he had already made urgent provision for what would happen next.

There was a screech of brakes as a Panda patrol car pulled up at the front of the building. The sergeant—Bob—who had been comforting May and Will, was in the driver's seat

"Let's go," said David, ushering the teenagers down the steps and into the back of the car.

"Where are we going?" demanded May.

"I think Mum's at home," came the reply.

"Then what's the urgency?" chipped in Will.

The question went unanswered as Bob switched on the blue lights and siren, crunched the car into first gear and stamped on the accelerator. A family of four smarted as the car leered towards the main road, missing them narrowly, and continued onward to the Pearce family home in Southwold.

The journey had been wordless for the less than three minutes it had taken. Consternation ruled the Pearces' faces as the car screeched to a halt adjacent to the front garden of the neatly-kept three-bedroom semi. The net curtains twitched in the houses opposite as the blue lights continued to blaze, and David Pearce flung the passenger door open and ran up the driveway, praying that his worst fears would be assuaged.

The white shutter door to the garage was fully closed, yet he could hear the sound of a car engine running inside.

He gripped the chrome handle and twisted it sharply to the right.

Bob, May and Will, now all out of the car, watched in dismay as the door swung fully open, and David Pearce was consumed by a thick grey cloud of smog, bending double and coughing profusely as the fumes entered his lungs.

"Oh Lord, no," said Bob, before running forward to assist.

As the clouds began to clear, the outline of the missing Panda car revealed itself. The debris of several broken garden pots lay strewn around. The front driver and passenger side windows were wound fully open.

Occupying the driver seat, unconscious with her head slumped fully forward, was WPC Jill Pearce, in full police uniform.

"Oh God, no, Jill," cried David as, still spluttering, he wrenched open the driver's door.

Switching off the engine and moving his wife carefully forward, he looked for signs of life. Bob had now squeezed in beside him, having radio-ed back to HQ for immediate assistance.

As David pinched her nose and gently smacked her face, Bob checked her wrist for a pulse.

The first good news of the afternoon came when Bob proclaimed, "she's alive!"

Concerned neighbours had begun swarming around the driveway. The feint sounds of emergency sirens seeped from across town.

As Will Pearce ran forward to join his father, his 15-year-old sister, in a state of deep trauma, could only gaze on helplessly.

CHAPTER 26

Tuesday 6th November 2001

Drew Hunter used the display light from his mobile phone to illuminate the lock to the Barton flat's front door. He turned the key, stepped through, and pulled the door shut again as quietly as he always did when arriving home after 3am. He groaned with relief as he placed down the black and orange Ministry of Sound record bag laden with vinyl, and removed his puffa jacket and Timberland boots.

Ordinarily, a late-night snack and a spliff would have been in order, but something was telling him to give that a miss tonight and head straight to the bedroom. He listened to the guidance, yawning as he went, and becoming alarmed to see illumination through the crack in the door.

Unsure whether this meant his woman had waited up or had fallen asleep with the light on, he proceeded quietly.

Technically, the latter option was correct—though not in the way Drew had been expecting. His senses sharpened as he regarded the record sleeve and envelope on the bed.

"Oh God, no! No! Maysie!"

Drew pounced on the bed, his worst fears devouring him. Wailing wildly, he leaned her head forward and cradled it in his arms.

***

"Mummy...I had a nightmare."

As Keith stirred and mumbled something incoherent beside her, Verity sat up in bed. Through the half-light of the waning moon seeping through the side of the curtains, she could just make out the silhouette of her young daughter standing at the foot of the bed, clutching her favourite teddy bear.

"What is it, sweet pea?" she asked in a croaky whisper, beckoning the child. Keith stirred and snorted again.

Hope stumbled into Verity's welcoming arms.

"Auntie Maysie fell asleep," the child whispered with wide, expressive eyes.

"I should hope she did," replied Verity. "It's the middle of the night!"

"No!" Hope responded belligerently. "I mean ...."

The child's protestations were interrupted by the sudden ringing of the house phone at the foot of the stairs. Any hopes of a restful night's sleep for Keith were now a dead loss.

"Who the fuck...?" Then, registering the presence of his daughter through bleary eyes, "Who the heck is that? What time is it?"

"It's...3.32," said Verity, checking the digital alarm clock. "You'd better see who it is."

Keith threw back the duvet. "This had better be fuc...it had better be good!"

Hope climbed into bed in his place as he stomped angrily down the stairs and yanked up the receiver.

"Drew? What...? What? Slow down.... *what?!*"

CHAPTER 27

Tuesday 6th November 2001

Max Zeall had received the same news as Verity and Keith, though at a more civilised hour. Keith had called him at 8.38am soon after receiving an update from Verity, who had arrived at the John Radcliffe Hospital a short while after Drew.

While Keith had stayed to tend to Hope, Verity had maintained as close a vigil as staff had permitted. This had amounted to several hours on a plastic chair in the corridor outside the Emergency Room, quaffing endless plastic cups of revolting coffee—more as a distraction than out of any desire for the beverage.

Though Verity was distraught and traumatised herself, she had recognised that her primary role was to support her cousin. Though May was still alive—clinically speaking at least—Drew had been blaming himself all morning for his inability to spot what were now some obvious signs. Though Verity had offered the obligatory platitudes, deep down she had also wondered how he could have been so blind when she herself had been able to detect for months that May had been spiralling into a very dark place.

This call had been bad enough. The one which immediately followed sank Max into an even deeper depression. Denroy, to whom he had entrusted his personal phone number, had called with the news that Milton William 'Bill" Cooper had been shot dead by police at his home the previous day. Seemingly, the man who had predicted the events of 9/11 just a few weeks before they had happened, and had then called out the US government—or at least the forces that control it—as being responsible, was too dangerous to be left alive. His death had occurred ten years to the day after the disappearance of the publishing magnate and Mossad spy Robert Maxwell.

Max had sighed and shaken his head without words. There was no need for any. This wasn't the radio show. And what was there to say anyway?

There were three rapid knocks on the front door. It seemed the momentous events of the day were just getting started.

This wasn't the postman. Hoisting himself up from his workstation, Max hurried to the door and peered through the peephole with his right eye.

Pulling aside the top and bottom deadlock bolts, he pulled the door towards him.

Into the room stepped the dishevelled frame of Shamim Amed, officially deemed "missing" since before the weekend.

Max pushed the door shut. The two men stared wordlessly at each other, some five feet apart.

Shamim reached into the right inside pocket of his black bomber jacket. He produced a device that looked something like a double-decker handgun.

Max instinctively smarted and prepared to take a defensive position. But Shamim held the device harmlessly to his side.

He broke the silence.

"Do you know what this is?"

"Yes," Max replied, as Shamim was sure he would. "I've seen it in pictures. It's a heart-attack gun. Developed by CIA black-ops. Though MI5 doubtless have their own. It fires a dart of shellfish toxins and frozen water. Once inside the body it melts, leaving only a small red mark where it entered."

The corners of Shamim's mouth upturned.

"Sounds about right. I think their idea was that I would use it on you."

"And ... you're not ... ?"

Max again smarted as Shamim stepped forward. Yet instead of taking any offensive action, he placed the device down on Max's workstation. He pulled out Max's office chair and, without invitation, sank down into it.

Max remained standing.

Shamim took a few moments to gather his composure. He took deep breaths as if preparing for a rigorous gym workout, before continuing with his story.

"My father was the Imam at Central Oxford Mosque in the 1980s. You knew that, right?"

Max nodded in the affirmative.

"Well ... he wasn't ... just that. He was also affiliated with The Order. Anyone in that position always is in the end. They have to be."

Shamim felt Max's intense eyes boring deeply into his.

"They promised him great wealth and privilege. He was a first-generation immigrant from Bangladesh. It was a very attractive offer. But it came at a price."

"They always do."

"Right. In this case, it involved him selling his own family into bondage. He was forced to give me up to a mind-control programme. I have vague childhood memories of experimentation taking place at Littlemore Hospital and at Dalton Barracks."

"Well, he wasn't 'forced.' There's always the magic word. 'No'!"

Shamim might have predicted the riposte.

"That's a fair point. Well, either way, that's what happened. I was put into a programme alongside my friend Hakeem. We became 'sleepers.' Programmed, but then put back into regular society ready for when—if ever—a mission might need to be completed. Well, you know how it works.

"I do."

"Well, last week I got a visit and I was told it was 'time'."

Max's piercing glare remained fixed. "And so...?" he asked.

Shamim let out a sigh.

"And so...I'm here today because I'm supposed to use this"—he beckoned towards the gun he had placed on the desk—"to kill you."

"But you're not? Because...?"

Another sigh.

"Because...all the time they were trying to programme me with the trigger phrase, I kept in mind the mantra that you yourself had taught me..."

"Which was...?"

"I call back my power and energy from all corners, people, places and situations that have been draining, siphoning or stealing from me—consciously or subconsciously, intentionally or unintentionally—from all realms, worlds and directions of time. I am safe, sovereign, and protected."

"You memorised it word-for-word."

"Seems the energetic vibrations of those words are strong enough to over-ride even the most insidious mind-control programmes."

As if subconsciously, Shamim brushed the gun yet further to the side as he continued.

"Also, 'all is Mind; reality is the illusion; Government is slavery; free your mind'!"

Max took his first steps towards his friend.

"I know a professional deprogrammer. We'll get you back on track."

"It's not me that's the problem any more. They took Hakeem. He's not as strong as me. He'll still be under their spell."

Max paused for contemplation.

"Then, as far as 'they' are concerned, you must be as well. You need to report back to 'them' that you've fulfilled your mission."

***

Placing a demanding Hope down, Keith ran frantically to the phone, fully expecting it to be an update from Verity at the hospital.

"Oh, Max?" He could scarcely disguise his surprise.

"Keith. There have been developments. I know who they're going to pin the attacks on Friday on. I'm going to need to lie low for a few days.

"Here's what's going to happen ..."

***

Verity was still not back at 216b. A tired and emotional Keith had laid out on the sitting room sofa to catch a rest, and had inadvertently fallen asleep. A bored and listless Hope had begun looking for things to do. Various of her toys and dolls were scattered across the floor, having already outlived their usefulness on this particular day. She considered picking up one of the square, hard-covered 'sensory' books with the fluffy inserts, but decided against it.

As she turned towards the telephone table in the hall, she was sure she noticed a quick flash of red light from around her eye level. She moved closer, pausing as she reached the table.

She crouched down beneath it and peered upwards. There, stuck firmly to the underside, was a small metallic disk. As she ran her finger curiously over its cold, smooth surface, the red LED light emitted another blink.

The five-year-old became suddenly scared. Whatever this thing was, she was sure it was nothing her parents had put there.

She ran straight over to wake her father.

CHAPTER 28

Sunday 10th August 1980

*"We got to keep it real with reality, and reality gon' keep it real
with us.
I remember them good old days.
Because, see, that's the child I was,
What made me the man I am today."*

*Ghostface Killah Featuring Mary J Blige: 'All That I Got
Is You.'*

*"When you're through with life,
And all hope is lost,
Hold out your hands,
'Cause friends will be friends,
Right till the end."*

Queen: 'Friends Will Be Friends.'

"I heard a rumour from Ground Control. Oh no, don't say
it's true. I heard a rumour from the Action Man ... no, no,
wait."

Keith Malcolm muttered under his breath as he
attempted to recall the precise lyrics from the strange

new song from David Bowie that he had heard played by Radio 1 all week. He made a mental note to be home early enough to catch the chart countdown with Tony Blackburn later that evening to find out where it would enter the Top 40.

Where was he, dammit?

His mind went back to the lyrics as he awaited the arrival of his friend. They'd agreed two o'clock. He wiped the sweat from his brow and squinted as he gazed up at the blazing sun. Today sure was a scorcher.

Now, how did it go again? "They got a message from the Action Man. I'm happy, hope you're happy too." Yes. That was it!

Looking up from the baked asphalt pavement where he had been entranced by the sight of a colony of red ants disappearing down one of the weed-laden cracks, he looked up to see that, at last, his friend had arrived.

Cycling swiftly towards him on his blue Raleigh mountain bike was a muscular young teenager dressed in a white T-shirt, slightly flared denim jeans and red Converse shoes. The bowl cut of his light-brown hair was concealed under a peaked white sun cap.

"What sort of time you call this?" Keith hollered.

The brakes screeched as the new arrival brought his bike to an abrupt halt just inches from Keith's feet. He glanced at his Casio digital watch and grinned back. "Two twelve. How about you?"

Phil Meritus climbed off his bike and wheeled it towards the clump of grass where his friend had left his, dropping it in the same place.

"This the one?" asked Keith.

"That's the one," Phil affirmed, squinting in the sunlight

The two 14-year-olds turned to Keith's right. There stood the crumbling, decaying shell˙ of a once grand building. Situated a few hundred yards into Osney Lane from its Becket Street junction, and adjacent to the train tracks, it had originally been constructed as a two-storey warehouse to hold packages destined for the Royal Mail trains.

Now, in 1980, it was over 100 years old, and its glory days were long past. Having lain abandoned since the early 1960s when a larger depot had been constructed further along the lane, its core frame had quickly deteriorated—almost as if the loneliness forced by the absence of human activity had caused it to fall sick.

The cement had become dry and powder-like, causing bricks to tumble to the ground at random, weeds and small tree shoots plugging the gaps. Dry rot and woodworm had afflicted the large wooden door on the upper floor from which packages had been raised and lowered by a winch in its distant past. The green paint on what remained of the door had long since peeled away.

As the imposing shape loomed ominously in front of them, an air of foreboding swept over Keith. His reservations seemed to have become immediately apparent to Phil.

"Not having second thoughts are you? Come on. We agreed."

"Something doesn't feel right, Phil. This place is bad news."

"Plane hijackings and IRA bombs are bad news. This is just a building. Don't be a pussy! Let's go."

Without waiting for a retort, Phil moved enthusiastically towards the remains of the barbed wire fence. It'll take more than this to keep me out, he thought to himself. More also, it would seem, than the battered wooden signpost proclaiming 'Danger! Keep Out!' with a skull and crossbones beneath for added impact.

Phil ducked to ease himself through the gap that had been conveniently cut in the wire by other intrepid parties, snagging his hat in the process. Once through, he found himself in thick grass two thirds his height, full of weeds with bricks and other assorted rubble lurking underneath.

He paused. The building looked even more dilapidated up close. This didn't bother him though. It only added to the thrill.

He turned around to see Keith still positioned cautiously on the other side of the wire.

"Will you come on?" he called towards him. "Are we doing this or what?"

Their friendship had always been this way. Keith's level-headed cautiousness had been countered by Phil's adventurous recklessness. Somehow, the contrast worked, and it seemed to bring out the best in each of them. While Keith's good sense had saved them from a fair few potential scrapes, Phil's zest for danger had seen Keith enjoy some exhilarating moments that he would never otherwise have experienced. Phil's simple observation that "life is for living" seemed overly mature for one so young.

By the time Keith had reached the point Phil was at before, his mate had already crossed the threshold of the building's facade. The wooden door had long since rotted away. To its right, an entire corner of the structure had crumbled into the pile of bricks that now lay there, layers of crushed drinks cans, discarded syringes and used condoms lying atop.

Phil stood still, waiting for his friend to catch him up. Once he had, the pair surveyed the wreckage that lay before them. More bricks and piles of debris. Jagged shards of dirty glass jutted from the corners of each broken window. Besides the air of menace that hadn't gone away, Keith was sure the place exuded an air of sadness; of forgotten-ness.

Almost as if it had feeling and had never fully gotten over having been abandoned in favour of a newer model.

To the left of them was a metal staircase, well rusted, which led to the upstairs level. Phil was already striding towards it before the protestations could leave Keith's mouth, and was almost at the top before Keith had placed his foot on the first rung.

The upper level retained more evidence of its past, as some shattered packing cases and mailbags lay strewn around. Keith looked up to see a large section of the exterior roof missing. Though today was hot and dry, the wooden planks beneath the gaping hole were bowing as the result of years of rainfall having taken their toll.

As Phil sauntered towards the right-hand broken window, Keith meandered to the left.

Phil peered out for an ariel view of the railway, just as a maintenance carriage creaked and thundered its way along the track towards the fuelling truck that lay beyond.

Suddenly, another noise entered his senses. The sickening crack of breaking wood, and the thunder of bricks and rubble falling to the level below.

Phil swung instantly around. In a cloud of dust, just about to disappear through the chasm that had opened up in a whole area of the upstairs floor, was his young friend. Keith was scrabbling desperately to cling on to anything that would hold him. His hands gripped the ends of two beams which had remained intact, but already he was struggling to support himself.

Without hesitation Phil had thrown himself on to his belly and was edging his way to where Keith was hanging by a metaphorical thread, his legs thrashing in wild panic below him.

"Grab my hand," he shouted, extending his right arm towards Keith, while keeping himself as far back from the chasm as he could in the process.

"Keith, give me your hand. You have to let go, just for a moment, so I can pull you up."

Though reluctant to relinquish his grip, Keith knew that following his friend's advice was the only chance he had. While gripping yet tighter with his left hand, he let go with the right.

No sooner had he reached forward as best he could, than Phil had locked hands with his and was beginning to haul his body towards him. Keith's right shoulder screamed with pain as he allowed his frame to be slowly pulled forward.

Seconds later, his T-shirt and jeans filthy with grime, and coughing and spitting out dust, he was out of the danger zone and immersed in a brotherly hug with the friend who had just saved his life.

Within ten minutes the pair had descended, climbed back through the wire, and reclaimed their bikes.

"Keith?"

"Yeah?"

"You know you can never breathe a word of this to my dad, right?"

"Course."

"You know what it'd be. An ass-kicking before a lecture all about his standing in the community, that kind of thing."

"Yeah, I know. Listen . . . thanks."

Phil smiled as he glanced across at his friend who, like him, was wheeling his bike back towards Oxpens Road rather than riding it.

"Friends for life . . . right?"

"Absolutely," replied Keith.

"Nothing could ever come between us now."

CHAPTER 29

Wednesday 7th November 2001

"He'd like to come and meet us,
But he thinks he'd blow our minds."
David Bowie: 'Starman.'
"But it's written in the starlight,
And every line in your palm.
We're fools to make war,
On our brothers in arms."

Dire Straits: 'Brothers In Arms.'

Verity and Keith had thought they'd discovered the true meaning of exhaustion when Hope had been born. Keith recalled, back in '96, examining the dark circles and crows' feet under his eyes, the wrinkles etched into his forehead, and his bloodshot eyes, and wondering how—or if—he would ever recover. He had been impressed to see his relative youthfulness return when life had got gradually easier as Hope had grown.

Now, as his degraded reflection stared reluctantly back at himself in the bathroom mirror, the 36 hours since Monday night had him feeling as if his recovery had all been in vain.

For most of that time he had been the custodian of Hope as Verity had insisted on remaining at May's bedside. She had finally returned home that morning looking as bedraggled as Keith himself had felt, and he had been happy to let her go to bed for as long as she had needed. After only four hours she had re-appeared downstairs complaining of dark dreams during the short amount of sleep she had grabbed, and saying that she preferred to remain awake. She had exited again to drop off Hope with Joy, it now being her turn to insist that Keith get some rest.

It was 3.30pm; this was now the plan, and Keith felt sure he would make a better job of it than Verity. In a T-shirt and grey pyjama bottoms he was about to make a headway to the bedroom when, with almost comedic timing, the phone began to ring.

Remembering that he had the house to himself, he allowed himself the luxury of a string of expletives. Tempting though it was to simply ignore the call, in times such as these it could be any kind of news on the other end. And whoever it was would doubtless keep trying and disturb his rest. Keith's foul-mouthed tirade continued and his pyjama bottoms flapped as he hurried down the creaky staircase.

He snatched up the receiver.

"Hello?"

No reply.

One more try.

"Hello?"

A short gap. Then the voice spoke.

"Hello, Keith."

Keith had heard accounts of the "life review" that newly-departed souls from the earthly realm experience at the moment of "death," where it is said that their whole life flashes before them. In the instant that followed, it felt to

Keith as if this was happening to him, as a montage of past experiences, memories and emotions all converged into an instantaneous crescendo.

Feeling suddenly dizzy, and not knowing if it was down to tiredness or the over-abundance of emotions, Keith sat down on the lowest stair, the receiver still clutched to his right ear.

"I knew you would call. I just didn't know when."

Keith strained to detect any of the background ambience that had been present on the previous calls. There was only silence.

The voice replied.

"Well, it had to be soon. Time is not on our side."

"Our?"

"We're on the same side, Keith."

Keith had pondered on many an occasion how he would handle an encounter such as this should it ever occur. Whatever possibilities his mind had entertained, he could never have imagined it would have occurred in such extreme circumstances.

"I'm happy that you answered. I can talk to you now that we're alone. Now that your unwanted eavesdroppers are no longer listening in.

"And how would you know about that?"

A pause. The caller seemed to be giving consideration to his reply.

"I know the sound of a phone tap, Keith. Lord knows I heard it enough times growing up.

"It's both a gift and a curse.

"You can choose your friends, but not your family. I'm connected for life as a consequence of mine. I still get 'information.' Even after all this time. Even here."

"And where is 'here'?"

Was that a sigh that Keith detected on the other end?

"That's not important any more. What is, is that you're all correct in what you've deduced is planned to happen less than 48 hours from now. You've figured out many pieces of the puzzle, but you're still lacking some of the vital parts."

With eyes closed, Keith rubbed the indent at the very top of his nose, an action which for some reason had always irked Verity and earned him a rebuke when done in her presence.

"You said we're on the same side. So why aren't you telling me what I'm missing?"

The caller's next comment both befuddled and infuriated Keith in equal measure.

"I've been to the underworld, Keith. You know that. I've been to places that no man should."

The fury started winning over.

"What the hell? Didn't you just say that we're short on time? But there's still time for you to talk in fucking riddles!"

A sense of affront?

"It's not a riddle, Keith. Listen to what I'm saying. I've been to the underworld. Literally, as well as metaphorically. That's the key to it all."

Keith continued to rub the bridge of his nose, now with eyes open for enhanced concentration.

The caller embellished his previous comment.

"A long time ago you, told me something without actually telling me. Because you couldn't. I accepted that. Now I'm returning the gesture. In the only way I can. In fulfilment of my spiritual obligations. To a friend. To a brother."

It sounded like more riddles. But Keith's beleaguered mind was starting to get the picture.

The caller offered more.

"Isn't that a wonderfully poetic example of duality in action? How something can exist as both one thing and its own polar opposite both at the same time? I guess that's why 'Jesus' and 'Lucifer' both equate to 444 in Sumerian Gematria. Maybe that's one to ask your new friend Daniela about.

"You know what's planned to happen. But I don't think you fully appreciate what's at stake. If there's one lesson I've learned through this...unusual life experience of mine, it's to never under-estimate the motivations of those who've grown up raised by satanists. You just can't apply the same measures and assumptions to them as we might to ourselves. There are certain depths to which the likes of us just wouldn't stoop. We couldn't. But when that failsafe switch is absent as a result of extreme inherited psychopathy...well, anything becomes fair game if it leads toward the end goal."

"The total and perpetual enslavement of all of humanity to those that consider themselves the rightful rulers of this earthly realm."

4,600 miles away the corners of the caller's lips upturned slightly as he recalled conversations of more than a decade previous.

"Good. Then, you won't be surprised to know just where this upcoming stunt is designed to lead.

"It will be used to capitalise fully on the fear and paranoia generated by the American event, and on the anti-Muslim rhetoric that's been carefully cultivated by the social engineers over the previous weeks. The trauma-tised public of Oxford will be so outraged that the horror has now arrived on their own doorstep—and that the "terrorists" have dared to desecrate one of the city's most iconic monuments—that they'll be literally begging the authorities to do whatever is needed to keep them safe. Whatever it takes.

"And when that solution takes the form of the entire city being placed in—to use one of their own favoured terms, a permanent state of "lockdown"—you'll see them literally begging to have their rights taken away and their freedom of movement deleted. All in the name of 'keeping them safe,' naturally. That one never fails."

For some reason an image of Norm came into Keith's mind.

The familiar voice continued.

"For some, the phrase 'what happens in Oxford stays in Oxford' might come to mind. Maybe that's true for the crowds that Drew plays to in those clubs every weekend. Except it doesn't in reality. You and I know that, Keith. First of all, so many stunts of this nature get cooked up in that place. The belly of the beast.

"Then, Oxford folk under a state of house arrest and enslavement today to a digital control grid of such severity it would make Orwell say, 'my god, I didn't go far enough,' expands out to the rest of the nation tomorrow. With the rest of the world not far behind.

"It's incredible what people are prepared to give up when they're being kept in a perpetual state of fear. I've seen it with my own eyes."

As Keith reflected on the way the conversation was unfolding, he concluded that this might just be the single most bizarre afternoon of his life so far.

Still, there was a question which had to be asked.

"Why? Why are you doing this?"

There was slight pause before the voice responded. What was happening at the other end? Contemplation? Resentment? Contempt?

"You really have to ask me that?

"I'm not a bad man, Keith. I'm a man who's made some very bad decisions. There's a difference. We're all flawed. My flaws have just been more on display than those of others. We all have the opportunity to atone for our mistakes. I've had long enough to reflect on it. That's what I'm doing here."

Keith sensed that the call was drawing to a close. And that this was likely to be the last one of its kind that he would ever receive.

The caller reiterated his previous point.

"Remember what I told you? I've been to the under-world. I've been to places that few others have, and I can tell you that this is the key to it all."

"That, and that the red pill is always the one to take. Never the blue. Remember that. Always the red."

Keith's eyes were closed again as he spoke what he suspected would be the last of his words the caller would ever hear.

"Is that all you have to say?"

"Pretty much. Except to say that I was very sorry to hear about May. I hope that she pulls through. I can fully understand her motives, and there's certainly no judgement from me. And pass on my regards to Max ... whatever he might now think of me."

" ... Goodbye."

" ... Goodbye, Keith. Be well."

Abruptly, the line went dead.

CHAPTER 30
Wednesday 7th November 2001

The disconcerting tones of dusk were beginning to set in as Keith, still reeling from the surreality of the phone call, and capitalising on his time alone, strode left off the High Street into Catte Street. Proceeding North he turned the corner, and caught his first glimpse of a building which, though decommissioned as a library some decades before, had stood as a proud emblem of the city's university institution for so long. But which, if certain parties were to have their way, would not stand for much longer.

The Rad Cam, as Oxford academia referred to it, loomed large, its majestic blue-ish dome accentuating the dark greyness of the late afternoon sky. Keith surveyed its circular yellow-ish stone exterior, the central section adorned with two rows of windows punctuated by pillars, and above them, a section housing balustrades. Memories of having read Dorothy L. Sayers' 1935 novel '*Gaudy Night*' while at school came flooding back, one of the plot's principal conversations having taken place on that rooftop.

As was ever the case, a handful of Chinese and Japanese tourists were milling about, a couple adjusting the flash functions on their cameras to try and secure a decently-lit shot in the rapidly darkening ambience. Otherwise, small groups of students with books under their arms and scarves flapping in the occasional flurries, dawdled past.

Keith wondered who else had been in this area recently, possibly standing on this very spot, of far more sinister intent than anyone presently there.

His mind raced through various possibilities. As did the conversation he had had a short while earlier. With this in mind, he fought to battle his tiredness and gain some mental clarity as he turned his head to look around.

East. West. Up. Down.

Down?

Keith moved forward a few steps and a little to his right, to further survey something which had caught his eye.

Moments later, accepting that there was nothing further he could do right there and then, but satisfied that he had seen all he had needed, he turned and headed back along Catte Street then right into the High Street.

As he walked from the Mitre Inn towards the imposing Carfax Tower, memories of events from ten years earlier filled his consciousness. Unwelcome ones. He fought to shake them off and quickened his pace as he took a left into St. Aldates and headed home.

Directly after Speedwell Street he found himself outside Thames Valley Police headquarters. He scoffed at the notion that there would be any point in tipping off those inside about what he and his friends had come to know, given that, even if he were to find an honest officer committed to doing the right thing, a firewall would immediately get applied once the message had travelled far enough up the chain of command.

Oaths of allegiance and the bonds of Brotherhood were the cement which held the infrastructure of Oxford together.

Instinctively, he glanced to his left. Though the evening had now set in, through the darkness he could still make out a curious sight.

The nearest of the white panda cars was rocking aggressively on its suspension. His contempt for this institution spurred him on to investigate further without fear of any consequence.

The car continued rocking. All around the windows were steamed up, but pressed tightly against the rear offside one were a pair of bare heels.

Keith yanked at the handle to the back door, surprised to find it unlocked.

Even more surprised were the car's occupants, as Aimee Hardwick's legs dropped out of the door along with a handful of random items—a pair of red panties, a black high-heeled shoe, an open handbag—as she let out a panicked scream.

Equally shocked was DI Sam Haine, positioned on top of her, his bare backside blocking any modesty Aimee might possibly have had left.

Haine turned his head from the business in hand to meet Keith's gaze.

Aimee's first instinct was to straighten her dishevelled hair.

Keith smirked.

"This is the part where you're going to tell me it's not what it looks like, right, Detective Inspector?"

While speaking, Keith had pulled from his jacket pocket the digital camera he routinely carried with him. His first attempt to rattle off a shot of the pair floundering desperately had resulted only in a close-up of the sole of Aimee's foot as she had raised her left leg unexpectedly.

The second was more successful, capturing Haine's face mid-protest.

"Insurance," smiled Keith. "You know how that all works, Inspector. Didn't you say you were going to 'nail' Max Zeall? Looks like you got to somebody else first."

Haine was speechless. Passion-killers don't get much heavier than this, he reflected.

Aimee had now pushed him off of her with her foot.

Keith was on a roll.

"Or—let me guess. You were chatting away, then you accidentally tripped, your hand accidentally opened the car door, She tripped also and fell on to the back seat, your belt broke and your trousers and pants fell down, Aimee caught her knickers on the door handle and they accidentally came off along with her shoes, you fell on top of her, accidentally entered her, and were desperately trying to get up when I arrived and opened the door. Sound about right?"

(Actually, Aimee was still fully dressed on her top half, making Keith's farcical account slightly more plausible.)

Outside of the car, a gust of wind had taken hold of a folded sheet of A4 paper protruding from Aimee's bag. The paper came to a rest as the gust pinned it against the wall to the right. While Haine hastened to replace his trousers Keith went to investigate.

His extreme concentration on the contents of the paper was broken by the click-clack of high heels, and he turned to see a newly-skirted Aimee Hardwick scurrying away, re-applying her hair-tie with one hand, her tights and knickers blowing in the wind as they trailed from the other.

He folded the paper, placed it carefully in his inside jacket pocket, and headed home.

CHAPTER 31

Thursday 8th November 2001

"In times of universal deceit, telling the truth becomes a revolutionary act."

George Orwell

The bastards were getting blatant now.

Dani smashed her fingers down on the play and record buttons of her cassette machine as Fun Boy Three's '*Tunnel of Love*' gave away to a less meaningful and more bland tune on Lux FM.

The ad was still playing, still voiced by Cas Passendale, except now the wording had changed. It simply stated, "the wait is almost over. Oxford will never be the same again." She wondered how—if the terrible event "they" had planned were allowed to occur—Lux would answer the question of just what that ad campaign had been all about, given that it couldn't be seen to be advertising anything in particular? Surely to God people would put two and two together and realise the station's complicity and foreknowledge? Or were "they" relying on the masses being simply too traumatised and fearful to be capable of thinking critically?

Or was it down to a level of hubris and self-assured arrogance that could only come from pure psychopaths? Certainly, her Uni studies had shown her that such people give no consideration to the likely consequences of their actions, and are incapable of feeling the shame or guilt that acts as a failsafe for *non*-psychopaths, thereby preventing them from engaging in such actions.

There was something else going on with the ads now, too.

At first, Dani had thought that she was imagining the feint bleeps that appeared to lie under the music bed, putting it down to tiredness ... or her condition. But when she identified the same strange sounds in two separate ads, she began to play back the tape recordings and scrutinise more closely. In her mind, she was able to separate the layers of audio—to block the music out from her consciousness so only the electronic sounds remained.

On the first occasion, she had scrabbled for a pencil and pad and begun scrawling. After playing the ad five more times, she slammed down the stop button and glanced at what was on the pad:

-. . .-- / .-- --- .-. .-.. .-.. -.. / --- .-. -.. . . .-.

The reluctant genius had come across Morse Code enough to recognise one of its broadcasts. She scoffed at the morbid mockery of using it in a city which had been made home to the fictional Inspector Morse.

All that remained was to translate the cypher into English.

She knew just the book to consult, but not where to find it.

Two minutes of frenetic searching later she had located it under her bed.

She tore the top page from the pad and went to work again with her pencil as she thumbed through the book.

'New World Order.'

Bastards!

The music following the Lux ads had changed nature, too. No more references to cameras and photography. Instead, songs evoking ideas of tunnels below ground leading to a highly eclectic hotchpotch of songs that would never ordinarily get airtime. Paul Johnson's '*Get Get Down*;' The Drifters' '*Under The Boardwalk*.' The theme from the movie '*The Deep*.' Even Elvis Presley's '*Way Down*.'

"Desperation," she muttered to herself, as she pulled her army surplus jacket over her trademark T-shirt and dungarees. The Doc Martens were already on her feet. Her keys jangled as she picked them up off her typically cluttered desk, and the door slammed as she hurried down the stairs.

"Dani? Are you going..." shouted a voice from the kitchen. But the front door had slammed before the last word could be heard.

The clues were now so clear, Dani considered, as she slammed the front gate shut and paced vigorously left along Helen Road. The threat was going to come from underground.

There must be a tunnel system below the Camera and that must be where the explosives would be placed. There would probably be a couple of Muslim "patsies" with fake explosives strapped to them, who would get seen by the public. They would take the rap, and would probably get blown up themselves and take the evidence with them. The real perpetrators would get away with it—just as they had in America, and the "terror" event would be used to justify...who knows what?

All that was on Dani's mind was communicating her conclusions to the others. Now suspicious of using the phone, she had decided a face-to-face with Verity and Keith was the first step. Though the long walk to Abingdon Road would not ordinarily faze her, time was of the essence, so a bus it would have to be.

Reaching the end of Helen Road, she swung left on to Botley Road. Though the morning rush hour had now cleared and traffic was up to around 30mph, this main artery route into the city centre remained characteristically busy, a mismatched array of cars, vans, trucks, cycles, motorbikes and red buses going their way in both directions.

Dani began to think through how she would present her findings to the others. Articulation was not her strong point, and her thoughts had a tendency to veer off in many directions.

Just as she had begun to process her ideas, she paused. Instinct had kicked in to over-ride all else.

Though wordless, if it could have spoken, it would have said "turn around, now!"

She heeded the psychic warning. As she turned, time seemed to speed up.

A white Ford Transit van which had appeared some distance away just a second earlier, had now mounted the pavement and was only inches away from mowing her down.

The sound of the engine revving merged with the nauseating screech of tyres. Dani jumped to her left, losing her footing as she did so, and sending herself crashing on to the hard concrete.

The action was enough to save her. The van's front left tyre landed only three inches from her boot. Unsurprisingly, the driver began to lose control. Other pedestrians swerved wildly to get out of the van's path as it careered on along the pavement.

The traffic on the road drew to a halt as alarmed drivers looked on. There was a sickening crunch as the van's nearside wing smashed into a bench, uprooting the bolts holding it into the tarmac.

A large section of the wing got wrenched away from the van and landed on the pavement. The van remained in motion. It veered violently from left to right, an un-natural sound screaming out from the engine.

Somehow, the driver managed to regain control and lurched the wheel to the right, sending the van off the pavement and back on to the road. With the traffic behind it now stationary, the driver had a stretch of road ahead towards Osney Bridge to gather up some speed.

Dani remained on the pavement. a searing pain seeping up from her right hip on to which she had fallen. Several pedestrians were now tending to her.

"Bloody maniac, driving like that" said a bald, stocky workman. "He couldn't have got closer to you if he'd tried."

"He did," answered Dani croakily, now realising that what she knew was known by other parties who wanted her out of the way. It was a classic attempt at an "accident."

"I've called the police … and an ambulance," said a young Asian student, mobile phone in hand. "Should be here soon."

"There's no need," countered Dani sharply. "There's no way I'm going to hospital."

"I got the registration, dear," said an elderly lady who had been gently stroking her hair

"So did I," answered Dani. "TO66 FOX."

***

A few miles to the North West the scenario was still the same. In a bed in the intensive Care Unit of the John Radcliffe Hospital, lay an emotionless, and seemingly

227

lifeless May Pearce, still entrenched in the deep coma she had been in since being discovered by Drew 80 hours previous.

Drew was there at her bedside, as he had been for most of the period, his face stinging from the torrent of tears that had flowed from his bloodshot eyes. With a lump in his throat he whispered what had become something of a personal mantra.

"I'm so sorry, Maysie. Come back to us. It's not your time to go."

Momentarily, he would whisper the words directly into her ear. No staff seemed to care. Aside from hourly checks of the machine to which she was connected via tubes under her nose, with the nurse scrawling figures on to a clipboard hung on the end of her bed, she remained unattended.

Verity had been sat next to Drew for the past hour, her sleep-deprived eyes as red as his.

She squeezed his hand as she raised from her chair.

"I have to go, cuz. So much to do. I'll check back in later."

Drew turned his head, a confused look in his eyes as he slowly processed the words she had just spoken.

"Oh … yeah. Sure … sure. You go, V. You get back to Hope. There's nothing more you can do here."

"She's at school, mate. But I have to get back to Keith."

Verity forced a smile as she scurried quickly out of the ward and through the hospital's sprawling warren of corridors towards the exit. She was no fan of such places. Childhood memories of her father having been rushed here with alcohol poisoning invaded her thoughts.

She worked to shake them off as she waited for the X3 bus.

Alighting at Lake Street, she began to walk the few hundred yards home, thoughts racing through her mind about what tomorrow would bring.

Instinct told her to look at her watch. 9:11. Of course it was.

She already knew something was wrong before she had reached the junction with Vicarage Road. Parked outside 216b, and causing a massive tailback of traffic behind them, were two police cars, blue lights blazing. As she neared the house, she saw that the front door was open. She heard the sounds of a fracas.

Suddenly the figure of Keith appeared at the doorway. He was being manhandled by two officers who were struggling to retain him. He had been handcuffed.

Verity began to run.

"What the hell's going on here? Keith, what's happening?"

A short, sharp buzz sounded. Keith let out a cry and wrenched his head back in agony. The officer re-attached the yellow taser gun to his belt. The officers then shoved a much less belligerent Keith towards the open door of one of the cars, pushing down his head and forcing him inside.

Before there was any chance of protest from Verity, two female officers had restrained her, and one struggled to fit a pair of handcuffs on her also.

"Verity Hunter. You are under arrest for the possession of Class A drugs with intent to supply. You do not have to say anything. But it may harm your defence if you do not mention when questioned something which you later rely on in court. Anything you do say may be given in evidence."

As she was led off to the second car, offering less resistance than Keith with no desire to be tasered herself, and as she watched two officers emerge from the door of 216b holding plastic "evidence" bags, the scenario became all too clear. This was a stitch-up orchestrated from on-high to keep them out of the way ahead of tomorrow's proceedings.

All so obvious.

CHAPTER 32

Thursday 8th November 2001

"You, me, or nobody is gonna hit as hard as life. But it ain't about how hard you hit. It's about how hard you can get hit and keep moving forward. How much you can take and keep moving forward."

Sylvester Stallone in 'Rocky.'

Not that he knew it, but following a couple of hours to "cool off" in a cold, dimly-lit cell that smelt of urine and bleach in equal measure, Keith now found himself occupying the same seat in interrogation room B at St. Aldates Police Station as Max Zeall had some eleven years previous when being taunted by DCI Nomas and DS Sam Haine. Virtually nothing had changed about the room in that time, save for more of the surface rippling and peeling away on the well-worn desk.

Though vexation had been bubbling up within him, left-brained level-headedness had won through, and Keith had realised there was little point in any displays of righteous indignation. Things don't work that way with fit-ups. Complete non co-operation was the only tool at his disposal.

Following seven minutes in the company of a stone-faced WPC, the door suddenly buzzed open, and in walked an equally stern-faced male officer along with a female counterpart. The man threw down a green manila folder bulging with papers before staring, it seemed, directly into Keith's soul. The woman, looking ridiculous in a loose-fitting grey suit that seemed to broadcast that it contained a woman who desperately wished she'd been born into a man's body, wore a slightly more amenable expression.

The WPC excused herself from the room while the male officer, sitting closest to the tape machine, inserted a fresh cassette and pressed the record button.

A bleep sounded as the red light flashed.

"This is Detective Inspector Cochon," spoke the officer, in a tone which would have been at home announcing arrivals at Oxford train station. "With me is Detective Sergeant Hundin. Today is Thursday 8th November 2001 at . . . " He glanced at his watch. "1.19pm. This interview is with Keith Malcolm."

Both the man and the woman now stared intently into Keith's eyes. Intimidation 101.

"Keith. A quantity of Class A drugs—cocaine and ecstasy—were recovered by officers earlier today from your home at 216b Abingdon Road. Can you explain how they came to be there?"

Fighting the urge to blurt out "because you treacherous bastards put them there," Keith instead opted to play it cautious. These traitors' favourite phrase "anything you say may be used in evidence against you" was about the truest statement they ever uttered.

"I don't answer questions" was his safe response. Delivered, for added antagonisation, with a tiny smile.

The man and woman looked at each other. The man seemed to nod slightly.

It was the woman's turn to speak.

"Look, Keith. We want to help you. We're only interested in getting to the truth of the matter here. Tell us where you got them. We want the big players here. Do you want to take the rap for them and let them get away with it? Tell us what you know. It will work out best for you in the end."

The smile remained on Keith's lips, purely because he found the predictability of this pair's well-rehearsed double-act so tiresome. Morecambe and Wise had nothing on these clowns. It was Good Cop/ Bad Cop 101, played for extra effect by bringing in a female officer to be the one "on his side."

"I don't answer questions."

Again, a traded glance between the pair.

"Keith. You and Verity are in big trouble. A substantial amount of gear was found at your house. This goes way beyond any claim of recreational use. We're talking intent to supply. We're talking some serious time for you both. I'm sure you don't find the thought of Verity going inside and Hope going into social care at all appealing."

Keith wore a poker face, the phrase "you bastards" dominating his mind.

The woman spoke.

"Have you ever been to the island of Lindisfarne, Keith?"

The man spoke.

"Who's your supplier, Keith? Give me the name."

The woman spoke.

"When's the last time you went to the circus, Keith? You like going to the circus?"

"Really?" he whispered silently to himself. "The '*Alice in Wonderland*' technique?"

It was a well-worn police cliché which he had seen acted out by Gene Hackman and Roy Scheider characters in '*The French Connection*,' and doubtless devised by behavioural scientists out of the Tavistock Institute or similar. One character appears reasonable and interested only in the facts, while the other chips in with completely unrelated and absurd-sounding questions, the intention being to confuse and confound the subject to such a degree that it scrambles their brain and they can no longer function rationally.

This pair really aren't too bright, Keith considered.

"Never been to Lindisfarne, but I hear it's very beautiful there," he replied, just for kicks.

The woman and the man looked abruptly at each other.

Right as they did, the buzz of the door sounded and in walked another male officer. He spoke in a matter-of-fact tone with no emotion in his voice.

"Keith Malcolm. You're being released with no charges. You're free to go."

Immediately the male officer at the table began to protest, but was evidently out-ranked.

"For the benefit of the tape, Mr. Keith Malcolm is being released from custody at 1.25pm," added the senior officer.

Not claiming to know what the hell was going on, but without pausing to try and find out, Keith hoisted himself up from the uncomfortable plastic chair, smiling at the visibly perturbed female as he did so. He couldn't resist a final dig.

"D'you know, I might just visit the circus this weekend. Oxford's such a marvellous city. Such culture. '*Alice in Wonderland*' *is* a textbook classic, wouldn't you agree, officers?"

He rapidly exited the room.

***

Not that he knew it, but it had been the nature of the conversation in Incident Room C, situated three doors along the corridor, which had secured Keith's freedom. There, Verity had faced a similar inquisition, in her case coming from two male officers.

The junior of the two had entered first. Detective Sergeant something-or-other. It was the arrival of the more senior officer which had secured Verity's fate.

She recognised him even before he had announced himself for the tape; Detective Inspector Sam Haine. They had crossed paths several years earlier when Verity had still been a reporter at Lux FM.

The procedure had gone along almost identical lines. The same questions and the same interrogation tactics. But Verity had seen '*The French Connection*' too. Furthermore, Keith had filled her in on all of Haine's indiscretions of the previous night. This, she quickly realised, would be the ace up her sleeve.

"Does this conversation really have to be recorded?" she asked, addressing Haine.

"Yes, it does. It's the law."

"And anything heard on the tape can be used as evidence of a crime?"

"Yes, it can."

The red light blinked away to Haine's right as he answered.

"Oh." It was Verity's turn to act. "So…would that include adultery?"

Verity thought that she detected Haine's immediate look of confusion become replaced by one of suppressed panic.

He chose to style it out.

"That has nothing to do with the conversation we're having here."

"Oh, but it does, Detective Inspector. You might recall that you and I crossed paths a few times back in the Neil Lowe days. Back then, though, it seemed officers didn't share such quite ... 'intimate' relationships with female reporters."

The colour seemed to drain from Haine's face as he started to realise where things were headed. Verity was relishing every second.

Haine turned to his subordinate.

"Sergeant, please give us a few moments."

His underling began to object.

"But sir, it's protocol to ... "

"Protocol or not, Sergeant, this is a direct order from a superior officer. Excuse yourself and give us a few moments."

Confused, the Sergeant did as instructed.

The tape continued to roll.

As Verity and Haine stared directly across the table at each-other, Verity was first to speak.

"That was a wise move. Let's see if your next is to be equally wise. Release Keith and myself from custody immediately, with no charges, or a souvenir of your little late-night encounter with Miss Aimee Hardwick goes straight to the Chief Superintendent. I doubt he would take a very accommodating view of that particular use of a police vehicle.

"Not only that, but a copy will also find its way to Mrs. Haine."

Far from appearing pale, Haine's face was now becoming distinctly flushed, as his challenged policeman's brain fought to process this turning of the tables. He had avoided interrogating Keith himself as a security measure.

He hadn't reckoned on such a gambit coming from Verity, the "softer" option.

"I know what you're thinking." Verity continued. "Keep these two here while I turn their house upside-down looking for that photo evidence. You can do that if you want, but you still won't find that SD card. You really think we'd be dumb enough to keep a piece of dynamite like that in the house? Best believe it's been safely stashed somewhere else, with instructions for it to be e-mailed to both the Super and Mrs. Haine if we're not back at home to make the call by 5pm this afternoon."

Haine's face grew redder as he stared Verity out and continued to consider his options.

"Either way, I'm sure it'll be a big hit on sex.com. It was a very clear shot of your greatest asset. Your face."

A few more seconds of silent staring were followed by a sudden flurry of movement as Haine jerked to his left, pressed the stop and eject buttons on the tape machine, and popped the cassette carefully into his inside jacket pocket. He marched silently out of the room.

Presently came the instructions for both Verity and Keith to be released without charge.

Neither were under any illusion that this marked an end to the challenges they faced, and accepted that 24/7 surveillance was virtually guaranteed. But, whereas the plan had clearly been to confine them to incarceration, they had at least regained their freedom of movement for the next 24 hours.

Haine clearly feared The Order, an organisation far from averse to using photographic evidence of indiscretions for strategic leverage.

But whatever consequences they might deliver paled in comparison to the wrath of Mrs. Haine.

CHAPTER 33

Friday 9th November 2001

"Number is the ruler of forms and ideas, and the cause of gods and demons."

Iamblichus, philosopher, C. 242-C. 325.

"Number rules the universe."

Pythagoras, C. 570bc-C. 495bc.

The Order's architects had been faced with a tough choice. Astrology, and particularly selenology, had always figured in their choice of dates for significant rituals.

The moon had disappointed on this occasion, diminishing into a waning crescent at only 39 per-cent illumination. The conspirators had had to let it go—a big ask in light of their obsessive-compulsive adherence to detail. On this occasion it was all about the ritual importance of the date. The plotters had almost orgasmed as they had pieced together the plan for "Britain's 9/11," having already selected the date some 33 years before.

Equally, their counterparts in the United States had chosen the date for their grand spectacle based on the importance of the numbers 9 and 11 in occult teachings—particularly those of Aleister Crowley, who had gained a mythical, God-like status among many secret societies and mystery schools. Crowley had explained the importance of the number 11, the occult arcanum 11 standing for "work with fire," when he had said:

"11 is the number of black magic(k) in itself, and therefore suitable for all types of operation...the unsacred number *par excellence* of the New Eon, the Eon of Horus."

This had become the reason for dark occultists opting to use 11-word phrases, such as Crowley's "do what thou wilt shall be the whole of the law." Satanists had also selected 11 for the official end-date of World War 1 on 11th November at 11am, and for the Apollo 11 "moon landing" hoax, and it was no accident that 11 had become the number of players on a soccer team, with the footballs themselves bearing an "alchemical wedding" of white hexa-grams and black pentagrams, five and six totalling eleven.

And little surprise that American Airlines Flight 11 was allegedly the first to crash into the WTC towers in the New York event.

Everything by the numbers.

And so, 9th November it had had to be...though the weather was proving as imperfect for the occasion as the moon phase. With the temperature barely above zero at almost 9am, a persistent drizzle had filled the air since pre-dawn, the haze hanging ominously over the City of Dreaming Spires.

Even at this hour, and in spite of the weather, Radcliffe Square was filled with a small gaggle of tourists, mainly American and Chinese, sheltered under umbrellas and snuggled into jackets, scarves and hats. The Chinese were pointing their cameras at anything and everything.

But there before them loomed the main object of their attention.

The blue-grey dome atop the Radcliffe Camera seemed to transcend the mist, rising majestically out of it, and standing imposingly, as if keeping vigil over the rest of the University quarter.

Some distance away, installed within one of the buildings lining the north side of Broad Street, were three individuals who fully expected this spectacle to remain the case for only a few minutes longer.

As Vic Kostta paced impatiently around behind them, Eugene Nicks and Fabian Lucas had positioned themselves at the second-floor window of a building cordially donated by other members of "the brotherhood."

Though, they had been reliably informed, they were far enough away from the impending chaos to remain safe from harm, their vantage point still allowed them a strategic view of the Camera's main dome and its central apex.

As he stared in anticipation, Lucas wondered why they hadn't devised one of the ads with the slogan "it will blow your top off!" Ah well. Too late now.

For his part, Nicks was finding amusement in his paralleling of Lee Harvey Oswald in his vantage point at the Texas Book Depository on the day of the JFK assassination—another Masonically-encoded date of 22/11. The only difference, Nicks reflected, being that Oswald had not carried out that event, whereas he, Nicks, was most certainly behind the one that, he fully anticipated, was imminent. (Drew, given the opportunity, meanwhile, would also have reminded him that INXS singer Michael Hutchence had been found dead on 22nd November four years earlier, in another music industry "suicide" that wasn't.)

As the digital watches of the Chinese tourists clicked over from 8:59 to 9:00, a singular bell atop University Church of St. Mary the Virgin, presiding over the south side of Radcliffe Square, began to faithfully chime nine times.

Among the sparse crowd were two women who were definitely not tourists, but had been doing their best to blend in as such.

Verity and Dani sported the Parkas, scarves and woolly hats worn by others, feeling slightly ridiculous in dark glasses on such a distinctly non-sunny morning, but certain that activity in the square would be getting very closely monitored. Both had accepted that, following the attempts to incarcerate and kill them respectively, they would have been followed on their bus journeys in. There would have been no way of avoiding it. Yet, still, there was no point in them standing out any more than they had to.

As they sauntered slowly around the perimeter of the Camera, they remained unsure of what exactly they were there to do. Whatever would happen within the next eleven minutes was in the hands of other parties, and outside of their power. Still, their presence may well be required depending on what would transpire.

Both had accepted that there was a chance they might not survive much beyond 9am; while Verity had bade a tearful goodbye to young Hope back at Joy's house, Dani had merely said "see you later, Mum, love you" as she had hurried out of Helen Road.

Dani aimed the vintage Canon camera liberated from her mother at her surroundings, and reeled off a couple of pointless shots as she and Verity ambled slowly around.

It was 9:06am as their boots trampled over the manhole cover on the south-west corner of the square at its entrance from St. Mary's Passage.

Unbeknown to the pair, some highly unusual activity was occurring several feet below their own.

CHAPTER 34

Friday 9th November 2001

"You may throw your rock and hide your hand,
Working in the dark against your fellow man.
But as sure as God made black and white,
What's done in the dark will be brought to the light."

Johnny Cash: 'God's Gonna Cut You Down.'

"If you can't fly then run; if you can't run then walk; if you
can't walk then crawl. But whatever you do you have to keep
moving forward."

Martin Luther King.

"He's told us not to blow it,
'Cause he knows it's all worthwhile."

David Bowie: 'Starman.'

"I've been to the underworld, Keith. You know that. I've been to places that no man should."

The words played over and over in Keith's mind, as if having been embedded by a master hypnotist.

"Listen to what I'm saying. I've been to the underworld. Literally as well as metaphorically. That's the key to it all. That's where it all happens."

And now it all made sense.

Evidently, other parties had been here very recently. But prior to them, who could pinpoint accurately the last time any human souls had occupied this particular point on Earth? Here, several feet underneath the historic facades of Oxford, in the dirt and the depth and the dank and the dark?

Keith had known only too well of the warren of tunnels reputed to exist below ground in this city. In recent times he had discovered the story of the Trill Mill stream, which disappeared below ground at the point of Oxford Castle, before weaving its way under the streets all the way to Paradise Square, then branching off to join the River Thames. A legend concerning a pair of Victorian-age explorers attempting to traverse it in a punt, and their skeletons being discovered decades later, had long since joined the canon of fables peddled by the area's ghost tour guides. Far more convincing had been the account of the same tunnel having been successfully navigated by T.E Lawrence of '*Lawrence of Arabia*' fame during his time at the University.

Similarly, tunnels lying below the University's Bodleian Library had become common knowledge relatively recently.

The tunnel motif had hit very close to home a little over a decade before. Now, it was even closer as Keith found himself in the terrifying blackness and claustrophobia of one which, available information had suggested, passed directly underneath the Radcliffe Camera.

It had felt like a descent into Hell itself…which had seemed an appropriate metaphor given recent events. It would have been an even more traumatising experience had he been in this netherworld alone. Yet, sharing the experience with him was a man who, appropriately enough, certain parties considered to be dead.

Max Zeall had been leading the way, equipped with a miner-style helmet with an in-built headlight, ever since the two, with the assistance of a pair of bolt cutters, had got to the other side of the metal-grilled gate which had so raised Keith's curiosity on the night he had gone on a recce of the area.

A little before dawn, the friends had descended several twists of the spiral stone staircase. Reaching an apparent dead end, further inspection of the floor had revealed a cast-iron lid. It had shown all the signs of having been removed recently—a notion confirmed by the relative ease with which they had been able to hoist it up.

Keith's high-powered flashlight, besides shocking hordes of rats into a frantic retreat, had illuminated a drop of perhaps five feet to the floor below.

Max had insisted on dropping down first and had led the way along the narrow passageway, evidently constructed at a time when men grew far shorter, as evidenced by their having to stoop continually.

The pair had been working blind—metaphorically as well as literally—through having no idea of how far exactly they would have to travel—nor what they would be looking for once they got there. If they ever did.

It had become clear when they had found what they had been seeking, however, when the first feature beyond stone walls, floor and ceiling suddenly showed up under the glow of Max's headlight.

"I think we've reached Ground Zero," Max whispered as he turned his head back towards Keith...before realising that there was little point in whispering in a place where they wouldn't be heard by another living soul even if they had screamed at the top of their lungs.

The tunnel had opened out into an expansive circular chamber, suggesting that they were now directly below the footprint of the Camera. Pretty much dead-centre was what struck Max as something of an altar...or a funeral pyre. Pieces of wood had been gathered together into what would have made an appropriate bonfire just four nights previous.

Balanced strategically atop the mass was a metal case about the size of a motor mechanic's toolbox.

So this was it, Keith reflected. Everything he and his friends had been anticipating was right here in front of him—as firm a validation of the efficacy of their collective decoding as could have been hoped for.

Evidently, the future fate of the people of this ancient city—and, inevitably, those of the wider world—hung in the balance with whatever was contained in this metal box. And he and Max were the only two living souls in a position to alter what was, in the minds of those who had placed it here, a foregone conclusion.

No pressure then.

Max took a few deep breaths, then instructed Keith to aim his spotlight at the apex of the pyre as, being the taller of the pair, he carefully leaned forward to inspect it.

A padlock held the lid of the box firmly to its main body.

Grateful that the pair had come well equipped, he slipped the rucksack off his back and, after a few moments of fumbling among its contents, retrieved the bolt cutters which had facilitated their way through the grille earlier.

Only too aware of the possible consequences of dislodging the box from its precarious position, he called

Keith over to steady it while he applied the cutters to the lock.

Despite the sub-zero temperature, both mens' brows were sweating.

Within seconds, the broken padlock lay discarded on the floor.

Max had—painfully slowly—opened the lid of the box.

Both men, illuminated by torchlight, now stared at what it contained.

In the centre was a slim glass cylinder, not dissimilar to a drinks flask. Protruding from its chrome lid were two wires—one red, one blue. Each ran down into a mass of what looked like kitchen foil.

And that was it. Keith found himself experiencing disappointment that there was not any kind of clock counting down the minutes and seconds until doomsday time, before rationality reminded him that this was the stuff of Hollywood movies.

The two men looked at the cylinder, then back at each other, before turning to the cylinder again.

In the absence of any counter, Max illuminated the display on his digital watch.

9:06am.

"Time is not our friend this morning," he said, no longer whispering. "You know what we have to do."

Keith let out a deep sigh as he stared into the eyes of the man with whom he had shared so many experiences of the type which few other souls—at least in these times—ever would.

"Max," he uttered with solemnity. " . . . if we're about to die . . . "

Max was having none of it and cut him off mid-flow.

"You talk like that and you'll bring it about! No-one's doing any dying! Not today, anyway."

Keith knew that he was right. Images of Verity and Hope flashed momentarily into his mind.

"Like I said," Max reiterated, "you know what we have to do.

"Now," he continued, beckoning with his head towards the cylinder, "what's it to be?"

Max had fumbled further in his rucksack, and was now holding in his hand a slim pair of wire-cutters.

Keith stared at the two differently-coloured wires protruding from the top of the cylinder.

Cutting one would almost certainly result in the instant deaths of, not just the two of them, but of who knew how many others depending on just how potent the contents of that container really were. That, and lead to the enslavement and subjugation of—potentially—generations.

Cutting the other would—potentially—prevent it all.

Max repeated the question.

"What's it to be, Keith?"

As he stared at the two wires for a few more seconds, but which felt like an eternity, another voice filled his mind.

It was the voice on the other end of the phone from two nights earlier.

" ... the red pill is always the one to take. Never the blue. Remember that. Always the red."

"Cut the red wire. Max."

Max hesitated.

"Cut the red wire, goddamit! Do it!"

In one swift motion the cutters had snipped the red wire in two.

The cold, misty Winter morning remained as silent and tranquil as it had been since dawn.

CHAPTER 35

Friday 9th November 2001

"Fantastic expectations.
Amazing revelations.
Finding everything and realising.
For everything a reason.
F.E.A.R. (You got the fear.)"

Ian Brown: 'F.E.A.R.'

"The secret to happiness is freedom. The secret to freedom is
courage'

Greek philosopher Thucydides.

"The physical body of Man must be polished on this Earth by
spiritual will."

Rudolf Steiner.

Above ground, everything was playing out just as it had
been meticulously planned.

Verity and Dani were still acting out their tourist
routine. Unbeknown to them, their movements were
being captured digitally. It was nothing they need have

taken personally, as activity was being monitored via a series of small spy cameras fitted into the top of the various lamp-posts which adorned Radcliffe Square. The footage they were capturing was being relayed remotely to a specially-constructed control room within the disused sector of Littlemore Mental Health Unit.

There, the content was being displayed on a bank of small screens arranged on the room's singular desk. If he had not been close to the heart of the action, Vic Kostta would have loved to have been sat there, presiding salivatingly over the scenes, like Blofeld in a James Bond movie.

But nothing could have kept him away from the scene of the crime today, the time when what he and his associates had planned for so very long was finally due to come to fruition.

In much the same way that Kostta and his fellow conspirators had been reliably informed that their vantage point in Broad Street was far enough away for them to remain safe, so they had been told that the cameras surreptitiously installed in the lamp-posts some weeks earlier under the guise of "routine maintenance," had been given sufficient reinforcements for them to survive the anticipated explosions. And even if one or two of them should be destroyed, it was highly unlikely that all would, ensuring that this event would be recorded and preserved for posterity.

9.09am. Dani's anxiety was at an all-time high, and she was a mere whisker away from a panic attack. Verity was none too settled herself, but could sense the nerves in her young friend's demeanour. She reached out to hold her gloved hand with her own.

"You OK, mate?"

Dani's response, muffled from under her scarf, was abrupt.

"We should split up. Go our separate ways. More chance of us seeing what's really going on that way."

The suggestion had surprised Verity.

"You think? I mean, you're sure? I really think we should stick together."

'No." The response remained sharp. "You go that way, I'll go this way."

Dani had turned on her heel before she had finished speaking. Then, as an afterthought, she turned back.

"Verity. If we don't ... I mean, if .... it's been a pleasure knowing you. Thank you."

Verity took a couple of paces forward, this time offering a reassuring hand on Dani's shoulder.

"Hey. We've got this. This is an experience that we're going to be looking back on years from now, and we're going to be grateful that we went through it. It'll be the making of us!"

Dani met Verity's smile briefly. Then, the moment searing itself too painfully into her consciousness, turned and hurried in the direction she had indicated.

As she watched her leave, Verity let out a sigh and checked her watch.

9.10am.

All too suddenly, her attention was caught by a flurry of movement to her right.

Quickly and erratically, a young man of Asian/Muslim appearance was running towards the Southern wing of the Radcliffe Camera. Not that Verity could have known this, but it was Max Zeall's friend Shamim. He was dressed in a turquoise shellsuit. On his back he wore a rucksack in fluorescent yellow.

This sight alone had been enough to alarm the ragtag group of tourists milling around. What occurred next was enough to strike pure terror into their hearts.

The young man opened his mouth and began to shout as his pace quickened.

"*Allahu Akbar! Allahu Akbar!*"

His cries were drowned out by screams from the tourists as they began to scatter in all directions, a masked Chinese couple tripping over themselves and tumbling violently to the ground in the process.

Enough time had passed for Daniela to have reached the north-western edge of the Camera, where the main entrance lay.

There, a similar scene had ensued. Another young Asian man had appeared out of nowhere and acted in exactly the same way. Dani had no way of knowing it, but this was Shamim's friend Hakeem, who had been "missing" for the best part of the previous week.

After reciting a similar double-cry of "*Allahu Akbar*," Hakeem, similarly adorned in a shellsuit with an identical backpack, had run all the way past the "Bodleian Libraries reader's card only" sign, and along the path towards the arched wooden door comprising the building's main entrance. Once there, in an act of pure theatre, he had emitted the cry one more time, before yanking violently on a piece of rope protruding from his backpack.

As she witnessed the spectacle, time seemed to slow down for Daniela. As she was perceiving it, the act of yanking the rope seemed to be taking an eternity. As it did, split-second images of all that she had done in her young life seemed to flash randomly into her mind.

The rope had been pulled fully, her consciousness confirmed. The act was complete.

Yet ... nothing.

"Normal" time restored, Dani stared instinctively at her watch.

9:11am.

The screams from the scattered tourists had now subsided, many of them having also witnessed the yanking of the rope and the anti-climax that had followed.

For his part, Hakeem was standing frozen to the spot, a "thousand-yard stare" look of dissociation etched firmly on to his face.

180 degrees around the Camera, there was similar stillness and silence as Verity had witnessed an almost-identical scenario to Dani's. Although a slight smile had appeared at the corners of Shamim's lips and—had anyone been close enough to scrutinise his expression—they would have recognised it as one of full cognition.

9:12am.

Across the rooftops, from their eagle's nest view in Broad Street, all the trio of conspirators knew was that something had gone desperately, desperately wrong.

CHAPTER 36

Friday 9th November 2001

"The point of 'predicting' a terror event is not to say after the fact, 'look how smart I am!' That is despicable. The point of it is to <u>prevent</u> it from happening. Your goal is to be wrong and make yourself wrong. That's the whole point. To be wrong is to be successful when you've identified something serious."

Dr. Webster Tarpley.

In the makeshift Littlemore control room, the small bank of screens had recorded the whole disappointing (from the point of view of those who had installed them) playout of events. In miniature monochrome silence, they continued to relay the activities of the tourists as, one by one, they began to disperse with varying degrees of urgency.

All with the exception of two young women in long coats, hats and scarves.

Of the two young Asian men, the one at the Camera's north-west wide remained glued to the spot in apparent paralysis. His counterpart at the Southern end was beginning to move, however; he was walking energetically towards the woman who was stood there watching him.

"You must be Verity," said Shamim with a reassuring smile, and still looking somewhat ridiculous in the shell suit and backpack. "I hope Keith told you about me."

"He did. And I'm very relieved he called it correct."

"We all are," Shamim replied, now directly in front of her. "I broke my programming. My friend Hakeem never did. But Keith and Max have evidently succeeded in their mission. We wouldn't be standing here chatting if they hadn't."

An image of Hope smiling was all that could come into Verity's mind.

"So . . . what now?"

Shamim's kind smile became replaced by an expression of gravity as he considered his response.

"Some very bad people are going to be very pissed off about what *hasn't* just happened."

Verity smarted as Shamim reached out to clutch her arm.

"Come. We have to find Max and Keith."

Before she was able to voice any objection, Shamim was shepherding Verity towards the gate through which Keith and Max had descended into their netherworld some hours before.

Some yards away, a traumatised Daniela had only been able to look on in a mixture of fascination and fear as Hakeem had suddenly snapped out of his thousand-yard stare trance and, seemingly switching back into full consciousness, pulled the rucksack from his back, discarded it on the lawn, and sprinted along the path away from the main entrance.

He had stopped momentarily to observe Dani, by now the only "tourist" remaining in the vicinity. He had met her expression of fear with one of sheer confusion, before continuing to sprint away from the square along Brasenose Lane.

The Chinese tourists had wasted no time with their mobile phones.

The wail of not-so-distant sirens filled the Oxford air.

No sooner had Hakeem exited the scene, than Dani's attention had been caught by three figures running swiftly in her direction. There was Verity, now minus hat, scarf and dark glasses, running in tandem with two distinctly grubby-looking men.

Shamim had evidently exited as quickly as his friend.

The flash of blue lights cut through the misty vapour of the November morning, as the sirens maintained their piercing screams.

"Time to make a quick exit," shouted Max.

Dani began to run towards the Catte Street entrance to the square following the lead of Max, Keith and Verity.

***

In Broad Street, the unfolding of events—or lack of them—had been equally noted by the three ariel observers, though with a different display of emotions.

Blind panic had set in in the case of Vic Kostta—panic at what repercussions the evident failure of the mission in which he had had so much confidence, would have for him. On Fabian Lucas's part, disappointment was more his emotional state. "Others" would be none too pleased at the failure of this operation. Questions would be asked and scapegoats would be sought.

As far as Eugene Nicks was concerned, treachery had been afoot. Vengeance had become his default emotion. But first, the primal state of self-preservation had taken hold. It was time to survive.

The expression in the eyes of the others seemed to ask, wordlessly, "what do we do?"

"We'll re-group at the Caves," instructed Nicks. "Right now. Let's go!"

No further encouragement was needed. With Kostta leading the way, the three hurried out of their bird's-nest vantage point, down the two flights of stairs, and out into the hustle and bustle of Broad Street.

To the western end, close to its junction with Turk Street, were sitting the two black Mercedes in which the three had arrived. Their drivers were sitting patiently, the engines running, awaiting further instructions.

Unbeknown to the trio, they had already been spotted and recognised by the rapidly-advancing foursome of Verity, Dani, Keith and Max, just a few yards behind.

Nicks was in no mood to take chances. The first driver received a rude awakening from the text message he was busy composing when he found the door being wrenched open, his seatbelt being unclipped, and himself being hauled out and dumped violently on the tarmac.

As Lucas hurried into the passenger seat, and Kostta into the rear, Nicks occupied the newly-vacated driver's position.

Within seconds the tyres screamed as the vehicle veered violently towards George Street.

Locals and tourists scattered in terror as the Mercedes roared onwards with zero regard for public safety.

Only seconds later, their senses were back on high alert as a second vehicle—a Ford Mondeo—sped off recklessly in its wake.

CHAPTER 37

Friday 9th November 2001

If the three from The Order had anticipated screams of terror that morning, they were to get them—though not from the place nor the circumstances they had expected.

The first was emitted by two female students walking in the centre of Broad Street close to the Martyr's Cross memorial. Cycles were the norm for this part of town, vehicle traffic comprising of only the occasional delivery vehicle. Top-of-the-range S-Class's gaining speed rapidly were something of a novelty.

The girls leapt to the side. The brakes on the Mercedes screamed. In the car, Nicks cursed violently at having had to use them. Other pedestrians had turned having noticed the fracas, and were already moving out of the way.

Hot on the heels of the Mercedes was the navy blue Mondeo. Keith had surrendered to his emotional exhaustion and was strapped into the passenger seat. Dani and Max had been left behind to fulfil whatever role they could.

At the wheel, Verity was finding herself taking risks she never normally would. Keith had already accepted that there was no point caring for the effects this pursuit would have on their beloved car. Hell, they might even lose their lives this morning after all. Either way, the architects of what he and his friends had just prevented could *not* be allowed to get away, and if they were to safely escape the city right now, that is what would surely happen.

The Mercedes reached the busy junction at the end of Broad Street, and veered recklessly to the left into Cornmarket Street, leaving deposits of its tyre rubber on the grubby pavement as it went. This was one of the city's two main shopping streets, both of which had been designated pedestrian-only zones, ironically by Nicks himself.

The street was full of shoppers, students and tourists. Most were sufficiently alerted by the din of the first car's engine to dive out of its path in time.

One was not. A delivery man from a meat firm was carrying a pig's carcass on his shoulder as he headed in the direction of a butcher's in the Covered Market. He was sufficiently distracted from the chaos around him by the music he was listening to through headphones to help numb the tedium of his job.

Nicks hauled the vehicle to the left to avoid a Chinese couple he was about to hit. In the process, the Mercedes' left wing slammed into the delivery man's midriff, sending him flying, then crashing back on to the hard concrete.

The carcass landed to the side of him with an unsettling splat.

The Mercedes ploughed on regardless.

Seconds later, Verity slowed down the Mondeo. In the passenger seat, Keith was appalled at the sight of what had just transpired. His every instinct urged him to jump out and tend to the man. A crowd had already gathered to help him, however, and an ambulance was evidently being called. If they stopped now the perpetrators would surely get away.

Verity knew this and worked to put it out of her mind as she continued the chase.

Having already been tossed around wildly, Lucas in the passenger seat and Kostta in the back, braced themselves for another involuntary white-knuckle experience as they anticipated a sharp left into the High Street.

Instead, the Mercedes continued straight over, past Carfax Tower to the right and into St. Aldates.

Nicks had evidently chosen Abingdon Road as the most direct route out of the city and on to the ring road. He had now begun blasting the horn to clear a path free of pedestrians and cyclists. The car roared past the Town Hall to its left, then, once beyond the junction with Speedwell Street, past St. Aldates Police Station, outside which DI Sam Haine had been enjoying the pleasure of Aimee Hardwick just 36 hours previous.

The din of the Mercedes' horn had been amplified by blasts from the Mondeo's, as Verity had remained in dogged pursuit.

Both cars flew over Folly Bridge, then continued straight along Abingdon Road, this route at least less busy and free of pedestrians in the road.

The chase was taking Verity past their own home. She instinctively glanced towards the light blue exterior of 216b, home of so many bizarre encounters, the front door still broken from the police's incursions of two nights previous.

As if on cue, a new sound suddenly alerted her senses. The wail of a police siren. She glanced at the driver's mirror to see the flash of blue lights a few vehicles back.

They had known this would happen. It would now be a case of outwitting the police at every turn.

"Not the average boring Friday morning then," she muttered to Keith sardonically.

She and Keith had actually given little thought to exactly how they would get the Mercedes to stop, or to what they would then do to apprehend the three.

Keith was regretting not having brought Max along for the ride.

Having attained a speed of 51mph, the S Class was now approaching the busy junction with Weirs Lane. The traffic lights were in the process of switching from amber to red.

Lucas and Kostta gazed in fear at the sight.

Nicks cursed, "fuck that" and, slowing down only slightly, sent the car careering across the intersection.

A line of eight vehicles had begun spilling out from Weirs Lane. The first two headed left. A taxi van was headed right.

The Asian driver had evidently remained oblivious to the powerful black machine bearing down upon him. At the last moment he turned.

A sickening crunch joined the sound of a groaning engine and the screams of a couple of onlookers as the front offside wing of the Mercedes smashed into the offside rear of the van, sending it spinning around to the right.

It had completed a full 360 degrees before it veered off the road on to the pavement and crunched into a low wall, the driver frozen in terror, but remarkably unhurt.

The traffic lights were switching back to green just as the Mondeo reached the junction, Verity acknowledged the chaos that had just ensued. The police siren was growing louder.

"What the fuck are we doing?" she shouted at Keith with incredulity.

"What we must," he replied, his vision fixed firmly ahead.

CHAPTER 38

Friday 9th November 2001

The Mercedes was nearing the junction with the Eastern bypass, from which Nicks was planning to gain access to the A40 and on to West Wycombe.

He glanced in his rear-view mirror, appalled to see the tenacious Mondeo still on his trail, and noting the blue lights bringing some colour to the drab Winter's morning behind it.

Suddenly, another stream of blue light appeared to his front right, accompanied by a cacophony of sirens. Two more police vehicles, a Panda car followed by a riot van, were looking to join the action, running a red light as they tore into Abingdon Road from the bypass.

Their drivers having noted the wanted vehicle to the right, they suddenly stopped. Other motorists hooted and wound down their windows to shout as the Mercedes ran the red light and spilled out on the bypass. Less than five seconds later, the stationary officers witnessed a Ford Mondeo making the same manoeuvre, followed doggedly by another police panda car.

The officer in the second panda couldn't help but find the scene vaguely comedic, like a scene from '*The Italian*

Job' or even a Benny Hill show. Either way, duty called, and so the panda, followed closely by the riot van, swerved back around and joined the chase. Other vehicles had slowed and stopped appropriately to allow them to gain their place.

The five vehicles were now thundering along the fast lane of the Eastern bypass, the din of the three sirens alerting any drivers up ahead and causing them to tuck back into the slow lane immediately, facilitating a clear path for the lead car.

Contempt consumed Nicks as he considered the officers now on his tail. Ignorant flatfoots who had no idea of what was really occurring on this fateful morning. Nor of the occult mockery that their own uniforms represented, the black and white checker design on their hats symbolising the Freemasonic infrastructure which controlled that institution, and sitting right over their third eye chakra, symbolising their higher consciousness having been completely surrendered to their unseen masters.

Nicks knew that he could pull rank on these "useful idiots" at any time. But there was hardly the opportunity now. There was the question of the occupants of the Mondeo. He knew they had the capacity to blow the whistle on the whole intricate plot if they were allowed to survive.

So they must not.

Consistently occupying the fast lane, the convoy had been able to reach speeds of almost 90mph as other vehicles had conveniently cleared a path.

They were now careering towards the Cowley flyover. The sprawling ugliness of the vast BMW plant loomed below. Originally Morris Motors, with car manufacturing going on to become a proud Oxford institution, in the 1970s this had been British Leyland, and Verity worked to clear a vision of her father from her mind as she remembered the times she had brought him his lunch when he had worked there.

Suddenly, her conscious mind snapped back into action.

Her eyes grew wide at the sight of the red brake lights of the Mercedes, only a few yards in front.

Instinctively she slammed her foot on the brake, sending herself and Keith lurching sharply forward.

Their seat belts snapped into action, and Keith yelped in shock and pain as a crack was emitted from his neck.

The tyres screeched and the engine wailed as Verity lost control of the Mondeo. As the brakes gripped the front wheels, the back section of the car lifted slightly. The pair momentarily feared it would up-end completely.

The rear wheels slammed back down. At the same time, the vehicle swung helplessly to the right, smashing into the grimy corrugated steel of the central barrier, sending both the barrier and the car's offside rear into a hideous tangle of mangled metal.

The offside rear tyre burst, pierced by a jagged shard of metal and rendering the car immobile.

Had this been a Roger Moore-era James Bond film, Keith might have quipped "women drivers!" But, being in such pain, he was in no mood for cheap gags.

His senses having been sharpened by the chase, the driver of the first Panda car noted the activity in front, and immediately slammed on his own brakes.

The other police drivers did the same.

Though having braked early, the driver of the van was unable to stop in time, and it smashed into the similarly-braking panda car in front, sending it, in turn, smashing into the first.

The car was shunted forward, stopping mere metres from the twisted wreck of the Mondeo and its traumatised occupants.

The occupants of the Mercedes were experiencing a different fate.

This car too had almost up-ended as Nicks had braked. It also swerved to the side, in this case to the left. The rear end crunched into the central barrier.

But the car remained in motion with Nicks no longer in any position of control. Still heading to the left, it traversed the slow lane, before hitting the soot-stained barrier.

Time seemed to slow down for the three occupants as the terrible truth of what they were experiencing became processed in their consciousness.

A section of the barrier gave way upon impact, and the car, continuing its spin, flew off the side of the flyover. As it did so, and in the couple of seconds available, the weight of the engine caused it to tip forward.

Each of the three were restrained in their seats as it tumbled at a 180-degree angle towards the west side of the Garsington Road roundabout.

A scream of 'Oh God, oh God!" came from the back seat.

Lucas remained silent, a look of sheer terror in his eyes.

Nicks' expression was one of reluctant acceptance.

The last thing the two front occupants experienced during their time in the earthly realm was a horrific clangour of crushed metal, breaking glass and an engine at breaking point, followed by unfathomable mental trauma and physical pain as the engine collapsed in on them, piercing their bodies as they remained helplessly pinned to their seats.

And with that, they were gone. Off to face what lay beyond.

There was a morbid irony in that it was down to budget cuts initiated by Nicks himself, that the barriers on that stretch of flyover had not been appropriately maintained. Had he signed off on the recommendations of the Council's Road Safety Department, he might have inadvertently saved his own life.

The car had hit the road—mercifully during a rare gap in the traffic with no further casualties involved—while still in a frontwards turn, and following the impact, had flipped over on to its roof. This had collapsed in on itself as the glass in all the windows had shattered.

As crowds of nearby workers had begun to assemble, the traffic on the flyover above had ground to a halt without any further casualties.

While Keith remained in the wreck of the Mondeo, moaning from the pain in his neck, Verity had exited and was standing at the missing section of barrier, staring down at the atrocity below. So too were four of the police officers, so dismayed by what they were seeing that they hadn't yet got around to arresting Verity—something she now accepted was unavoidable.

All sounds from what used to be the S-Class had now ceased save for the gentle trickling of diesel from the fuel pipe.

All traffic on the roundabout was now stationary. Onlookers were desperately gabbling into their mobile phones. While most were keeping their distance out of fear that the vehicle might explode, a couple of workers from the Cowley plant were approaching cautiously.

They were alerted to a new movement. Through what had been the nearside rear window, now a twisted mass of fractured metal, a bloodied arm appeared. Then another.

Painfully slowly, Kostta was using every shred of energy that remained in his body to haul himself through the available aperture. His skin was getting cut to shreds by the shards of glass he was being forced down upon.

Agonisingly, he managed to pull his whole body through, before collapsing in a bloody, exhausted mess.

The two workers rushed to his assistance, kneeling down and bracing themselves for the extent of his injuries. Kostta, however, was in no mood for any kind of assistance. Left-brained survival mode had kicked in, and it somehow drove him to haul himself on to his knees. The workers grabbed an arm each and helped him to his feet.

No gratitude was offered, however, as Kostta, once upright, shook them off and shouted at them to stay away.

Verity and the officers continued to observe from their vantage point above. The uncanny silence of the scene had been pierced by the distant blaring of another police siren.

To the onlookers, Kostta was barely recognisable as a man. His blood-soaked clothes hung off his body in tatters. His head was marinated in fresh blood. Small slivers of glass were embedded in his face.

He stumbled pathetically as he attempted to run away, at all cost, from the scene.

The police siren grew louder.

With each step more agonising than the last, Kostta somehow managed, in what felt to him like an eternity, to lumber his way to the left-hand exit from the horror site on to Garsington Road.

No-one could have been certain as to who next became the most alarmed—Kostta himself, or DI Sam Haine at the wheel of the unmarked Audi, blue lights and siren blazing.

As it tore down Garsington Road towards the round-about, a figure suddenly appeared in the Audi's windscreen.

Haine's eyes grew wide as he slammed on the brakes.

Kostta's eyes were like a deer's in headlights.

The black metal of the Audi thudded into Kostta's body, sending it flying several feet in the air before it landed, with a grotesque thud, on to the tarmac.

The Audi swerved left and right before slamming into one of the flyover's supporting walls.

Haine was immediately engulfed by the car's airbag.

Cowley, Oxford. Where cars are made and lives are bettered.

But also, evidently, destroyed.

9th November 2001. A date when collateral damage was inevitably caused. But when the lives and freedoms of untold millions were saved.

No pain, no gain.

EPILOGUE

Monday 31st December 2001

"They fear love because it creates a world they can't control."
George Orwell: '1984.'

"Strange, isn't it? Each man's life touches so many other lives.
And when he isn't around he leaves an awful hole, doesn't he?"

Clarence in 'It's A Wonderful Life.'

For a network with such a track-record of influence and power, like a decapitated beast, The Order had certainly shown one of its organisational weaknesses following the demises of Nicks and Lucas.

Its members having been strategically embedded within every niche of Oxford society, was showing itself to be of little consequence now that the top level of the pyramid had been removed. Those occupying other levels were entirely devoid of any kind of "order" without instructions filtering down from above, as they had been so used to. Similarly, any other "sleeper" assassins who might have been embedded within city society were harmless—for the moment—now that Kostta had taken with him the trigger codes to activate their programming.

The meetings at West Wycombe caves had continued at the hands of a few of the underlings, however, and many of the firmly-established rituals maintained. Various attempts at a power grab had been made by some of the more ambitious and narcissistic members. Those with less lofty ambitions had ensured that the usual traditions were adhered to, with any new member requiring the approval of at least 51 per cent of the others in a leadership vote.

By the end of 2001, no such election had yet taken place, however, and The Order continued to symbolically lick its wounds. It had been injured badly, going from the excitement of being poised for its greatest moment, to the devastation of realising the plan had been foiled by a laughably small group of individuals, whose value systems stood diametrically opposed to their own. Its initiates were used to getting their own way. Encountering those who could not in any way be bought off, blackmailed or threatened into compliance was a dynamic that none were used to dealing with.

The people of Oxford—and ultimately the rest of the nation—remained blissfully oblivious to how close they had come to having their natural-born rights and freedoms taken away on the back of an outrageous and monumental scam. They had continued about their business, and seven weeks later, on the last day of 2001, hundreds of thousands were preparing to party, as tradition dictated, without a single troubling care on their minds.

The six folk who had prevented their worst nightmare from manifesting had never sought any glory for their efforts. All they had wished for was that the masses would get themselves clued up with the knowledge which they themselves had taken the personal responsibility to attain.

Max had stayed true to his word to Shamim, and had worked to get his friend Hakeem de-programmed by a former handler from a multi-generational bloodline family embroiled in such activities. The handler had been able to reverse-engineer the mental damage, allowing Hakeem to reclaim a semblance of normality.

No "official" action had been taken following the nightmare at the Cowley flyover. DI Sam Haine, nursing his whiplash, and with his having unwittingly caused the death of one of the most valued assets of The Order on his conscience, had known that his only option was to pull rank over the other police in attendance—those whose only sworn allegiances had been to the Queen rather than to any other parties—and to do his best to clean up the terrible situation.

In spite of the protestations of the rank-and-file officers in attendance, Haine had insisted that Verity and Keith be allowed to leave the scene with no charges, pointing out that the event had been a terrible accident that nobody could have foreseen.

Though several of the officers had challenged his call, maintaining that the pair should be detained on dangerous driving charges, Haine had belligerently reminded them of their place. Though he knew they could launch official complaints against him, he doubted any of them, ultimately, would have the moral fortitude to do so.

The passage of time proved him to have called it correctly.

Haine knew that his own inadvertent killing of Kostta would prove to be nothing more than a minor setback, "legally" speaking. He had anticipated that outcome accurately, too. Whereas any regular member of society would have faced a manslaughter charge, with the "special" privileges his job title and badge afforded, he walked away with a three-month suspension on full pay pending an internal enquiry...which he knew would end up ruling in his favour.

Of far more concern to Haine had been how the events of 9th November would affect his standing with The Order. Though now without a nominal head, it would only be a matter of time before a new leader would emerge. And The Order bore grudges. It played the long game. It had been known to carry out killings of retribution *years* after a member had done something to mark their own cards.

Haine would—metaphorically speaking—be sleeping with one eye open for whatever remained of his life.

***

Though the outrage in Oxford had been thwarted, the fallout from the earlier one in the United States had continued to leave its legacy. The dark occultists behind it had been salivating over the warmongering in the Middle East that they would "justify" under the "War on Terror" that had followed in its wake. Accordingly, Northern Alliance forces had conquered the Afghan capital, Kabul, on 14th November. Three weeks later, the Taliban, (which had morphed out of the Mujahadeen, in morbid irony, a creation of the CIA to advance the American government's agendas in the Middle East,) had surrendered its final stronghold in Kandahar.

Eleven days after that had seen the "Battle of Tora Bora." Somehow, mainstream newsreaders around the world had been able to keep a straight face while reporting that, in this daring raid, "9/11 mastermind" Osama bin-Laden had miraculously escaped the carnage and gone into hiding elsewhere in the mountain caves—presumably dragging his dialysis drip device behind him all the way.

Those with the will and the ability to do their own research, however, knew that bin-Laden was already dead by this point. Gravely ill even at the time the attacks of September 11th were pinned on him, he had succumbed to his kidney disorder earlier in December, passing away in an American hospital in Dubai, a fact reported on at the time by a handful of Middle-Eastern newspapers, but—naturally—ignored by the Rothschild-owned Reuters and Associated Press "news" agencies, and therefore by default, the entirety of the western world's media.

Though the residents of Oxford had narrowly escaped a "suicide bombing" of their own, those in Haifa, Israel, had not been so fortunate when, on 2nd December, a "Hamas militant" had detonated a bomb, killing himself and 15 others on a bus.

***

At just after nine in the evening on 31st December, as the hordes began to descend on the bars and clubs of the city centre, three friends sat at one of the tables in the bustling Angel & Greyhound pub, formerly Parker's Wine Bar, on St. Clements. To the others in the bar, they appeared as regular punters. None could have had any idea that, were it not for the care and action of these three, none of them would be here this evening, but would rather be held in house arrest under martial law in a scene straight out of one of the nightmarish, dystopian movies that they so enjoyed viewing at the cinema.

Though the friends had met on a few occasions in the previous weeks at one of their respective homes, this was the first time any of them had been out in a social situation. Though all knew that the real "new year's eve" would not occur until March, it had seemed as good a date as any to try and unwind and celebrate the freedom of association that they had been able to retain for themselves, along with everyone else.

Absent was Drew Hunter who, ordinarily, would be gearing up for his biggest night of the year at one of the clubs in Oxford or beyond. This year was different, though. He had not played a gig since Bonfire Night, his evenings consisting either of sombre, marijuana-fuelled reflections at home, or holding vigil beside May's bed in the Intensive Care Unit at the JR.

Keith Malcolm dodged the gyrating hordes as he manoeuvred towards the corner table with a tray of drinks—a pint of Stella each for himself and Max, and a rum and coke for Verity.

"Don't you miss all this, babe?" Verity smiled at him as he passed the drinks around the table.

"Not really, no," he replied wryly, just as a rowdy cheer went up from a crowd of young males positioned near the bar.

As the three took the first sips of their drinks, a raised voice from one of the other small crowds in the room entered their consciousness.

"That fuckin' bin-Laden should be strung up by his balls."

Verity rolled her eyes. "They'll probably delay announcing that he's actually dead for another ten years," she muttered. "And when they do, that lot'll buy it hook, line and sinker."

"Probably wait until some future president needs a boost in his approval ratings, right?" added Keith.

Max chipped in.

"Guys, didn't we tell ourselves that this was going to be a 'cheerful' gathering? Remember that part?"

"I know. But it's just so difficult, Max! Without doom and gloom, what else do we have?"

All three chuckled lightly.

"The death of George Harrison was genuinely sorrowful," added Verity.

The former Beatle had succumbed to cancer at the end of November, never the same since the vicious knife attack at his Henley-on-Thames home two years earlier, which had surely been intended to kill him.

"Well, as he said himself, 'all things must pass'," said Keith.

"Oh, I do have *some* good news," Verity piped up excitedly. "Mum's dumped Norm!"

A huge cheer raised up from the table, alarming others around.

In rapid turn, the attention of the friends was caught by a loud wolf-whistle from the young men leaning against the bar. A young woman had entered.

Though Daniela Mots looked almost unrecognisable from her regular appearance, her three friends placed her instantly.

Gone were the National Health glasses, replaced, evidently, with invisible contact lenses. There was no T-shirt or dungarees; instead she wore a low-cut black top and a pair of tight-fitting black trousers. The Doc Martens had been replaced by a pair of fashionable black boots with silver tassles.

As the gazes of the young men at the bar remained fixed on her backside, Dani glanced directly in Max's direction, a smile that seemed to say "see what you're missing?" etched firmly on her lips.

Keith's gaze, likewise, was fixed on Dani's lower half—a fact which had not escaped Verity's ever-vigilant eye.

Max remained speechless as she approached the table. Verity did the talking.

"Dani! You look . . . amazing!"

"Thanks," Dani replied. "Thought I'd make a bit of an effort as it's New Year's Eve. Hi Verity. Keith ... Max."

"Uhhh, yeah ... You look great, Dani. Get you a drink?" said a shocked Max eventually.

"I'll have a Babycham, please. You're only young once, right?"

Max Zeall wasn't often rendered speechless, but on this occasion he was, excusing himself to head to the bar.

Dani seated herself next to Verity.

"You're pretty popular tonight," grinned Verity, signalling towards the lads at the bar.

"You think?" Dani replied, apparently innocently, but with a twinkle in her blue eyes.

Suddenly, Verity felt a vibration at her waist. She recognised it straight away as the ring of her Nokia mobile, strapped to her trouser belt.

Surveying the display ID, she accepted the call immediately.

"Drew. Wh'appen .... Wha? ... F'real?! .... "

Dani stared across at Verity, noticing her eyes growing wider as the conversation progressed. Keith stared on anxiously.

As Max returned to the table with Dani's drink, Verity suddenly pushed back her chair and stood up.

"Gotta go. I'll explain later. You guys have a great evening. I'll talk to you soon."

Before the others were able to protest or enquire further, Verity was out of the bar and on to St. Clements, ready to hail the first taxi cab that would take her.

***

The traffic in and out of the John Radcliffe Hospital grounds was bedlam. Verity's taxi became sandwiched between two ambulances. Chaotic as this scene was, it would no doubt become worse as the evening wore on, bringing multiple casualties of excessive alcohol consumption.

She checked her phone again, as she had for the entire journey from St. Clements. There was a new text from Drew simply asking "where are U?"

Her right-hand thumb darted wildly around the keypad as she messaged back, "hold on. 5 mins."

Verity tossed a ten pound note to the driver with a hasty thanks, and, without waiting for change, was out of the taxi and in to the JR's main entrance in seconds. She was more than familiar with the route to the ICU by now, and raced up the stairwell to the first floor. The claustrophobic fear of lifts had always made her avoid them.

By the time she had reached the ICU reception she was sweating and panting. Stood at the reception entrance was Drew. His default facial expression for the past weeks had been one of desperation. As Verity got closer she noted that he was wearing a new one—was that a feint hint of jubilation cloaked under a protective layer of caution?

"What's the latest?" Verity asked breathlessly.

"She's awake and responsive!" This time Drew allowed himself a smile.

A bald, stern-faced doctor in a blue medical suit hurried out of the ICU ward, a clipboard full of notes under his arm.

"Doctor! How is she? Can we see her?"

The doctor's expression remained grave, despite the apparent hopefulness of his words.

"You can. Just for a few minutes. But be warned. She's been drifting in and out of consciousness and is very confused and disorientated. "She has a collapsed lung so we've put her on a ventilator. "

Drew sighed heavily.

"The overdose slowed the nerve cells in the brain. The oxygen, sugar, and other substances necessary for proper brain function have decreased. She's lost almost a stone."

Armed with this caveat, the cousins were permitted access to the ward. Once inside, they headed straight to the familiar bed. Filling in notes on the clipboard which hung on the end of it was a senior nurse.

Propped up against two pillows, clear tubes running from under her nose to paraphernalia beside the bed, was a semi-conscious May Pearce.

As the doctor had warned, she had clearly lost weight. Her face was gaunt, the cheek bones jutting out prominently. Her hair was unkempt, and much longer than she ordinarily kept it. She looked tired and confused.

Verity took the lead. "Hey, sister! Look who's here!"

The nurse stood vigil some feet back, observing guardedly as Verity crouched down beside her friend's bed. A hug was out of the question given the breathing tubes, so Verity gently pushed back May's hair from her forehead.

"You gave us such a scare," she whispered. "I thank God—literally—that you've come back to us."

May stared at Verity, her apparent lack of response worrying her for a moment.

Then she spoke, her voice little more than a quiet croak.

"I didn't want to. That was the whole point! I couldn't even get that right!"

May began to cry.

Drew stepped forward and crouched down on the opposite side of her bed.

"Don't you talk like that, angel. Don't ever talk like that. You coming back to us is a blessing, and you're going to see just how much you're valued."

Though a television had been broadcasting at low level since their arrival, something compelled all three to glance at the screen at the exact same moment.

As was so often the case at this time of the year, the movie 'It's A Wonderful Life' was nearing its end. Clarence, guardian angel to James Stewart's suicidal character, was showing him a vision of what the world would have been like had he never been born. Had he not been there to save his younger brother Harry from drowning when they were children, Harry would not have gone on to thwart an attack on a transport ship full of American troops, thus saving hundreds of lives.

It was as if the Universe had synchronistically decreed that this portion of the film should be showing at this exact moment.

Though the TV was on low volume, the three could make out James Stewart's words.

"I want to live again. I want to live again. I want to live again. Please God, let me live again."

Drew and Verity turned to May. She was still crying, only this time there seemed to be some measure of relief in the tears.

"I saw my Mum and Dad, Drew. I saw them. Mum spoke to me."

"What ... what did she say?"

"She said ... she said I had to come back. It's not my time. I still have work to do."

Tears were filling Verity's eyes also.

"She wasn't kidding. Don't you realise that if it wasn't for you, none of us might be here now, and thousands of people might be dead? Wasn't it you who first identified the Camera as the target? And remind me again who it was who identified 9th November as the date and interpreted the clue in that weird Prince record?"

Drew looked at Verity, then back at May.

"It was you, Maysie. We couldn't have done it without you."

As May's tired mind worked to process the words, some life energy appeared to show on her face.

"So, you did it? You stopped it?"

Verity tightened her hold on May's hand as she spoke.

"*We* stopped it, Maysie. You've been a part of it all along."

'*It's a Wonderful Life*' was on to the part where, granted another chance to live his life—this time with full gratitude to Creation—James Stewart runs through the snowy streets shouting "Merry Christmas" to all and sundry.

"So ... we put them down? the danger's gone?"

"You bet. Yes, Maysie, we put them down."

As Drew stroked May's forehead, Verity turned to the side and mouthed, almost silently.

" ... For now."

THE END